Books by Julie Midnight

Monstrous Hearts

Wolf's Wife

Wolf's Bane

Wolf's Kin

Wolf's Bane

MONSTROUS HEARTS
BOOK TWO

Julie Midnight

HELLCATPRESS

ISBN: 978-1-7367836-1-0

Any references to historical events, real people, or real places are used fictitiously. Names, characters, and places are products of the author's imagination.

Front cover image by Julie Midnight
Book design by Daniel Young

Printed by Kindle Direct Publishing in the United States

First Printing Edition 2021

Hellcat Press LLC
www.hellcatpressllc.com

Table of Contents

A Taste of Lost Things

Hist, now. Hist! Listen closely and you'll find a story that only the trees and blood-soaked soil would remember. There's a girl out here in these woods, a girl who looks ordinary at first glance. You've seen her kind before: raised with a pampered childhood and gliding through life in new cars and good careers. The type that never needs to worry about money.

Ah, but don't envy this girl in her little house surrounded by towering pines. She has scars, this one, hidden deep beneath her freshly-showered skin while she picks an outfit for the evening. Her mother went mad and abandoned her as a child when she was old enough to remember what happened but too young to understand why. Her last lover came into her life as bright and otherworldly as a star, and then proved to be a spider that wrapped her in a web and fed without ever being sated.

And yet the girl doesn't seem sad now, does she? That soft smile as she lets the bath towel fall from her... How her hands musingly trail over the bite marks on her heavy, red-tipped breasts, and then the bruises on her hips and thighs. Behind her, the man in the bed shifts and begins to lazily stroke his cock. Even before she turns to look, she knows what he's doing, and her smile widens.

"I have to leave in twenty minutes," she says, fingers deft as they twist her hair into a neat updo.

It's an invitation. Perhaps a challenge as well. She doesn't even have time to reach for a bobby pin from the dressing table before he's on her.

His breaths sound like growls from a beast as he takes her from behind; hers are quieter, rising whenever his slow, hard rhythm jolts her against the table. There's a fresh sheen of sweat on her skin when he catches the back of her neck with his teeth and pushes in deep. It makes her yelp and writhe, already anticipating his cock unloading into her, and in response he bites harder and pins her still with his weight. His shuddering climax draws her into one, and for long, breathless moments, the girl remembers what it was like to have the savage abandon of a beast.

Oh yes, this girl is something more than human, even once the flush of sex fades from her skin and she puts on a shimmering dress with a neck high enough to hide the love bite left behind. She knows strange things live in the shadows of the mundane world. Magic, the supernatural... Call it what you will. She knows it, and the man does, too.

He lingers close by, now, hands skimming along her bare arms while she fusses with earrings before a full-length mirror. The sky outside shows streaks of lavender from the approaching dusk. The girl is already late for the party, but hesitates even so, meeting the man's gaze through their reflections in the mirror.

"You can join me." She tries to sound casual instead of hopeful.

He's taller than she, and tucks her head into the hollow of his throat so that his response rumbles in her ear. "Not tonight."

It's the same answer as he always gives. He holds her close in those endless nocturnal hours when she wakes from nightmares and can't stop shaking. He makes her shake for much sweeter reasons with that clever tongue and those teasing teeth. He's even spilled blood for her. Yet he's never joined her life of cocktails and caviar. The shadowy otherworld that she's glimpsed—where witches spin spells and beasts carry the dreams of men—is his birth realm, and he only knows how to look human.

She accepts the answer but can't help twisting around to nuzzle for one final kiss. His mouth is hot, hungry, and her heart clenches at what's about to happen. But the girl has survived the wounds of loss before, and this will be but a papercut in comparison. She steps back, ankles trembling in their high heels even as her gaze remains steady. She loves watching him change, loves it even as she hates not being able to do the same.

It's like watching firelight flicker, a sense of movement too fast to truly grasp. The hard muscle and hot skin that had only minutes before rutted her senseless now shifts into a thick black pelt. Teeth flash in the warm lamplight. Green eyes sharpen into a piercing yellow, and only their feral gleam remains the same as what had been the man gives a quick shake from muzzle to tail.

A black wolf now circles around the girl on rangy limbs, panting easily and nuzzling as if to say he hasn't forgotten her even with the lure of the forest just outside. Tears shine in her eyes, but she smiles while kneeling down to bury her face and hands in the wolf's coarse fur.

"Be safe," she murmurs, knowing his ears will catch the words. Knowing he can still understand them. "And come back to me."

The wolf nudges her, all cold nose and velvet tongue. Then he's gone like a shadow, out through the opened sliding door and into the shrouded wilderness. The girl watches him disappear in the gloom, hands fisted in her lap. When she stands up again, her jewelry feels heavy as chains. She knows wildness, you see, and used to live it, too, running at his side as a she-wolf. It haunts her to stay behind among humans, and for all that it's been months since she last shared a night with the black wolf, she still grieves as one would grieve over a death.

Yet the girl doesn't realize how the past may become more than memory. Sometimes, the past may come alive. A comforting thought, no? Well... It depends on what returns to life. This girl, whose name is Alice, has many ghosts indeed— her mother's madness is never far from her mind. Her last lover's name is never far from her lips. And on the liminal path she walks between the mundane world and its furtive shadow, anything might happen.

No, do not envy poor Alice, for she's about to find out how the past has teeth sharper than any wolf's.

CHAPTER ONE

STEPPING INTO THE PAST

Alice kept a pleasant expression on her face while mingling with the other guests at her father's anniversary party. It was uncanny, the feeling of having stepped back into early girlhood. Then, she had liked pretending that she'd hardened into a doll, with porcelain cheeks that could never sag free of a smile and luminous eyes that engaged at a glance. That her fragile aura instinctively sensed by others was an effect of nature, of having ceramic bones fired into brittle elegance and a mouth silent from being mere paint.

Now, an adult in present day, she knew her body was solid meat, with a beating heart and a heavy brain. Tender flesh showed more than impassive clay. She had more scars now, too, and felt vulnerable at exposing herself to so many familiar gazes. How differently did she appear to them? How strained her smile? How haunted her eyes?

They all appeared the same, moving in currents of crisp suits and elegant dresses. Gold glittered against throats or around wrists. Champagne sparkled in crystal glasses. Conversations murmured, constant and polite, with an occasional peal of laughter rising above the live pianist.

Many of the faces lit with vague recognition as she offered greetings in passing. Why, it was Alice, Tom's daughter come back into the fold after five years away. What had pulled her to the city? Something to do with trying to make a career in the arts, wasn't it?

Alice avoided the questions in their eyes by continuing her aimless circuit through the rooms. In-depth conversations... No, those hadn't yet returned to her. She no longer knew how to act like the well-schooled teenager she'd been when these people had last seen her, majoring in veterinary science and so sure of her life ahead. In truth, she had felt as dead-eyed and posed as a piece of taxidermy, but that very state had allowed her to hide all feelings. Now she was like an exposed nerve, raw and vulnerable and *alive*, and trying to fit into her old role felt painful.

Needing something to do, she sipped at her champagne, half-expecting to taste the sparkling cider she'd always been given as a girl. Sweetness bubbled over her tongue; warmth sank into her throat. The sound of her father's voice drew her attention, and she looked over to find him relaxed and happy, his arm around her stepmother's waist. Denise, always in her element around people, chattered excitedly with a woman in a navy chiffon dress. Both of their neatly coiffed heads gleamed with jeweled hair pins.

Something clutched at Alice's heart. Wistfulness, perhaps? A sense of feeling so far removed from these people—her very own family—that she might as well have viewed them through a telescope.

Just then, her father's gaze found her. After a dip of his head to excuse himself from the conversation, he approached Alice. Her fingers tightened around the stem of her glass.

"Hi, Dad." Her smile felt no different from when she faced a stranger.

His, however, had cooled. "Alice. I haven't seen you speaking with many people."

She hesitated, wondering whether to push at things, and then admitted, "I'm not sure what to say. Everyone thinks I moved to the city to be an artist."

"That's what I told them and they don't need to know more."

Hard-earned knowledge, that, back from when the disappearance of Alice's mother had shattered their lives. People pried through their show of concern and then whispered details among themselves, vying to see who had the juiciest bit to share. Had Tom's smile turned spiteful when his wife's name had been spoken aloud? Did he look like an innocent man? A grieving one? So many unanswered questions... After all, a woman doesn't simply *vanish*.

Accounts morphed into rumors, and rumors into convictions. The sheer hell Tom Corrigan had gone through in those first years was likely why he had hardened into someone so fiercely dull in his hobbies and so painfully conscious of attention and demeanor. He guarded against embarrassment and discredit to his family with iron rigidity. A knight who couldn't bend in his armor.

Even now, Alice looked at her glass rather than try matching gazes with him. In some ways, she felt very sorry for her father, yet she remained terrified of that hardness, especially since she had spent the past five years crossing his personal crusade by living with Magdalene.

Magdalene.

Thinking of her still drove Alice's heart into a frenzy. At times, she woke up believing she was back in their apartment in the city, and that the morning was about to begin with the smell of used cigarettes and stale coffee. That her sleep-crusted eyes would discover a notebook rubbed soft from anxious fingers, not one word written in its pristine pages.

But oh, those early days... Compared to the careful, sterile existence she'd known, Magdalene had burned as brightly as a star. She had stood up to Alice's father, laughing in his face at his cold reserve and sheen of manners. She had been strange, different, *alive*, and the chance to bask in her light—to share her intoxicating life—proved too alluring to resist.

And so Alice, sweet little fool, had stepped into the camouflaged cage and locked the door behind her. Even now, watching her father break his mask long enough to rub at his eyes, she still understood how that had caught her so completely.

"We've talked about this," said her father, looking at her once more. "You're fully welcome here, but if you want our support, you need to stop dwelling on what happened and get your life back on track. I'll even find a therapist if you want professional help in moving on from... your last relationship. But as far as I'm concerned, that was then and this is now. The past is just that—the past. Tonight, we're all here to celebrate. Right?"

Alice nodded, voice quiet. "Right."

Something softened in his expression. "It's the only way through things, Alice. One day, you'll understand."

Before she could think up a dutiful response, Aunt Fiona exclaimed from half a room away and came gliding toward them. "If it isn't our Ally!"

Alice's mouth snapped into a smile, as did her father's, and he drifted away to check on the rest of his guests just as Fiona threw out both hands to clasp Alice's own free one.

"Look at you! You fully grew into yourself. Will you really be twenty-five in another month? I feel so old."

"You're not old at all," said Alice, feeling her smile grow warm. Fiona had always been the most cordial member of the family, sparkling in conversation and blithe about anything demanding depth. The rainbow of their family's plain prism.

She waved away Alice's compliment, but it hadn't been a kind lie. Her aunt appeared unchanged, with the same gold bangles marching up her wrists and the same taste in olive-colored clothing that matched her eyes. That green gaze scrutinized Alice while Fiona pulled her to a nearby couch.

Potted plants surrounded them with wide, waxy leaves, offering the illusion of privacy, and Fiona started in as soon as they sat on the white, overstuffed cushions. "You're living close to your father again, aren't you? He said you moved in about a month ago."

Alice nodded. "A house in Calico Creek."

"Never heard of it."

"It's a small town about forty-five minutes from here. Up in the foothills."

"You're right in the forest? My God, it sounds horrible. I remember trying a cabin in the Sierras one year as a summer vacation. As soon as we drove up, we saw a bear rooting in the woodshed. It only got worse from there." Then Fiona shot the nearest waiter a significant glance. He responded obediently, offering his tray of champagne.

Alice kept her half-empty glass, already feeling flushed in the cheeks from the warm, stuffy air. She found herself wondering if Colton had yet caught something, ripping open its pelt to get at the tender meat beneath. They never had problems with pests; no raccoon or bobcat wished to linger near a wolf's home.

After a sip, Fiona pivoted into a new topic. "What have you been doing since coming back here? Tom's mentioned how he wants you to find a more suitable career than the fine arts. I think it's horrible that he'll cut off his money unless you go back to school, but my brother always has been stiff-necked about that."

"It's only fair. It's his money, not mine."

Fiona regarded her. "You're always so agreeable about things. You have been since you were a child. I specifically remember how, on your fifth birthday, the bakery made a mistake with the cake. It was chocolate beneath the frosting when everyone knew yellow was your favorite. But you just sat there, looking at your slice. No sign of tears or an oncoming tantrum. All you did was pick up your fork and start eating it. I almost checked you for angel wings right then and there."

Alice nodded, remembering that and the reason behind it as well. Even as she sipped at the champagne, keeping her pleasant expression fixed in place, a memory slid into her mind.

It was the spitting of hot butter that always came to her first. A frenzied, spiteful sound that made her want to cover her ears. Then the muttering of her mother, ominous and fitful like a cat's growl. She was out of sight in the kitchen, busy cooking something. Something special for Alice, she'd said.

Alice now shook her head, trying to chase away the rest before it enveloped her thoughts like a fog. But then the smell of cigarette smoke drifted in through some nearby windows, encouraging more of the memory, drawing her into the haze that swirled around her mother as she came over to where Alice sat at the table. A cigarette hung heavy in her mouth as she shoved a plate of scrambled eggs in front of Alice, eyes distracted. "Eat it all. It's important to have a big breakfast."

As Alice blinked at the eggs, their yellow bright against the blue glaze of the plate, her face wrinkled in disgust. They looked wrong, all runny and glistening instead of dry and bumpy like when her father made them. There were even bits of eggshell poking up from the curds. And it was *lunchtime*. Daddy always gave her a sandwich and goldfish crackers for lunch.

When she made no move to eat, her mother blew smoke from her nostrils like an angry bull snorting out a breath. "Go on. I made it for you."

"I don't wanna."

"*Eat it.*"

"No."

Then her mother grabbed the plate and flung it to the floor. Ceramic shattered, leaving behind yellow streaks of egg and plate shards jagged as teeth. The sharp noise made Alice jump, made her face scrunch up again—this time in tears.

Her mother was also crying, both of their voices rising in wordless shrieks. When her mother smacked the tabletop with both hands, Alice shrank back, hiccuping for breath as her mother leaned in and screamed inches from her face.

"You ungrateful, snot-filled brat. Why can't you just do what you're told?"

Then she fled the room, and only the smoke from her cigarette lingered as Alice hunched into a ball, hoping to shrink herself enough to disappear entirely.

But she couldn't, and forever afterwards carefully ate anything set before her. To refuse something made people mad or sad. To say what she thought caused problems. It was much easier to just follow along, and smile, and pretend everything was fine.

For awhile, she believed it was the best way to get through life. And then she had met...

A laugh cut through Alice's distracted thoughts, one that froze her expression. It sounded again, and now her hand broke into a sweat against the champagne glass. She knew it, that laugh. Once upon a time, it had stirred the hair by her ear in the sweet, dark hours of night, and she had craved it as she had craved nothing else. A soft chuckle, reluctant and all the more likable for it. Throaty instead of shrill. Entrancing.

It was Magdalene's laugh.

Alice's gaze darted among the nearest clusters of people. It wasn't possible. Magdalene was dead and she had seen the corpse herself. She must have misheard. It must have come from a stranger. A weird coincidence brought on by her night-long dwelling of the past and those—

Her thoughts faded at the sight of a woman standing a few yards away with her back to her. A sharp-angled body dressed in sleek black, hair that was the same cut and color... Head tilted at that slight angle that Magdalene had always used when she listened to someone but not very closely...

Panic prickled behind Alice's ribs, as cutting as a childhood fear, and she suddenly needed to see this woman's face in the way of looking beneath the bed to make sure nothing hid there. Once she did, embarrassment would burn through her for questioning whether the stranger could have been Magdalene. Yet right at that moment, no amount of rational thought could have convinced her to look away and feel safe. It was so *uncanny*...

The chiming of a spoon against glass startled her. Fiona made a pleased noise and straightened in her seat. "Time to hear Tom make an awful toast while surrounded by family. You better hurry up and join them."

"I think I'll just..." Alice craned her neck, trying to find that woman again, but she had seemingly disappeared into thin air.

Then Fiona caught her by the arm and drew her up from the couch. Not wanting to rip herself free like a sulky toddler, Alice let herself be led along to where people had gathered on the deck. Lanterns strung through the air glittered on her father and stepmother as they stood in the center. Fleur, Alice's twelve-year-old sister, was there as well, reading on her phone until Denise noticed and murmured something to her. A baleful glance was the girl's only resistance before she put it away and looked up with a fixed smile.

Fiona stopped at the crowd's edge, leaving Alice to walk alone to her father's side. As he smiled at her, she responded with one of her own but still couldn't meet his gaze. And when his arm settled around her shoulders, she remained stiff, looking out at the guests. She didn't know what they saw in return.

They stood there, all of them, beaming under the lights as if the very shadows couldn't reach them. Yet Alice wished with all her heart for one of those shadows to appear, the one with sharp fangs and a lolling tongue. The one who slipped into her bed as silently as a hunter and tasted at every part of her body as if nothing else would ever sate him. As her father's words slid past her unheard, she pressed her tongue against her own blunt, pitiful teeth and remembered how she had once run at that shadow's side, moonlight to his night.

It was just after midnight when Alice returned home. Already, she breathed a little easier to be in land that was wild but for pockets of civilization left over from historical gold mining. Pumas prowled abandoned tunnels and streams smoothed away signs of placer mining. Sugar pines towered above abandoned shacks half-eaten by scrubby undergrowth. Timeworn outcroppings of limestone had lost their scars from being bitten into by pickaxe and shovel. Nature slowly reclaimed itself.

The crisp air of an autumn night brought prickles to Alice's skin as she stepped out of her car, but she relished in it. A few kicks of her feet and her high heels were cast aside. Her sore toes wriggled at their new freedom even while she ripped her hair free of its bun, suddenly impatient with herself. She left her clutch in the car and her keys beneath the fronds of a potted fern. The forest waited and so did another, and she went to them both.

She walked carefully against the fallen pine needles and loose earth, breath quickening in excitement. He would find her before she found him; he always did. An owl screeched somewhere in the distance. The trees sighed. The waxing moon hardly penetrated the thickness of the woods, and some of that innate human fear of being alone in the dark touched her. Alice stopped by a fallen tree, the bulk of its massive trunk an instinctive comfort.

It was as far as she got before hands grabbed her from behind. The shock of it drove her to gasp, but already she recognized the possessive way those rough fingers moved along her body, and she giggled even before a tongue licked the curve of her ear.

"Colton," she breathed, twisting around to look.

She could never grow used to him, and even now reached out in wonder. Dirt scraped beneath her fingers; blood coated his jaw. He reeked of fur and sweat and musk. There was nothing of the refined about him, nothing in common with the cufflinks and cologne of the men at the party.

She had a heartbeat to feel his arm snake around her, one large hand sliding past the small of her back to grab at the heavy flesh of her ass, and then his fingers were pressing up between the cleft of her cheeks. She jerked at the pressure, hips instinctively arching in response, and grabbed at his shoulders just before he lifted her up. The hard muscles of his chest and stomach rubbed against the thin silk of her dress as their noses brushed.

The weak moonlight wasn't enough to pick out his features, but when she locked her legs around him and breathed his name again, she caught the way his eyes glowed in response.

Then he was... No, not kissing. That was too tame a term for it. His mouth *devoured* hers, hungry and hard and impatient. The tang of iron spread over her tongue. He had hunted. She nuzzled forward to take in more of his savagery, savoring those sharp teeth and that sweet tongue. How could pink champagne compare to this?

He teased the breath away from her until she had to break off, panting against his mouth. "What was it?"

"Hare." His voice was dark and as rough as the rest of him.

Then he kissed her again, briefly. "You had caramel."

"Yes."

He was fully erect, now, heavy against her lower stomach, and she wriggled impatiently, desperate to feel him *in* her. He nipped along the sensitive skin on her neck, stoking her need with every passing second. Her fingernails were now scratching at his shoulders while she rocked her hips again, knowing he would feel how wet she already was. Hoping it would be enough to draw out his frenzy.

He moved with that predator's quickness, pinning her face-down against the fallen trunk, leaving her to pant helplessly while rough bark scraped at the front of her dress. The sensation of his hands pushing the fabric up past her hips left her hissing his name, and he rumbled in reply while drawing her panties down. Cold air rushed against her aching cunt a moment before a hot tongue licked her slick seam, and her voice rose.

She gasped out breaths there in the dark, the inability to touch him turning her eagerness into something agonizing. He knew it and teased, straightening up to rub his erect cock against her spread thighs, letting her feel its weight against the cleft of her cheeks. When she whined wordlessly, the head nudged at her swollen folds, just enough to tantalize. Then his hand slowly ran up her spine, as if marveling at the softness of her bared skin. She arched into his touch, her own hands digging into the moss on the trunk, and at that, his fingers tangled in her hair and he thrust in all way, drawing her voice into a yowl. Caught in his grip, her next breath came out as a laugh, and she met every rock of his hips with one of her own.

Hot muscle stretched against her exposed body; dirt and sweat scraped against her own clean, perfumed skin, leaving it muddied. A hand slid around her throat, pressing against the tender flesh just enough to hint at a threat. Like catching sight of eyes glowing in the dark. He always tested her, trying to see what she liked and what she flinched from. She only hummed, wanting her pleasure to vibrate against his fingers. She loved his teeth as much as his tongue, and when she hummed again, his touch turned feather-light, tracing the pulse pounding against her skin.

He had enough will to drop his hand to the fallen trunk and brace himself as the rhythm of his breath changed. His hips now jolted hers, spearing her with each thrust until she was reduced to shuddering gasps. His mouth found the side of her neck, and then she was caught by his teeth, caught by his weight while his cock bucked deep inside her. He growled through his climax, teeth digging in, one hand tight against the flesh of her hip. A few breaths, and he shifted against her, fingers sliding over her hip and pushing into her slick folds. The rasp of those calluses against her clit ignited her own release, and she panted while he licked the marks of his teeth from her skin.

Her dress was ruined. There were leaves in her hair and the bangles on her wrist had slipped off, lost among wood beetles and ferns. She wasn't even sure what had happened to her panties.

She had never felt more alive.

Later, Alice settled herself in bed with the feral creature that was her lover, curling against him as he dozed. Her fingers were now gentle as they stroked his thick, dark hair, finding burrs that had been overlooked in her earlier desperation. When she began plucking them free, he gave her a sleepy growl.

"I should start checking you for ticks, too. October is when they really come out."

"Didn't get any. I'd know it."

"I'm still looking you over tomorrow morning."

That drew another rumble from him, but she could tell his warning growls from ones that were all bluff, and knew he'd enjoy the extra attention even if he'd never admit it.

Wolf's wife. The words rang through her head in a sneering voice, a familiar voice. Magdalene had once spat those syllables at her like poison, the beautiful pelt clutched in her hands as she threatened it with the nearby fire. Alice still remembered how the fur had bristled at the tips from the heat. The memory often burrowed into nightmares until she woke up shaking, her jaws locked shut even as her dream-self's screaming rang through her head. Dreams were supposed to offer the impossible, and yet she never managed to save the pelt from being flung into the flames.

The feeling of a hand sliding up her spine startled Alice. Her fingers stiffened against the hair beneath them, and she realized Colton's eyes were open. Watching her.

"You miss running with me at nights." Then his thumb stroked over her cheek and came away wet with tears.

It shamed her still, that painful day when she had watched the pelt blacken in the fire, unable to save it. She nuzzled close until she couldn't see his face. "She *took* it from me. I agreed to everything else in some way, but not that. It was the first time I ever fought against her, and I couldn't do anything."

Then she waited, unsure if he would respond. They had never spoken about the loss of the pelt, or what had happened afterward. Colton knew Magdalene had burned it while making Alice watch. Alice knew the savage teeth that had mauled Magdalene to death had been his. Why discuss it? He always preferred actions to words, and she hadn't wanted to think about it at all.

Yet it wasn't guilt that had driven her to silence during these past months, but a desperation to move forward. To forget how she had loved Magdalene so very much, burning herself in that bright, caustic flame, always complicit in giving up more and more of herself in the hopes that it would be enough. And then—too much given away, too much burned to ash, and what remained was a weedy sort of devotion. A weariness with rotting roots.

How could she ever explain how that—not Magdalene's grisly death, and not the fact that she slept in the murderer's bed every night—was what filled her with shame?

Colton's voice rumbled against her. "So the pelt is gone. It was a stolen thing, a witch's empty dream. You brought it to life, Alice, not the other way around. There's wildness in you. Even the woman couldn't stamp it out."

She laughed, a whisper of breath against his neck. "I've never heard you say Magdalene's name, not even once."

"You always know who I mean. And you know what I mean right now." His hand slid along her back again, soothing the tension in the muscles there. "You lick blood from my teeth and giggle like it's chocolate. Even if you can't run as a wolf, it's still there in you."

They were simple words, soothing in their very bluntness. Her grief didn't leave, but its edges dulled enough for her to relax, his heartbeat strong and steady against her ear.

Later, just as she drifted toward sleep, Magdalene's laugh rang at the edge of her hearing. Alice jerked as if she'd been slapped, too muzzy-headed to even properly respond, but then Colton's arm tightened around her and the heat of his body settled more firmly against hers. She fell limp again, losing herself in him. The last thing she was aware of was the lingering tang of iron on her tongue.

CHAPTER TWO

REOPENED WOUNDS

The day began with a sunrise cold and grey, wind shaking the sides of the little house and making the surrounding pines sigh. Alice stirred first, shifting against the warm pressure of Colton's body. Daylight revealed as much dried mud on her as there was on him, and where the sheets weren't dirtied, they were shredded. A beast in her bed, and she knew just how to rouse him.

She nuzzled down the hard lines of his body, quickly finding his morning erection. It was sticky from the dried remnants of last night's rutting and overwhelmingly musky. The first lap of her tongue against the head drew a growl from him but nothing else. His heavy sack was just as filthy, and she mouthed at it without hesitation, lips curling around him in a wicked grin when she felt him wake up. By the time his hand found her hair, she was licking the wrinkled skin there smooth, feeling his balls twitch against her eager mouth.

This was different than the primal domination of last night. This was lazy, tender, his fingers tracing over the curves of her body as if to memorize them. He knew how to be wicked, himself, occasionally tweaking one of her nipples to make her gasp against him. Every time his balls flexed, her mouth followed, sucking at first one shape and then the other.

When a growl slipped into his breathing, she shifted enough to rub her cheek against his straining cock. "No ticks there, anyway."

Even as his fingers tightened in her hair, keeping her in place, his gaze remained relaxed, amused. "If you think you're done now..."

She smiled against his cock, feeling it twitch in response. "Not at all. But your shift starts in half an hour and you haven't even showered."

He lathered her hair with shampoo while she sucked him clean, tongue polishing every inch of his shaft. Even while his hips thrust against her face, he was careful not to let soap suds trail into her eyes. It was absurd. It was playful, something that still surprised her about him.

Afterward, while he dressed for work, she pulled on a robe to cook something he could eat one-handed while driving. This wasn't the first time they'd done this, and she had perfected making a fried egg sandwich in under ten minutes. Smoked gouda to keep the bacon in place, tomato and lettuce to cut the richness, and mustard on the toasted bread to brighten it all. She had just finished wrapping the sandwich in parchment

paper to keep it from dripping when he came out of the
bedroom, shrugging on his coat.

She met him at the front door, licking a trace of melted
cheese from one thumb.

"Make one for yourself?" he said. He already sounded
distant, all attention on checking his pockets for his keys.

"You already gave me breakfast."

His focus snapped back to her, and she bit back a laugh at
the thunderclap of surprise on his face. Her lewdness always
startled him—the hunter met with something that enjoyed
being hunted. Then his eyes took on a hunger that stirred a
sweet ache between her hips, and she didn't resist when he
pulled her in for a long, hard kiss. When they broke off, she was
panting and he had to rearrange himself through his jeans.

"Minx," he said, sounding unaffected.

She just smiled, handing over the sandwich. "Be safe. And
come back to me."

Alone, she started the coffee pot and set about stripping the
bed. Colton was hard on sheets, and she noted ripped areas
that would need to be mended once the mud had been washed
off. The heady aroma of brewing coffee drew her back to the
kitchen, where she slipped a leftover fried egg onto the last slice
of bread and ate it in bites while cleaning the pan and counter.
She'd have to make another loaf. There was also black fur
threatening to invade the kitchen; in some ways, living with a
man who changed into a wolf invited a mixture of the
mundane and the bizarre. He left hair everywhere.

Such tedious tasks, and yet she enjoyed living like this, with the domestic lull of the day balancing the wild abandon of night. Wolf's wife, indeed.

She had cleaned half the hardwood floors when a knock came at the door. Alice glanced up, toes flexing against the wood as it sounded again, hard and impatient. Odd, that. A mile of forest separated the house from the highway. If someone had come here, it was to see her.

Mop still in hand, she approached the door and peered through the spyhole. Her breath choked in her throat when she saw who waited on the other side. Darby Reeves. One of Magdalene's writer friends.

Panic shuddered through Alice, bringing with it an urge to slam the deadbolt in place and slink away. Her past was something that needed to stay buried, not be upturned into fresh earth. Even so, her hand hesitated against the lock. Was hiding truly the better answer? Darby had come over for a reason. Would it be more dangerous to hear what it was or to remain ignorant?

To live with a wild beast is to take on both its boldness and its wariness. To understand when one is the hunter or the hunted. Better to flash threatening teeth or to slip away to safety? Both have their uses. Yes, through beasts, one soon learns the wisdom of survival.

When Darby knocked a third time, Alice acted, heart pounding as she opened the door. "Hello, Darby. It's been a while."

Lips red as a warning twisted in a sneer. "Eight months, to be exact. It would've been only six if you had gone to Magdalene's funeral. But you didn't."

Harsh words, angry words. The type meant to club at a conscience. Alice was surprised that she didn't flinch. Her voice even remained steady as she said, "We broke up earlier that day. I was mourning over her before everyone else, if you want to be *exact* about it."

That crimson mouth straightened out again, and the rest of Darby's face creased in sudden wariness. She hadn't expected that answer. She hadn't expected a fight.

Alice was painfully aware of how meek and colorless she must have appeared to Magdalene's friends, and wondered what other differences Darby might now see in her. Whatever they were, they left the other girl tongue-tied and scuffing her combat boots against the doormat. Obviously, she wished for Alice to ask why she'd come.

But Alice had learned a few tricks from Colton, and the effectiveness of silence was one of them. She waited, patience itself while Darby squirmed against the unfriendly weather. The other girl had dressed for urban traveling, wearing an artfully ripped-up jacket, a mesh shirt, and thin pleather leggings, none of which offered protection against the gloom of looming trees. When wind howled against the house, her shoulders flinched.

Finally, Darby scoffed and gave in. "Are we just going to stare at each other, or are you going to let me in?"

"I haven't decided. It's pretty galling that you showed up here after everything you've said about me."

"Shouldn't have Googled yourself if you didn't want to know about it."

Alice's fingers flexed against the door as she considered slamming it in the other girl's face. The media frenzy over Magdalene's death had meant Magdalene had been everywhere and unavoidable—as had Darby, who had been constantly interviewed about her. Dear Darby, one of the last people to see Magdalene Bishop in her final weeks, and so someone who had taken on the roles of immaculate witness and anguished cryptographer for the late author's last, mysterious actions. And my, how she had relished her duties, spinning narratives for journalists that twisted facts into something as fictional as one of her steampunk novels.

Alice still shook with rage if she allowed herself to think about it. Despite all she had gone through, she was now labeled as the selfish lover who had used Magdalene, the rich bitch who had drifted into artistic circles without having the talent to reach them on her own. A parasite feeding off someone else's genius. It was Darby herself who had referred to her as a heartworm. As if Magdalene had even had a heart by the end. Perhaps she'd been born without one; Alice still couldn't decide on that.

"Why are you here?" said Alice, already tired of facing the other girl and the memories stirred up by her presence.

"I want to talk inside. It's fucking cold out here."

Even now, Alice was unwilling to ply petty cruelty toward another, and after a final, grudging moment, she opened the door wider and stepped aside. "Do you want coffee?"

Darby appraised everything in sight while Alice led her into the kitchen, her gaze sharp and bright in the way of writers absorbing every detail as potential story fodder. Silence simmered between them, broken only by the clink of ceramic against the countertop as Alice took down a second mug and poured steaming coffee into it. She didn't bother asking how Darby liked it, remembering well enough to get out the milk.

As she added a few glugs to the mug, she said, "How's Rob?"

"Fine. You think the death of his childhood friend would have fucked him up, but he doesn't care." Then Darby settled into one of the chairs at the kitchen table. "Do you care what happened to her?"

It was a question Alice had long wrestled with. Every time she thought back to the sight of Magdalene's mutilated body, horror shuddered through her. It had been a vicious death and she wasn't enough of a coward to pretend otherwise. Still, she sometimes wondered what she herself might have looked like if Magdalene's savagings had been teeth on flesh instead of words in minds.

Did that excuse Colton's actions? Or her own lack of guilt? She didn't know. All she felt sure about was that not one ounce of glee filled her over what had happened. When weariness ebbed like waves pulling back from the shore, what remained sparkling on the foam-flecked sand of her thoughts was a bright and painful relief. The finality of something ending, of something being gone for good.

"When I think about it, all I can feel is tiredness," she said, finally. "I was tired when I left her, and I was tired when I found out she'd died. She was brilliant at writing. She seemed otherworldly at times. And she was very hard to live with."

"Sounds selfish to me. She dies and all you can think about is yourself."

Something in the words drew Alice's attention, and for the first time, she truly looked at the other girl. Darby's skin, always pale, now looked bloodless. The dark circles beneath her eyes were as ugly and purple as bruises, and the shape of her mouth, always so smug, now crooked toward bitterness. She looked unwell, as though nights were sleepless and days were bleak. She looked like she lived with grief.

Unsure of what to say, Alice brought over the steaming mugs in silence.

Darby took hers with a nod, still looking around. "Really going for the homespun wifey thing, huh? Checkered curtains, watercolor paintings..."

"They're made from coffee." If she was going to be sneered at, it might as well have been over the right things.

Darby caught the implication. "You did them?"

Alice watched her gaze travel over the framed pieces again, taking in the landscapes and still lifes of flowers and fruit with renewed interest.

"Who's the guy?" said Darby, pointing at the one nearest to them. It was Alice's favorite painting of Colton, where she'd gotten his eyes just right.

"Someone I know." Alice kept her voice light, but her reluctant manners hardened into pure hostility at the possibility that Darby would now prod at and insult Colton. It was time to get to the point. "Why are you here, Darby?"

Darby wrinkled her nose at the cup of coffee and pushed it aside. "I'm writing a biography on Magdalene. I want to show the world what it lost."

A book. Of course. "Why you?"

"Why not me? Now that she's dead, it can only be a secondhand narrative, anyway. And... I know what she went through with her art. I know what it's like, aching to write while the words stick in your heart until it suffocates. I can't think of anything worse than to have your life end like that—a blank fucking page. People pity her. She deserves more."

And with that, the traces of grief on Darby's face made complete sense. "You loved her."

Darby raised her chin. "Sure, and I'm not ashamed of it."

Well, and how was that shocking? Magdalene had woven people's thoughts and feelings into paeans of praise for her with as much skill and care as she had put into her literary efforts. In that past dark winter, when she had gone off with Darby and Rob and had left Alice to wait alone in the cabin, how hard would it have been to coax Darby's heart to beat to the rhythm of hers?

A new feeling wormed its way into Alice: reluctant sympathy. "You think she loved you."

"She *did* love me." Darby's tone dared her to challenge that. When Alice didn't, she added, "Her story needs to be told, and that's why I'm doing this. I'm willing to be her defender in death since no one was in life."

Alice sipped at her coffee to quell the laugh that wanted to come out. What kind of bullshit had Magdalene told her in their time spent together? When Alice felt sure her mouth wouldn't twist into a bitter smile, she said, "And how do I figure into this? Do you want an interview?"

"No, I don't need one."

Something about that pricked at the edges of Alice's mind. The first breath of danger, so faint that it could be doubted.

Before she could respond, Darby sighed. "Fuck it, I'll just put it out there. You own the cabin where she spent the final months of her life. You own the property next to the area of the river where she planned to drown herself. Where she was... Found."

Alice watched the muscles in her throat spasm, as if the word hurt too much to say. Suicide could be seen as darkly romantic. An animal attack, though, horrified with its ugliness. It reminded one that a body wasn't a vessel for a tortured soul but instead simple meat that could be torn apart and eaten.

"The area where she was mauled to death," said Alice, quietly. The words gave her no pleasure but no pain, either.

Darby winced. "Yeah. So I want to visit it—the cabin. Spend a few nights inside to see what it's like. I need your permission to stay there."

"No." The word flashed out of Alice's mouth. The cabin was as ugly to her as a scar and just as tender. The idea of anyone walking around in it left her feeling sick. Trying to sound calmer, she repeated, "No, I won't give my permission."

Darby didn't look deterred. She didn't even look surprised. Rather, she smiled, a slow one that said, *I knew you'd say that.* "I think you will."

Then Darby reached into her messenger bag and pulled out a thick sheaf of paper. With one glance, Alice knew it was a printed manuscript, and once more that sense of danger crept over her. When Darby slapped it onto the table between them, she couldn't keep from flinching.

"Go ahead and take it. It's your copy to read. I marked places you'll find *really* interesting."

Alice kept her expression neutral while flipping to the first red arrow label highlighting whatever it was that Darby wished her to see. She scanned over a few sentences, breath growing shallow at the mention of her mother's name. When she looked up dumbly, Darby was already pulling a red folder from her bag and handing it over. It was stuffed so full that paper stuck out from the edges.

"Just so you can't say I'm making shit up."

The folder contained newspaper articles, ones that looked printed out from archives. Headlines dug at old, half-remembered memories like a terrier at a rat hole.

Woman missing in Eldorado National Forest.

Ten years later, Ruth Corrigan remains unfound...

Numbly, Alice thumbed through more pages and found what looked like medical reports. The name on them was Franny Harford—Alice's grandmother. Darby had probed deep into her family's past.

"How did you get these?" The words slipped out of her, too shocked to sound anything but weak.

"Why does that matter? I have them, and I used them."

Alice's stomach twisted then, and she shoved it all away from her.

Darby pushed it back. "Keep them. They're yours. I also made digital copies in case you try to break into my house and steal the originals."

"Do you really think I'm that crazy?"

"After what I found out about your family? Sure. Magdalene mentioned you were pretty fucked up, but I didn't realize how bad until I looked into things. Your grandmother used to stick pins in herself, did you know that? And she'd put leeches on your mom as a kid. Your mom wasn't much better; she liked to burn herself with cigarettes. Did you know she was hospitalized three times?"

"And it's all in the book for everyone to see," said Alice, clutching at her mug to keep her fingers from trembling.

"Sure. Otherwise, people wouldn't understand where you came from. Right now you're just a trust fund baby. After this comes out, people are going to *really* see you."

She didn't have to look up to know that Darby's expression had changed. Triumph radiated from her, and Alice hated how helpless she felt in response. Even Magdalene had avoided writing Alice's past into a book, at least until the very end of their relationship. And when Alice had found out, she had finally snapped, forgetting fear and familiarity and instead seeking out Colton in that wild, uncaring forest, the wolf pelt giving her anger teeth and claws.

Yet she didn't feel fierce now. She felt panicked, and bewildered, and ready to cry rather than bite.

Darby's voice slid around her heart like a garrote, cutting in with each word. "This is just me scraping the surface. You think you were treated unfairly in the media when Magdalene died? This will fuck up your life for good."

"You're blackmailing me into giving you permission to visit the cabin, is that it?" God, she had even slipped back into asking for confirmation, as if her words alone couldn't possibly be right without another to correct or approve them.

She looked up in time to catch Darby's smile. "If you give me access to the cabin, I'll let you have the final say on anything about you that goes into the book. We'll do up a contract and everything. If you refuse, I'll reveal every dirty secret you have and make you look like the biggest bitch alive."

Alice's gaze dropped back to her coffee.

Darby gave her a breath of silence before saying, "Well?"

Alice didn't want to answer. She wanted to claw Darby's face off. Tremors of rage and panic rolled through her. To have her sordid family history mutilated and restitched for a reader's hungry eyes... Or to lash her willpower to another's, something she'd sworn never to do again.

"I hope you're not thinking that I won't go through with it. Or that I don't know anything really embarrassing. Free example: I found out you became a bedwetter for a few years after your mom disappeared. Is that why you're obsessed with cleaning everything in sight like you're a '50s housewife? This manuscript is only a first draft. I could imply that in the rewrites."

The final word had barely left Darby's mouth when Alice threw the mug of scalding coffee at the wall beside the other girl's head. Ceramic shattered in bright, brittle violence. Darby's eyes widened—but not in fear. Glee filled her face as dark trails ran down the white tile.

"That's definitely going in. Your mom liked breaking things, too."

"Get out." Alice was still too close to unthinking reactions to keep the growl from her voice.

The other girl stood from her chair casually, as if she'd been the one to decide it was time to leave. "I'll let you have a few days to think things over. It'll give me more time to look up your loverboy."

Darby then glanced at the painting in a wordless threat of how she had already figured out that much about Colton.

Alice should have said nothing. The last thing Darby needed was more information, no matter what type. But a smile crept over her face before she could stop it, the hot, feral one that sprang into life whenever she tasted blood on him. And when she spoke, her voice held as much malice as Darby's. "He won't be afraid of you."

For the first time, Darby's confidence faltered. Something—doubt, perhaps?—flashed in her eyes, and her fingers briefly tightened against the strap of her bag. But she recovered all too quickly. "Even if he isn't, you are."

There was no way to respond to that without lying, and so Alice fell silent while seeing the other girl to the door. She watched from the porch as Darby got in her car and then rolled down the window. "I know you'll run to Daddy and his lawyers. That's okay. I already talked to mine. Sorry, Alice, but you can't mop up your past like it never happened."

It took everything Alice had to keep her chin held high as the car started up and eased away on the rough-cut road. Once the taillights disappeared among the dark trunks of the trees, though, she started shivering and couldn't stop.

For the longest time afterward, she sat there on the steps while her fingers ached with the faint memory of claws.

CHAPTER THREE

THE TENDERNESS OF WOLVES

An hour after Darby's visit, Alice's trembling had dwindled to a dull headache that throbbed behind her eyes. Probably, she should have been looking into lawyers to see if Darby's threat had a solid foundation. Probably, she should have thumbed through that damned manuscript to see what else had been put in there.

Instead, she shoved the armful of papers into the back of a closet, piling them onto a few packing boxes and covering them up with muck boots. Then she cleaned. The mop slapped against the floor. The bristles of the scrub brush tore at the sink. Even the soft dust cloth hissed as it wiped over surfaces. A fury of domesticity against the sudden intrusion of the unknown.

Throughout it all, Darby's words filled her head, uncovering memories in the way of a sledgehammer cracking apart cement to reveal worms writhing in the forgotten earth beneath. Alice remembered broken plates and the ragged note in her mother's voice whenever she yelled. How her body would tense just before she exploded. The strange things she would fixate on... Like the wristwatch Alice's father had always worn.

It hadn't been anything special, but from the dulled leather of the band and the muted gleam of the metal hands, anyone could tell it was old, loved, and depended upon. Alice remembered how, one day, her father had come out of the bedroom with a puzzled frown, and when he'd picked her up and kissed her goodbye, his wrist had been bare. Later, Alice had been strapped in her booster seat and dabbing chubby, careful fingers into blue and yellow paint, pleased with how she could make streaks of green appear on the paper like magic, when her mother appeared and casually set the wristwatch on the nearby kitchen counter.

There was a hammer in her other hand, and as she raised it, aiming the heavy, rusted iron of the head at the watch, she growled, "Always ticking. Tick, tick, ticking. Even at night, it never stops."

Then she swung the hammer down, and a great *crack* echoed throughout the room, startling Alice enough to send her hands jerking along the paper and leaving shocked strokes of blue.

Alice didn't remember how her father had reacted after finding his destroyed watch, or her mother's explanation for doing it, if there had even been one. What remained burned in her mind were those beautiful little gears left crushed and still, and the cracked face that had popped free. Her father's watch, something he wore every day. Now just a broken, useless thing.

Alice realized her eyesight had blurred over from the memory. Even so, she continued scrubbing at the sink, the bristles of the brush vicious in a way she never allowed herself to be.

A pearl of fear lived deep within, polished throughout the years as her uncertain child's heart had hardened into a weary adult's: that she would be a source of misery to whatever loved ones she had. Contrary to what Darby claimed, she had tried so hard for Magdalene even once her adoration faded into something tired and weedy. Her own complaints—smothered. Her angry words—choked back. All that self-binding rooted in the fear that if she ever opened her mouth to scream at her lover, her mother's voice would come out.

Something ran through her maternal line. The gentle phrase for it was a history of mental illness, but Alice had learned a little more after inheriting her grandmother's cabin. Wolf pelts that came alive, Colton's dark hints about what he had seen while working odd jobs for Franny Harford... Witchhood ran through the women of Alice's family, and she didn't know what that meant. Madness, certainly, from what she remembered of her mother. But how did it begin? From birth? Did it creep up with the years as the heart toughened with experiences, failures, love found and love lost? What sparked that slow spiral down, and had it already happened in Alice's head?

The previous night flashed through her thoughts like lightning. How she'd heard Magdalene's laugh. How she'd even believed for a split second that she'd seen her. What had *that* been? Painful memories resurfacing, or the first hints of her mind turning as treacherous as her mother's?

Beasts have instincts to guide their senses. A sound like a predator's footstep will send them flying. A scent on the wind will pull them into patient stalking. They are unburdened by thoughts too self-aware, by brains too painfully absorbed with their own existence. They may jump at shadows, but never will they question whether those shadows are a real threat or a false scare. In the quick, brutal life of a wild thing, doubt holds no sway.

Eventually, a familiar noise broke through Alice's frantic cleaning. A truck's engine rumbled to a stop in the driveway. She blinked, one cramped hand frozen against where it had been scrubbing at the streaks of soot on the hearth. Colton was already back? A glance out the window revealed a sky dark with dusk. Hours had somehow slipped past.

The scrape of a key in the lock roused her further, and suddenly she realized how it would all appear. A house that breathed chilly air. Laundry left to mold in the washer. A forgotten batch of bread dough in a kitchen that had nothing else except dregs of coffee.

She tried scrambling up off hands and knees, but her muscles had gone stiff and sore from all the work put to them, and she only managed to push herself upright before Colton stepped inside.

"Alice?"

She couldn't see him, not while he was still in the short hallway leading from the front door, but there was an abruptness to his voice that stoked her panic.

Words streamed out of her mouth as she snatched at some kindling to light it. "I'm sorry! I lost track of time. I was cleaning and I just..."

The match shook in her tired hand, refusing to catch, and she was still crouched on the hearth when he appeared, now silent.

Shame kept her head down and drove her voice high. "I can have soup ready in half an hour. And I'll make biscuits. Biscuits cook quickly. I—"

Hands caught hers. Stilled them. The warm, callused fingers against her own drew her a little away from the panic, enough so that she could look up at him. He was studying her knuckles, scraped and reddened from bumping brick and wood.

As his thumb lightly brushed her raw skin, he said, "You always clean like this when you're upset. On the date your mother disappeared, you scrubbed the walls from floor to fucking ceiling."

That had been back in the city, in the sleek apartment that had been a place of limbo for her and Colton while they'd searched for something in forestland. He'd caught her straining on a ladder, frustrated that the double-paned window in the ceiling had trapped a layer of dust that couldn't be reached from either side.

Alice sighed, unresisting when he coaxed the kindling from her grip. "I didn't realize I was that predictable."

"Something happened. Your fear is in every room."

After a hesitation, she nodded.

"Tell me while I build a fire."

"But what about dinner? You probably haven't eaten since the sandwich this morning."

His eyes gleamed with amusement. "Alice. I've gone two weeks without food. Skipping a meal won't kill me. Unless you're hungry?"

She wasn't, but wanted some wine and said so. Her hands clutched at the glass while Colton lit the kindling in quick, efficient movements. His silences held depth, complexity. They could be tasted in the air as easily as she could taste the sweet white on her tongue.

This one was borne of patience, but after a large gulp that drained half her glass, the words came out of her in a rush. "One of Magdalene's friends came by."

He looked over. There was no trace of surprise on his face.

"You smelled her in here, didn't you?" Her fingers fidgeted with the stem of the glass before she added, "She and her husband were the ones Magdalene stayed with. You know, during those two weeks when we had the cabin to ourselves. I don't know if you ever actually saw her."

"Sure, outside the grocery store. Pink hair. Laughed like a horse."

She blinked, startled. "I thought you were busy shopping."

"The store has windows."

"And you just happened to notice me."

"I notice everything about you, Alice." The rasp in his voice never went away, but sometimes it grew tender. Like a hot tongue against a bruise.

It brought a smile to her face, but she didn't relax until he settled next to her. As flames crackled over the logs, she dropped her head against the hollow of his throat, her free hand working at the buttons of his flannel shirt until she could stroke at the hair dusting the hard muscles of his chest. He smelled like cut wood and sweat from his shift at the sawmill, and she loved it.

In return, he pushed up her sweater, baring her back and the sore muscles there. As his fingers eased away the last knots of tension, he said, "What did she want?"

"She's writing a biography on Magdalene." A lingering shiver ran through her, and then she gave in and let all her fears unspool. "It'll include her final weeks, so Darby wants to see the cabin. Stay in it. She's looked up things about me that she can put into the book just to make sure I agree to it."

"What happened with your mother." It wasn't a question.

"And details about my grandmother, too." Then Alice smiled a little and looked up at him. "But she didn't find out that she was a witch."

He didn't smile back. "Fucking blackmail. No wonder you panicked."

"I didn't give her an answer. I don't need to. There's nothing she can do that hasn't already happened to me."

They were words that she thought would be reassuring, but Colton's eyes held a peculiar flatness that appeared whenever he calculated at something.

A little alarmed, Alice said, "Are you thinking of killing her?"

He studied her. "Do you want me to?"

Ah, there was his feral nature, for all that he lounged on the couch like a normal man tired from a day of hard labor. Green irises shifted yellow in the firelight, free of any guilt or conflict from the thought of tearing into another throat. Ending a human life held no weight, not to him. It was simply a hunt, and he had been through many of those. Alice knew how easily he could sleep while covered in blood.

And yet it wasn't fear that kept her from answering right away. Some part of her resisted bone-deep to the idea of turning him into her personal monster, something to be sent out whenever she was too cowardly to face problems. It would be an act of arrogance on her part, trying to put those dangerous teeth under her will. It would be using him in a way.

"That's not why I'm with you," she said, quietly, looking him full in the face. "The fact that you'll kill for me. Besides, I don't want Darby dead. I just want to be left alone."

His head tilted, and she had the feeling her answer had surprised him. Then the color of his eyes darkened back to their usual green, and he smiled a little. "Just the sex is good enough, hm?"

"There's nothing 'just' about it." She relaxed against him once more, back to stroking along his hot skin, and his rumble of a laugh vibrated against her fingers.

For some time she fell silent, sipping at the sweet wine and letting the warmth of his body lull her. She felt herself grow heavy, unguarded, and stopped looking at the shadowed corners of the room. As the light from the fire danced over them both, words slipped from her. "You once said you knew my grandmother was a witch."

He nuzzled at her temple, a silent way of confirming her words.

"Well, how does someone turn into one? Is it like the old superstitions, where a witch gets her power from the Devil and has a mark on her body from him licking her while consummating their pact?"

"That's just human fear." Colton sounded amused. "A witch is as natural as a wolf."

"Then how do you tell one from a human?"

"A witch can survive anything except water or fire. Whatever else they can or can't do is on them."

Her thoughts felt pleasantly fuzzy from the wine and the heat of his body, enough so that his cryptic response was lost on her. "I don't understand."

There was a grumble from him over having to use more words, but he elaborated. "Spells, rituals, all those things—they're just tools. They're not part of a witch's nature. A witch is *empty* unless she feeds off the land around her. Or people."

"Or animals," said Alice, thinking of the wolf pelt.

When the answer was obvious, Colton never said it. In his silence, she spoke up again. "So witches are evil."

"Not always."

Wine made her tenacious. "You just said that they suck things away from others."

"You kill to stay alive. It's the same as hunting. I catch rabbits cute enough to be stuffed toys. Does that make me evil?"

His point wasn't lost on Alice, but her ever-burning curiosity in him flared into life. "No. But what about you? What *are* you, Colton?"

"Something of a wolf, something of a man."

When she groaned, she felt him smile against her cheek, and was sure he'd change the topic.

He did. "Witches need to ground themselves in something. Find a balance between taking and giving. Otherwise..."

"They'll go insane?" said Alice, slowly, the fear rising in her again.

She was looking down at her glass, but his hand caught her chin and tilted it until her gaze rose to his face. "Is this it, then? The root of your fear?"

Despite the wine, her mouth had gone dry. "Yes. How would I know if I'm a witch or not? You once said I wasn't, but that was before I used the pelt."

When he didn't immediately answer, she tensed again. He felt it and smoothed a hand along her back before saying, "You're not like most. You seemed starving, not empty, and you wanted to help me instead of feed. But then you made the pelt come alive, and that left me unsure. You might be a witch. You might not be. Shouldn't matter either way."

Alice shook her head, wishing she could feel as calm about it. "I don't want to end up like my mother. Or my grandmother. If it was being a witch that drove them both mad... At least my mother just disappeared. My grandmother started making little figurines out of snail shells and rat bones. We think she ate them and then used the remains. My mother would send a check every month, and my father continued that after she disappeared, but not a single one was ever cashed. She had money for food but ate vermin instead."

She took another swallow of wine, mulling over the strangeness of a woman she'd never known, and then added, "And all those clothes in the cabin. They were in different sizes and styles. That's something you'd see in a serial killer's house. I remember it was even searched by the police after being tied to an unsolved disappearance. They never found anything. No bodies. No bones, even."

"Probably ground into meal and used for the rose bushes in the back."

When Alice looked at him, Colton steadily met her startled gaze. "She fed on people, Alice."

She sucked in a breath, head spinning like she'd had several glasses of wine instead of just one. "And my mother? Would she have been like that, too?"

His arm tightened around her as if to keep her steady. "Never met her. Couldn't say for sure. If she was, she would've stopped to be with your father."

"But it didn't work. She got away and still went mad in the end. And now there's only me." It was almost as if she could see the generations of her maternal line nestled together like the growth rings of one massive trunk, the rotten roots slowly poisoning the rest of the tree.

Colton's thumb traced the curve of her cheek, drawing her back. "You won't end up like them. You're different."

"What if I'm not? What if I just spiral down and disappear into the woods, too?"

"You won't, Alice."

She looked at him, this strange, bewildering creature. "Why?"

He studied her, reflected firelight dancing in his eyes. "Really want to know?"

"Yes."

His nose brushed against hers. "Because whenever you start fighting against yourself, I'll fuck you back into your senses."

It was so unexpected that she laughed, a hard one that sent wine spilling from the glass. It soaked through her sweatshirt, but she only laughed again and set the glass aside while his teeth nipped at her ear. The panic that had prickled throughout her now evaporated in a flash of heat, and her voice came out a bit breathless. "Not the sweetest promise, but I'll take it."

The hand against her bare skin slid down again, tracing the sensitive dimples in her lower back as his gaze took on a lazy smolder. "You're the sweet one, not me."

Her response was to pull off her sweatshirt. She wasn't wearing a bra beneath it, and the spilled wine had already hardened her nipples. He growled softly at the sight, and again while her fingers slid over his fly, playing with the metal teeth and then tracing the bulge in the denim there. When the fabric grew strained, she unzipped it and reached in.

He let her pull his hardening cock free, but when she bent to lap at the head, he moved with that feral quickness. She found herself sprawled on her back and pinned on the couch while he loomed over her.

"No. How I like."

She hummed at his roughness, lifting her hips so he could tug off the rest of her clothes. He ignored the movement, instead licking the wine from her breasts. The contrast between the chilled wine and his hot mouth was enough to make her gasp, and when his teeth tugged at a nipple, her breaths quickened into panting. He teased, the near-pain of bites stoked by his tongue into sweet agony.

Her fingers dug into whatever part of him she could reach; the hard strength of his shoulders, the muscles in his arms, the hair that bristled up the back of his head. Each time her nails bit into his skin, he gave her a pleased rumble in return, and even in her haze, she marveled at how he enjoyed her desperation.

The sensitive flesh of her breasts felt inflamed when he finally moved down, the ghostly sensation of his teeth lingering with each breath even as he tasted at the skin along her ribs and stomach. She already felt herself brimming on the edge of release, the warmth of the wine mingling with a heavy need that left her twitching her hips again. But when her hands left him to pinch at her aching nipples, he stopped and pinned her wrists above her head with one large hand.

Their noses brushed again as she groaned. "I'm so close."

"I could draw you out more." The heavy insistence of his cock prodded at her through the denim of her jeans.

"No, I need it now." She nuzzled at his mouth but he pulled back just enough to prevent a kiss.

At his sly expression, she groaned again, falling limp even while her limbs shook with lust. "You love this, don't you?"

"Don't you?" He sounded amused, but his hand flexed against her wrists, and she had the feeling that sometimes he still wasn't certain of her, that her lack of fear stupefied him, this predator who lived by tracking terror.

Her mouth curled into a smile. "Completely."

Then she arched her back, a movement that left her nipples brushing against him, daring him to ignore such sweet targets. It drew a growl from him, and then he *was* kissing her, hand sliding down from hers to rip at her jeans. Her laugh was swallowed by his mouth, and then she truly was lost in him.

Later, he untangled himself to add wood to the fire. The warm light flickered over the sheen of sweat on his skin. It was only after sex that he ever seemed to truly relax, as if the natural law of *kill or be killed* slipped away into the shadows for a time and took his wariness with it. As Alice watched him coax the flames back into life, something much deeper than lust squeezed at her thoughts.

She and Colton had never pledged devotion to each other. Even an "I love you" had remained unsaid. What they had was something feral and slicked in blood. Something that beat like a heart and seared like molten rock deep beneath rigid crusts of earth. What did a promise have to do with such wildness? He had once said that he would stay until they grew tired of each other, and she, just freed of Magdalene's forever, hadn't wished for anything more binding. And yet the idea of losing him now...

Anguish cut through her so sharply that it must have reached her scent, for Colton looked over with alert eyes. When he approached, she pushed herself up to nuzzle at the dark hair that ran over his lower stomach, very glad he didn't like words. She couldn't begin to explain the tumult in her heart... But she could still show how deeply she felt for him.

He caught the back of her head, perhaps to stop her and ask what was wrong, but now she was the insistent one, kissing along the vein that ran from his hip to his cock. He was sticky from their drying fluids, and she took him into her mouth to suck him clean. Salt and musk filled her senses as she worshipped him with every slide of her tongue. Feral, unashamed, pride straining in every thick inch... Sometimes she wondered whether her reverence of his savage abandon all came from the deep ache to have those teeth leave scars behind once he decided to slip off to the forest and return to living as the wolf he truly was.

She had so many already, ugly keloids marking where the tender flesh of her heart had been cut into, cut away, and left misshapen as scar tissue grew lumpy and hard in the spaces remaining. Even the oldest ones still made her flinch. What would it be like to have some that were precious instead?

When she broke off with a final lap at the head of his cock, he was already hard again, heavy against her while she planted kisses down its length, knowing he could feel how she smiled whenever a growl slipped into his breaths.

His fat sack was just as filthy, and at the first touch of her tongue, his fingers twisted in her hair. When he swore under his breath, she hummed in response, gently mouthing at one ball and then the other through their thick, wrinkled skin. As she continued to suck and kiss, worshipping him with every movement of her mouth, his free hand started rubbing his cock. Primal excitement left her flushed and panting against him, clinging to his hips while urging him on with every press of her lips. The hand in her hair tightened even as the rhythm of his breathing changed. She knew he was there, and followed his balls with her mouth as they drew up tight.

His growls rumbled into her bone deep, and then wet heat striped her neck and shoulder. It wasn't shock that made her laugh, but delight. Yes, let them be filthy beasts in the dark of night. Let them dwell in the joy of the unashamed. Nothing he did was too grotesque for her, and nothing she did was too broken for him.

She was already sucking again when his next shot of seed caught in her hair. The hand at her head tugged her back, then, forcing her to arch her back to keep her balance. The movement exposed her breasts to his final load, and the next breath that came out of her was a satisfied hum.

It was answered by his own quiet laugh, and now his fingers slid to the nape of her neck, coaxing her to look up at him. Marked as she was, she met his gaze without shame and saw him marvel at her reaction. As if she were the entrancing, mysterious creature of the two, not him.

His panting had already eased away, and his voice sounded as steady as always when he spoke. "If you ever lose yourself, I'll bring you back. Understand? No matter what."

CHAPTER FOUR

CIGARETTE BURNS

Thousands of lights glittered through the fog that drifted past the windows. Alice blinked, realizing she was back in her apartment in the city. The white walls and geometric furniture looked as hard and cold as always, and fake logs crackled with fake flames in the gas-powered fireplace, too weak to generate any heat toward her place on the couch.

Across from her sat Magdalene, her black dress and boots stark against the bone-colored upholstery of the chair. Her eyes looked honey gold as she tilted the glass of wine in her hand, swirling the garnet-colored liquid in a way that mimicked the twisting in Alice's stomach.

"It needs something," she said, her lipstick as vivid as a gash.

Alice swallowed hard, aware of how her fingers were curled into fists in her lap. "What?"

Magdalene gestured with her other hand, which held an unlit cigarette. "It's too bare in here. It throws off the balance."

Alice glanced around, feeling dizzy from how the angles of the walls seemed to stretch and leer at her. "Maybe a rug?"

"I was thinking a pelt."

Alice's gaze shot back to Magdalene just in time to see the other woman smile.

"Yes, a wolf pelt. I think black would be perfect."

Then she drank from the glass and wine poured from her throat, for a gaping wound had suddenly appeared in it. Even as Alice gasped, the thin ruby of the wine thickened into a bright red. Magdalene kept smiling.

Rivers of blood ran from her neck and spread over the floor, reaching for Alice's feet. Alice tried jerking back, but she seemed frozen in place, unable to do anything as it welled ever closer.

Magdalene watched while ducking her head to light a cigarette. Her wound gaped and breathed out smoke. "Is something wrong?"

Alice just shrieked, thrashing against whatever held her in place.

Then Magdalene stood, stretching like a cat. As she approached, blood continued to pour from her throat, soaking her dress until the points of her nipples showed through.

Her fingers felt like claws as she caught Alice's shoulders, pinning her back against the couch. The cigarette's cherry glowed inches away from her mouth.

"You never mind blood on him. I think you're being fickle, Alice."

"You died," hissed Alice, trying to wrench free of Magdalene's grip. Every movement on her part drew a fresh gush of blood from the other woman's ruined throat, drenching them both. "You can't hurt me anymore. You're *dead*."

At that, Magdalene paused, taking the cigarette from her mouth to flick away ash. The grey motes stun where they landed on Alice's cheek, and she flinched even as Magdalene's fingers dug in to keep her still, the cigarette now burning close to her neck. "Oh, Alice, you're smarter than that. Only fools believe that something dead is something gone."

Alice felt herself locking up, limbs heavy as though Magdalene's very touch turned her into stone. The feeling of the other woman leaning in gave her a final, desperate lurch of energy, and she wrenched herself from head to toe.

Light plunged into dark, and for one wretched moment, she wasn't sure whether she fell or lunged upright. She felt herself panting, and then felt sheets crumpled around her. A mockingbird's nightsong drifted through the air, and so did the smell of pine sap.

A dream. She'd only been dreaming. The haze of sleep cleared a little more, and she remembered how Colton had woken her up earlier, teasing her into enough consciousness for her to mumble a goodbye before he'd left on an early work shift.

A glance at the clock revealed it was just after four, and she reluctantly sank back against the mattress to wait for sunrise and its reassuring brightness. She slept fitfully through those final hours, smelling cigarette smoke whenever she began to drop off the edge of consciousness.

Morning found her bleary-eyed and shuffling for coffee. Even the potency of a brewing pot of the stuff couldn't shake her lethargy, and it wasn't until she reached for the carafe that she grew aware of an irritated, pulling sensation on her arm. She finished filling her cup full and rubbed the sleep from her eyes before glancing down. Then she froze.

Cigarette burns marked her arm. Five of them. Dark red, perfectly round, and mercilessly highlighted in the bright morning sunshine. When she brushed fingers over them, still in disbelief, she felt the answering flares of pain, felt the raised, tender patches of skin. How...?

Images from her nightmare slipped back into her mind. She quickly shoved them away, heart racing. Dreams didn't bleed into real life. They couldn't. Yet somehow these burns had happened.

Her mind raced for explanations while she stumbled to the bathroom to cover up the marks. There were really only two possibilities—that Colton had done it to her, which she immediately ruled out as ridiculous, or that she had done it to herself. Was *that* just as ridiculous? Even as she wrapped gauze around the burns to protect them from the sleeve of her robe, horror crept along her spine over the idea that she might be hurting herself without remembering it. Although even that didn't make sense; neither she nor Colton smoked. There weren't any cigarettes in the house to burn herself with...

Not unless a pack lingered in the moving box left sealed shut after she and Colton had settled into the house—the one filled with all that was left of Magdalene's belongings. In the final flurry of days before Alice had moved out of the apartment, she hadn't paid much attention to what had been shoveled out of Magdalene's safe and desk. It was just possible that cigarettes were among the things.

After tying off the gauze, she drifted to the same closet where she'd stuffed Darby's papers, now shoving them out of the way to pull the box out into the open. It was a strange place to keep it, there among the rarely used boots and rain slickers, but she hadn't been able to bring herself to put anything of Magdalene's in the bedroom.

The box was as she'd left it. Without ceremony, she ripped off the silver tape that kept the flaps shut, fingers clumsy with dread. She didn't know what to expect as she opened it and looked inside.

Magdalene's parents had taken all her rewards for *The Chrysalis*. Half-written drafts and story ideas remained locked up in bitter court battles between them and Magdalene's publishers. What Alice had been left with were things unwanted or things that only she knew about. Her fingers still held reverence as they sifted through letters and prose pieces that Magdalene had written to her in those early, golden days, but it was of the careful type that came with handling an

ancient crossbow or a ceremonial dagger—an artifact from
another time that could still kill.

She also found the notebook of scribblings that had turned
into *The Chrysalis*, and was surprised no one had taken it. She
thumbed through pages that bore coffee stains and still smelled
faintly of tobacco. Magdalene's handwriting was long and
spidery, each stroke biting into the page. Alice remembered
how she had liked using fountain pens, and how elegant they
had seemed compared to Alice's own cheap ballpoints, the
ends of the plastic caps chewed from her nervous teeth.

Then something fell out of the notebook, fluttering into
the box, and when Alice reached in for it, her fingers brushed
over Magdalene's most precious possession: a photo of the girl
she'd always called Indigo. Indigo, her first and only muse.
Indigo, a high school sweetheart turned eternal tragedy.

Alice had seen the picture before but had never studied it,
always aware of Magdalene's protectiveness toward Indigo's
memory. She glanced over it now, wondering at this girl who
had so bewitched Magdalene. A hard smile played over her lips
as she took in the flawless skin and wild red hair, the wide blue
eyes that held depths as vast and empty as abandoned quarries.
To think that she had been jealous of this dead girl and
Magdalene's obsession with her.

Underneath the photo waited a packet bound in black
ribbon. Alice recognized what they were—more letters from
Magdalene, but this time to Indigo. Ones that had been
retrieved by Magdalene on the night of the girl's funeral. Once,

when Magdalene had been very drunk, she had admitted to Alice that she'd climbed a tree and crawled through a window to get inside Indigo's room and search for those letters. That she had hoped to be caught and have the secret relationship spill out into the open.

But she hadn't been, not even while spending the entire night there on the bedroom floor, reading through each letter. And at dawn, she had slipped away unnoticed with the last traces of night, leaving the rest of the world to mourn Indigo as Liberty Bower, a pretty, happy girl who had died with her boyfriend on their way back from prom.

When Alice had first learned about this painful part of Magdalene's past, she had cried for her. She had also cried over Indigo having lost her life and her true love. Now she simply wondered if pity would have been more appropriate. Had Magdalene's devotion ever been softer? Kinder? One might blame bitterness and loss for her behavior toward Alice, but an inferior replacement had far less expectations to bear than a perfect muse. Alice had been expected to fail; Indigo had probably been held up as someone who never could.

And if there was one thing Magdalene had excelled at outside of writing, it was making people feel just what she wished them to. A treasure to her—or a piece of shit stuck to her shoe. The guardian to her secrets, or the backstabber with the bloodied knife. Her second heart that gave her a reason to live, or a toy to play with.

Alice's gaze flickered to the fat manuscript beside the box. Darby's ode to a woman she felt she better understood than anyone else ever had. Yes, Magdalene had certainly crooned enough words to make her feel like a treasure. And before Darby saw any other side to her, Magdalene had gone—first back to the cabin with Alice, and then away to the morgue as a rotting body.

Was it really any wonder, the lengths to which Darby was going? Magdalene must have seemed like a shooting star to her.

Slowly, Alice pulled the manuscript onto her lap. Her fingers hesitated at the first red label that marked a section relevant to her, but then she quickly flipped to it and began reading. Her mouth went dry as she found out just how deeply Darby had dug into her family's past, but she forced herself to move to the next marked page, and then the one after that. She didn't bother going through Darby's notes to check what she read; she had her own memories to weigh how much was truth and how much was falsehood. And even Colton had admitted to the extent of her grandmother's darkness and possibly her mother's, too.

When she came to a page that told of how her mother had liked putting cigarettes out on her arm, Alice finally shoved the manuscript away and rubbed at her eyes, unsure of whether they ached from lack of sleep or from tears. Were the burns made by her own hand? Time had slipped by so strangely for her the day before. She had blamed it on the shock of Darby's visit, but perhaps she should have blamed her own mind instead...

Her focus returned to the packing box, and she pushed aside a few more notebooks, determined to reach the bottom and find out for good whether any cigarettes were there. And then, between a dried-up stick of gum and ink cartridges for a fountain pen, she found a pack.

She knew it was Magdalene's favorite brand even before she lifted it out and saw the gold lion logo. The earthy smell of tobacco drifted up to her face, muted with age. The top of the pack wasn't quite shut, all but inviting her to take a peek inside and see how many cigarettes were left. After a deep breath, she did.

Five were missing. Five burns were on her arm. Alice's hands started shaking, and she quickly dropped the pack into the box.

Her movements grew more frantic as she fought with the cardboard flaps to re-tape them shut. Back into the closet went the box, shoved in the furthest corner. The manuscript went with it and then Alice slammed the door shut and sat on the floor, panting as if she'd been wrestling with something alive.

Eventually, her hand crept back to her bandaged arm. It wouldn't be enough, ignoring Darby. If she had become so fragile as to come undone at the mere threat of blackmail, what would happen when the book was actually published?

Give in and let her see the cabin, whispered a voice deep in her mind, one that reminded her of Magdalene's.

Some part of her still resisted, still wished to fight. Not against Darby, no—that was a lost cause. But what about Darby's husband, Rob? Alice had never felt any warmer toward him than she had toward Darby—her perception of Rob was of a man absorbed in himself and his art. But he was certainly as bullish as Darby. Some of the fights she had witnessed between them... And in the end, Rob had usually gotten his way. If Darby's obsession with Magdalene rankled at him, then perhaps he also wanted her to give up this crusade.

Or perhaps he found it all amusing. Alice felt sick as she remembered some of the other things he had found entertaining, and quickly pushed the memories from her mind. She couldn't know for sure how he felt, not until she found out.

It was worth a try.

She didn't have his phone number but remembered where he worked—at some commercial photography studio. She called there, pacing around the house while waiting for the office assistant to put her through.

"I'm sorry, ma'am, but he's working from home today." The assistant's voice had a polite chill that warned Alice not to ask for any personal information.

She didn't need to, instead finding the address from the cover page of Darby's manuscript. After logging it into her phone, she showered and dressed, taking her time in putting herself together. Hair pulled into a French twist, understated gold in her ears, a stark dress and a starker wool coat against the autumn chill... She wasn't about to make the same mistake she had with Darby in looking like a little mouse that could be pushed around.

It was a two-and-a-half-hour drive to Rob and Darby's and she spent it entirely in silence. Panic flickered through her whenever the burns pulled at her skin, spurring her forward through the snarls of traffic around toll booths and bridges. The roads grew cramped between towering buildings that swallowed the sun; the air gained the tinge of smog and salt. People walked, smoked, played music on the corners and begged for change in the shadows. She smelled coffee, frying food from street carts, and sewage from sewer systems overwhelmed by recent rains. It was a city that teemed with life of all strains, a constant dance of the senses.

A smile touched Alice's lips as she remembered how Colton would give a surly twitch of his shoulders to the view of the city through the windows of her apartment. But he had never complained out loud, and when she'd asked if he hated urban living, he'd only grimaced and said, "Elk live in large herds. Not wolves."

Her next question had been whether there were elk that could change into humans, too, and his expression had turned long-suffering. Then she'd started giggling, unresisting when he'd pulled her close with that predator's quickness, teeth tender instead of fatal as they'd tested the soft area of her throat where her laughter hummed.

The memory reminded her of what she was determined to fight for, determined to *save*, and she drove faster, now intent on seeing Rob. Her hands remained white-knuckled while she found the right street and turned down it. It was a quiet neighborhood made up of houses that were artifacts of history. They stood there two or even three stories tall, ornate woodwork modernized with coats of cheerful paint. Weary with age, they all leaned along the hill they'd been built on, cramped and uneven like a mouthful of crooked teeth.

She parked on the street, already spotting Rob on the balcony of their house, cigarette in hand. He looked the same as she'd remembered: dark hair short yet styled, and a blocky head held up by a thick neck and sloped shoulders in the way that had always reminded her of a buffalo. Clothing understated, hands sensitive. Black-framed glasses shrunk the appearance of his eyes a tad, just enough to emphasize the hyper-focused stare he would give the rare thing that actually caught his attention. He glanced over her while she got out of the car, but when she called his name, his focus cleared.

Different emotions ran through his face as she looked up at him, shading her eyes against the noon sun. When he spoke, his voice sounded the same, too, a dark purr that always held a hint of smugness, as if his photographer's eye saw through to souls and laughed at what was found. "Darby's out and I have no fucking clue where."

With that handful of words, Alice realized he knew everything. "I'm here because of her, but I'd rather talk to you."

"Why?"

The same old Rob. Annoyed that he couldn't watch from a distance and instead had to be pulled into the thick of things. Alice stepped closer to the balcony, feeling her chance slip away by the second. "She visited me yesterday, and I'm worried about how much of what she said is true."

Rob took another drag and then ran a thumb over his left eyebrow, as if he already felt a headache growing. "Ask her about all that."

"She wants a yes or no from me, nothing else."

Laughter burst out from the other side of the street. Nothing more than a group of girls in their lace shirts and ripped jeans, oblivious while they slid down the steep, uneven sidewalk, but it still reminded them both that they were speaking out in the open where anyone could overhear.

For one wretched moment, Alice was sure Rob would refuse to talk any further. But then he sighed and straightened up from where he leaned on the railing. "You better come in."

Alice hurried for the small porch before he could change his mind, the first hints of hope stirring over making it that far. She wasn't sure what sort of conversation waited for her, but she knew she would have to put up a fight. At the front door, she ran her tongue over her teeth, trying to remember how to snap and bite. Then it opened, and she stepped inside.

CHAPTER FIVE

GRAVE DIRT

Despite the vintage exterior, the decor inside Rob and Darby's house looked much like Alice's old apartment. She glanced around, taking in the severe angles of the ultra-modern lights and furniture. Every room that Rob led her through appeared pristine and unlived in. Hardwood floors unscuffed, carpets smooth and fresh. The only immediate difference proved to be framed prints hanging from the walls—Rob's work. He liked taking black-and-white photographs of people, oftentimes even strangers on the street who agreed to spontaneous portraits. Not all were unfamiliar, though; when Rob waved Alice into the studio, she found a large print of Magdalene waiting on the wall.

Rob could be an asshole, but he knew how to coax out the essence of a person and capture it. In the photo, Magdalene's eyes were a striking mix of light and shadow, haunted and haunting and uncomfortable in the way they bore into the viewer. A cigarette hung from the corner of a sneering mouth, but Rob had somehow gotten the lighting to emphasize the lushness of her lower lip through the smoke.

Alice couldn't look at it for long, and Rob noticed.

"She really fucked you up, didn't she?" He sounded amused while sitting at one of the desks in the room—his, going by the photography paraphernalia that littered the surface. His gaze traveled over her while he flicked his cigarette at a nearby ashtray.

She didn't like his attention; it felt too cold and curious, like a scalpel slitting open skin to find what waited inside. But he was also the first one who had ever implied having an awareness of Magdalene's darker nature, and Alice found herself asking, "Do you miss her?"

He thought about it, smoke trailing between them. "I always saw her as a rock skipping across water. Destined to sink, but oh, the ripples she made before she disappeared. Once you knew her well, you enjoyed what she did, but never who she was."

At Alice's startled look, he added, "Don't pretend to be clueless. You were with her for years and looked like a ghost by the end. We both know how she ran through people, using them up and wearing them down. Hell, I was her only friend who never wound up in therapy. Or dead."

The frankness was so startling that Alice didn't know what to say. "How did you manage it?"

"Ego and balls. She'd feed off anyone, but the sensitive, wounded girls who reminded her of Indigo got it the worst."

She must have reacted in some way to Indigo's name, because Rob straightened up in his chair. "Magdalene told you about her?"

"Yes."

He blew out a lungful of smoke, studying her with more interest. "I'm surprised even while I'm not. Surprised because Magdalene rarely talked about her... And unsurprised because there's a fragile quality to you that Indigo also had. You're like this sweet little doll that will break and be all the more beautiful as shards. Magdalene loved that shit."

Alice never knew what to say when artists slid into distracted, abstract conversation, and so she now remained silent.

Rob eyed her again. "Do you remember the nights we spent together? Entheogens would leave Magdalene talking for fucking hours about the connections of the universe and time warping in on itself, always dancing around the ways Indigo could somehow come alive again. Half the time, Darby would be in the bathroom having the shits because she never adjusted to mescaline well. But you... You would just go limp and pliable, open to any suggestion. Like being a doll was your secret nature."

Alice glanced away, not trusting herself to immediately respond. She'd hoped Rob wouldn't go into any of that, especially because she remembered enough to feel shame scald her at the mere mention. "Why are you bringing this up?"

"Because we're talking about Magdalene and her effect on people. On Darby. On you."

"While you stood off to the side and took photos." The bitterness in her words surprised her, but Rob just looked interested again.

"Sometimes I'd be in the middle of things." Then he shrugged and offered that indulgent smile he used with anyone who flared up at him over his art. "You probably remember that, since you won't even fully look at me."

She did, and hated how she had always agreed to let Magdalene drag her to those psychonaut parties, and how whatever they took—pill, shot glass of liquid, smoke—left her flushed and confused and looking to Magdalene for guidance.

In a low voice, she said, "I think it was a test from her. She liked watching us fuck. She liked seeing in my face that I'd do it only for her and not because I wanted to. Funny how words were never enough. I always had to *prove* it."

Realizing her cheeks stung with heat, she turned away to avoid his gaze. Silence simmered as her restless steps took her to Darby's side of the room. The walls there were painted turquoise and littered with photos of Magdalene. Some looked like Rob's work, but others were missing his cool, precise touch and instead held a rawness that made Alice wonder if Darby had taken them.

She suddenly remembered the first time she had admitted to Magdalene that she liked painting—just a little, just as a secret hobby that bore results too crude and embarrassing to show to anyone. Magdalene had given her an indulgent smile while insisting on seeing them, and then had crooned over each one as if it had been a striking masterpiece instead of simple splatters of coffee. Something had rushed through Alice, then, sweet and immediate like a cube of sugar dissolving on the tongue. And so she'd flung herself after that feeling again and again until it became habit to seek Magdalene's approval, until it became the very course of nature itself.

How many times had Rob seen this happen? How could he have let his wife fall into such a trap? Alice nearly turned around to ask him, but a larger part of her insisted it was better to stoke his goodwill over his irritation. Instead, she kept studying Darby's space, trying to figure out the other girl.

An antique writing desk overflowed with paper and books. Just enough space remained clear for a vintage typewriter to sit and preen. Off to the side nestled an office cabinet with the doors open to reveal a modern workspace. The corkboard above the desk interested Alice the most, though, and she stepped closer to study it. Handwritten notes were pinned all over its surface like dead butterflies, the delicate paper crumpled from obsessive fingers. Most were scribbled too illegibly for her to read, but she did recognize one as the address of her cabin. The number "31" was written above it and circled.

"What does this mean?" she said, looking over at Rob.

"She doesn't tell me anything." Then he stubbed out his cigarette and rose from his chair. "All I can tell you is what I guessed on my own."

Alice locked her muscles to keep from flinching away as he approached, but he only studied the corkboard with her, his expression losing some of its smugness. "She's fixated on Magdalene. Everyone fucking sees that. And I've known about her biography idea for awhile. She came up with it after the funeral. But I learned how you play into it only because I caught her nosing through my files. She could've just asked to see the photos. The fact that she didn't made me wonder what the hell she planned."

"Photos?" repeated Alice, cold fingers suddenly clutching at her heart. This wasn't at all what she'd expected. At the look on Rob's face, she guessed the answer and fumbled for a nearby chair before her legs gave out.

His voice drifted at the edge of her thoughts. "The ones from the nights we spent together."

Alice tried to keep her voice from shaking. "She didn't show me those."

"She looked for them after seeing you. My best guess is that when you said no to the cabin idea, she decided to bring out bigger arsenal than a missing mom and a fucked-up grandma."

"And you let her have them?" Despite her best efforts, her words rose in panic. "God, Rob, she wants to ruin me. You of all people know that not everyone waves away things like that.

Magdalene told me enough about the town you both grew up in."

Rob scoffed and lit a fresh cigarette. "Do you know how many times she's screamed at me for not taking Magdalene's death like she thinks I should? Do you know what she'd do if I tried to prevent this? It's not worth it."

When Alice shook her head, he added, "*You're* the one who can stop it, and you already know how to. The cabin."

Silence descended then. Alice found herself looking everywhere but at him while a question burned in her mind. Eventually, she forced herself to say it. "How bad are they? The photos?"

"Explicit and you're recognizable in them." There was no trace of apology in his voice.

She felt ready to throw up. "She can't publish those in the book. Is she planning to show them to my family?"

"She will if she finds them. She hasn't yet."

"How can you be sure?"

Rob hesitated and then reached for a manila envelope on his desk. "Because I did. Prints and the negatives."

The relief felt so sweet as to be agonizing as Alice reached for the envelope with greedy fingers, mentally thanking him for being enough of a prick to shoot his boudoir photography with film cameras instead of digital.

But Rob only stepped back, expression flat.

"Rob?"

"You'll get them if you let her into the cabin."

Her hand fell back to her side. "You're in on this, too?"

"I just want my life back. She's fucking obsessed with visiting that place. Hopefully seeing it and finishing the book gets Magdalene out of her system." Then he slapped the envelope back on the table.

Alice couldn't stop staring at it. Rob was used to soft urban living and had the body to show for it. But she remembered that he'd been strong from a naturally burly build. She wasn't sure she could snatch the envelope and make it to her car without him catching her but felt desperate enough to try anyway.

Her fingers had just curled into claws when he sighed, lines of frustration appearing on his forehead over her lack of response. "Just let her see the damn thing."

"Or what?" Anger left her savage, and she spat out the words at him. "You'll show my parents what I look like while sucking your cock? Maybe I don't care about that anymore."

It was a lie, but he didn't have to know that.

Surprise glinted in his eyes. Then he relaxed again. "If you didn't care, you wouldn't be so desperate to have them. Besides, your family is only one part to this. Darby told me you're living with a guy and pretending your time with Magdalene never existed. *That* would have to hurt, him seeing the photos and finding out just who you really are."

Her heart clenched. "You wouldn't risk being punched out by an angry boyfriend."

"My face isn't in these. Yours is."

"He'd still kill you."

"Me but not you?"

It was a desperate needling to see who flinched away first. Where was the chink in the armor? Where was the Achilles' heel? They each had their own, but who would be the first to find the other's?

Alice pressed her lips together in a tight line, trying to get back under control. "I'm not afraid of him. I never have been."

"But you're afraid of losing him."

She sucked in a breath, feeling her face tighten, and knew right then that she had lost.

"Abandonment," repeated Rob, triumph clear in his voice. "Magdalene said it was a thing with you. Does he know how you used to live?"

"He knows my last relationship was with a woman, yes." Another blunder on her part.

Rob didn't hesitate to pounce on it. "Then seeing a man balls deep in you wouldn't be high on his list of expectations."

If she tried saying anything else, the words would dissolve into tears of sheer rage. When she remained quiet, arms folded to keep her hands from trembling, he rubbed his face. "Look, I want my life back and I want Darby to have hers back, too. Show her the fucking cabin, or I'll release the photos."

Something weak yet stubborn rose within her, like the worn nubs of teeth in jaws that still remembered how to bite. "How do I know you really have any photos? That envelope could be filled with anything. I'm not going to give in to a bluff."

Rob scoffed but put his cigarette in his mouth to reach for the envelope. As soon as his hand pulled out the glossy prints, she lunged. Her desperate fingers crumpled two before he wrenched the rest out of reach. "Christ, are you serious?"

She only snatched at the photos again, ready to claw his face off if it meant grabbing them. This time, Rob caught the fine wool of her coat and revealed that strength of his, shoving her hard enough to send her sprawling. Her back hit the floor just before her head, leaving her breathless and stunned as she looked up at him.

He adjusted his glasses, all traces of amusement gone from his face. "Stop fucking around, all right? Darby's going to ask again once she finds something else to stick you with. If you don't agree, I'll release the photos myself."

"You—" was the only thing she managed to say before he pulled her upright, dragging her toward the front door. She hated the feeling of his hands on her and struggled enough to break free just as they reached the threshold. She ended up on the porch and he just inside the doorway, and for a long moment they stared at each other. Again, surprise flashed across Rob's face. He'd truly expected her to break then and there.

"I won't do it," she said, voice cracking.

But he had already recovered enough to offer a small smirk in return. "We'll find out for sure, right?"

At that, Alice turned away, unable to look at him any longer. As she walked down to her car, she hardly felt the shocked throbbing in the parts of her body that had hit the floor the hardest. Instead, all that filled her thoughts was how that slender thread of escape had snapped. She was trapped.

Back home, she agonized over what to tell Colton. The inexplicable burns on her arms had been overwhelmed by the danger of the photos, yet both seemed impossible to reveal.

She was in strange waters now, for Magdalene's fixed attention had offered security in its own way. Alice could never have been her muse but never her devil either. Magdalene had often called her beautiful like a fractured mirror, one of those strange insult-compliments that she'd always given. At the time, it had been a comfort. An assurance that even at her worst, Alice would remain loved. Or at least wanted...

Damn Rob to hell. He'd seen the core of her as surely as Darby and Magdalene had, just more coldly with his photographer's gaze. She didn't want to lose Colton to past stupidity or current madness. And if it was inevitable, why not stall the bitter end for as long as possible? Why not snatch at the bits of happiness that still glittered and keep them close until they dulled to nothing?

At last, she bandaged her arm, practicing lies until her voice stopped shivering with shame. Then she made sure to light a fire against the chill, and to finish making the bed, and to check what bills needed to be paid. A varnish of domesticity to hide the sickly guilt that beat like a second heart. She even had dinner ready when Colton came home from work.

She reached for plates just as he slipped up from behind, pinning her body against his to taste the side of her neck. Tree sap and musk filled her senses as her hands shifted to instead reach behind her, stroking up along his hair. The heat of his body melted the tension that had snarled throughout every limb, and she twisted to nuzzle at him, wanting one of those rough kisses. Wanting a final taste of that dangerous mouth while her own was still honest.

His tongue teased hers, lulling her into dropping the back of her head against him. It left her neck exposed and strong fingers found the tender flesh there, stroking along the pulse pounding beneath vulnerable skin.

Then his hand ran over her shoulder and continued down, stopping when it found the bandaging on her arm. Alice stiffened a moment before he broke off the kiss. When she felt him shift to look, she turned breathless for a different reason and quickly said, "It's just a burn. I brushed the oven rack while reaching in."

"How bad is it?" His fingers ran over the gauze as if he considered pulling it off to look.

Alice covered his hand with hers and angled her face for another kiss. "It's fine."

He accepted it, but she knew she was still too quiet during dinner, picking at her food rather than eating it. Chicken breasts stuffed with cranberries and chestnuts was a favorite meal, but fear turned each bite into a flavorless lump that had to be choked down.

Afterward, he looked over at her while they washed the plates. "Something's troubling you."

She nodded, aware that it would be useless to claim otherwise.

"Tell me while I get the wine."

It felt like her heart withered and died while she shook her head. "It's all right. I just need to think over some things."

It was the first time she'd ever shut him out rather than bare herself in full, and she hated it. Surprise flashed across his face, but he took it with nothing more than a nod.

Later that night, in bed and their skins slick with sweat, she stroked his hair and listened to his slow, easy breathing as he slept. Tears prickled in her eyes as she lay there, afraid of staying silent and afraid of shaking him awake to confess what had been happening.

Eventually, she must have slipped into sleep as well, for she found herself standing in the attic of her grandmother's cabin. Blinding sunlight shone through the round window and birds screeched somewhere outside, panicked.

Alice blinked, trying to clear her eyes while the dim shapes of forgotten furniture and useless relics slowly hardened into clarity.

"It took you long enough." A familiar voice dripped into her ears like honey.

Alice jerked, her vision clearing in a flash, and found herself facing Magdalene and her smile. She still wore the same blood-soaked dress, but her throat looked whole while she tapped fingers against the large trunk between them. Alice recognized it as the one that had held the wolf pelt that had given her so many sweet nights of running in the forest with Colton.

Shivers wracked her body even before Magdalene spoke. "Open it. It's for you."

Alice shook her head, struck mute, but when Magdalene's elegant, clever hands snapped the lock and pulled up the lid, she found herself stepping closer even as the metallic tang of blood filled the air.

Instead of the tanned grey-and-white fur that she remembered, the trunk's plush interior cradled a black pelt. Blood streamed as if it had been freshly peeled off. Yellow eyes stared at her, now clouded over in death. Alice shrieked, fingers clawing at her own face as Magdalene laughed. The sound filled her head, drowning out her own screams as the first of the flies landed on lifeless fur.

She woke up shaking, pulse pounding so hard that it felt like her heart would burst. Even as she gasped for breath, she grabbed at Colton, absurdly sure she was about to touch a bloody, lifeless body. He shifted beneath her fingers, whole and strong and real, and she clung to him, trying not to cry.

It was the first of many sleepless nights.

CHAPTER SIX

A SELF-CONSTRUCTED CAGE

Strange, isn't it, being in a self-constructed cage? The girl constantly tests the bars in her mind in the way of a tongue poking at an aching tooth. Are they still there? Are they still too close together to slip free?

They are and the girl doesn't know what to do. She recognizes the easiest key to use on the locked door—to give in to the wills of others, crawling or dancing or pretending as they wish. *Give in and stay quiet.* That is how she lived most of her life before the black wolf slipped in and showed her how to savage and howl. When one learns to bite, how can one then unlearn it?

Yet the girl has lost her fine pelt. While she can no longer pretend her old life fits, those nights of moon and fur remain far out of reach. What key can she find among ashes and scorched hide?

The key of resistance. Let them expose her vulnerabilities. Let them cut up her past and restitch it as they see fit. Let them test her family's patience and her lover's willingness to take her ugliness. But can she stand it? Can she risk losing everything to repulsion?

The girl crouches in her cage and shakes, watching the past bleed into the present. If she will not pick one or the other, then she must wait until a new key reveals itself. She must endure until, hopefully, it is not too late.

Alice knew it was impossible to remain furtive without Colton noticing. To stop eating and instead push at the food on her plate because her stomach churned. To go from gleefully cleaning him in the shower to pretending she had a headache and needed more sleep, arm curled against her body to make sure the bandaging stayed in place. Soon enough, his frustration thickened the air in the way of heavy clouds gathering into a thunderstorm, but he remained as silent as she.

Although no further burns appeared on any part of her body, Alice began to hear footsteps throughout the day, the same angry tread as when Magdalene had paced back and forth, frustrated by words that refused to leave her mind. Alice often smelled cigarette smoke, too, although the pack remained untouched in the cardboard box each time she looked. And once, while alone in the house and brewing a pot of mid-morning coffee, she even found a carton of cream waiting on the counter. She never took her coffee with anything, but Magdalene had always insisted on filling her cup half-full with it.

Alice began to pace herself, waiting for Darby to call and offer her one final chance to give in. Trying to decide what her answer would be when that ultimatum came. In the meantime, she read through the manuscript again and again, hands shaking while imagining her father's reaction to so much of her sordid history being revealed. Worse, she could see how her mother's early behavior now mimicked her own. Sleepless nights, paranoia clinging to her bones, hearing and seeing things... With Darby and Rob's threats hanging over her head, she even began to understand why the ticking of a clock had been such torment to her mother.

And of course, there were the nightmares. Magdalene always loomed in them, bearing down on Alice like a wrathful star, and one night it simply became too much for her to hide. She woke up clawing at the sheets, shrieking at the feeling of blood running down her hair and shoulders from where Magdalene had tried fitting a freshly-skinned pelt over her.

Then an arm hard with muscle caught her writhing body, and Colton's voice rumbled against her ear, thick with sleep yet steady. "Easy. Easy, you're safe."

She just whimpered, fumbling for the bedside lamp before he stretched over her to turn it on. Light revealed her to be drenched in sweat instead of blood, and at that, she fell limp and shaking.

"What's wrong?" He pulled her close, and she wanted nothing more than to melt in him.

She ducked her head into the hollow of his throat, unable to keep her voice steady. "Just a nightmare."

"Another one." It wasn't a question.

She nodded, still shivering.

"What about?"

"I don't..."

"You do remember. Your fear's growing in your scent, not fading."

When she didn't say anything, he caught her chin. His hand remained gentle as he tipped her head toward his, but his stare was nothing less than a challenge.

"You're lying to me. Been lying for a week now. Ever since the human visited."

Alice dropped her gaze from his and licked lips gone very dry.

"You don't eat. You don't sleep. We've fucked twice in the last week. You can't even look at me. What's wrong?"

When it became obvious that she intended to remain silent, his hand tightened against her face, and the rasp in his voice turned desperate. "Alice. Talk to me."

Her chin trembled with suppressed tears. "I can't. I'm sorry."

"Why not?"

"I..."

"Why?"

"I'm too scared." The words wrenched themselves out of her as a sob as some of Rob's photos flashed through her mind. Too scared of what he would think, too scared of what would happen.

There was a long pause from him, and suddenly she couldn't take how poisonous she felt in his presence. He held her like something precious, something to be adored, and still she lied to him. His muscles bunched in tension as she pulled free, and his snarl was one of pure frustration, but he let her slide out of bed and leave, silent while she shrugged on a robe and stumbled for the doorway. Every part of her burned; her eyes with tears, her cheeks with shame, and her body with lingering memories.

A headache throbbed at her temples as she looked at the nearest clock. Hours until dawn. She stayed up anyway, sitting in the kitchen with a mug of tea as the tension within her grew muddied with weariness. As her overtired brain drew up snatches of her mother's erratic behavior and stubborn silences to compare with her own, she painted with the dregs at the bottom of the mug, needing something to do while she worried.

Did anything about her mother make more sense, now seeming right and reasonable as her own madness seeped in? Had any of it flickered into clarity like learning enough of a language for inane sounds to crystallize into beautiful words?

Alice didn't feel like it had at all. Instead, an increasing panic overtook her. Everything had spun out of her control, even her own reactions.

Her brush flickered over the paper in sharp strokes as she painted the face that haunted her dreams. The sharp cheeks and angular jaw. The eyes that could never settle on being just one color. The mysterious tilt of those lips, secretive and knowing. Alice wasn't sure whether to laugh or cry that she still remembered Magdalene's features well enough to paint them, and accurately, too.

Perhaps the truth was that this was all inevitable, merely hurried on by Darby's vengefulness and obsession. Perhaps she would never be free of Magdalene, and those empty spaces would never be filled in. The idea turned her entire being into knots of anguish, and her strokes became violent as she brought to life the woman she had never fully understood. The brush hairs grew splayed from the abuse. Coffee splattered over the table's surface.

Heedless, Alice drove herself to exhaustion, intent on drawing Magdalene from her head in the way of venom from a bite. Desperate for some sense of control restored to her life. Desperate to give herself an ending more hopeful than the bitter idea that she *had* been a doll all along, and now she was merely a broken one. And the entire time, those eyes seemed to mock her...

Eventually, Alice realized she'd stopped painting. She blinked with sleep-crusted eyes, one cheek pressed against the cool surface of the table. Then a hand brushed hair from the other side of her face. For one blissful moment, sleep blurred her awareness too much for her to remember anything even as she recognized Colton's touch and moved into it with a hum.

Then it all came flooding back, and she jerked upright, flushing. "It's already morning?"

What a foolish question, for sunlight streamed through the windows. A foolish question, but Colton still nodded. He had already dressed for work, hair damp from a shower.

Her heart lurched as she rose from the chair. "I can make something to take with you."

"Forget it. Just wanted to be sure you knew I'd gone off to the mill."

Instead of leaving her to wake up with no way of knowing whether he had left for work or had left for good. Even while angry, he'd decided not to put her through hours of panic over the possibility that she'd been abandoned.

Tears welled in her eyes, and the words tumbled out before she could stop them. "It was about Magdalene. The nightmare I had last night."

At that, the frown lines on his forehead deepened, and his eyes lost some of their distance. When his gaze dropped to the table, she pushed the painting toward him.

He turned it around to look at it. "What about her?"

Oh, how she wished to spit out the words. To admit everything that clawed at her thoughts, day in and day out. At least she would feel clean in her honesty. Strands of hair had fallen back into her face, and she distractedly reached up to push them aside while fumbling for the courage to reveal it all.

Then she gasped, seeing that her furious painting and restless sleeping had loosened the bandage enough to reveal the cigarette marks. Before she could even think to hide her arm, Colton snarled and caught her hand. "The fuck is this?"

His grip on her wrist was painless but unyielding, and she had no choice but to sit there and watch his expression as he realized she'd lied to him.

"A burn from the oven?" he said, rage thick in his voice.

"I..."

"Are you doing this to yourself?"

Her throat choked up as she realized she truly didn't know the answer.

Then he looked at her, and her heart shattered like porcelain. His expression... That seething mix of concern, confusion, and suspicion. How many times had she seen her father stare at her mother in that way?

"I'm so sorry," she managed. "I never wanted to do this. To be like this."

"To be like what?" A growl slipped into his words.

Crazy. Erratic. A misery in your life.

But she was already crying too hard to answer, breath hitching in her chest. When he swore to himself, she twisted her wrist free of his grip. "Just go. You'll be late for work."

"Fuck the mill. I won't leave while you're like this."

And she didn't want him to see her while she was like this. Already, she could hear a shrill note in her voice that had also been in her mother's. "It's all right. I'll be fine."

"Fine?" Now he sounded incredulous, and that hurt more than the most savage bite.

"Colton, please." Her voice cracked on the last word.

He swore again, but this time she refused to look up, and after several agonizing moments, he left the kitchen. Then the door slammed, and in another heartbeat or two, his truck roared away. The tears streaming down her face felt hot enough to scald her skin.

Salt tracks still marked her cheeks when she poured her second cup of coffee for the morning. Just as she sipped at it, her phone rang.

Her stepmother's voice sounded bright, cheerful, and from an entirely different world. "How are you, honey?"

Alice's expression shifted into something pleasant, a hardwired reaction to such questions. "Fine, thanks."

"I didn't call too early?"

"Not at all."

"Good. I would have felt horrible over waking you up. Anyway, I have a big favor to ask. Fleur just now told me she volunteered to take cupcakes to her school's harvest festival tomorrow and that the flavor and decoration has to fit the autumn theme. Fleur's never baked anything so complicated, and I'm such a bad cook that I set eggs on fire when I try boiling them. Is there any way you can come over today and help make…"

Alice waited patiently until her stepmother's voice came back, the words imbued with doubt. "Apple pie cupcakes with cinnamon buttercream frosting. She found the recipe on Pinterest."

Cupcakes were fussy little things. Alice knew Denise would have trouble trying to make them. And getting out of the house would probably do her more good than crying in bed for the rest of the day. "I'm happy to help. Text me the recipe and I'll come over with all the ingredients."

"You're an angel. Does eleven work for you?"

"Sure."

"Fantastic. See you then, sweetheart." Denise made kissing noises before hanging up.

After setting the phone aside, Alice looked out the nearest window, taking in the cinnamon-colored trunks and bright green needles of the trees that marked the beginning of the forest. The sight left her feeling like she stood at a grave, but she made herself stand up to start getting ready.

Before leaving, she made a shepherd's pie. The notes for reheating it came easily enough, but then she found herself staring at the blank space left on the paper, struggling to put into words everything she wanted to tell Colton. In the end, only one sentence seemed honest enough. *I love you.*

She spent the forty-five minute drive in silence. Her ears popped several times as rugged mountains sank into gentle humps of land covered in wild grass and weeds. The winding road straightened out, smoothed out. Human architecture no longer cowered in the shadow of giant pines and instead row upon row of houses covered the hills, white walls and red roofs clear even at a distance. Shopping centers sprawled close to the road, calling at drivers with bright signs. It wasn't the asphalt jungle of a city, but civilization still reigned, and Alice already found herself missing the forest. The low hills and wide skies made her feel vulnerable and exposed.

In the light of day and without a vibrant party inside it, her father and stepmother's house looked plain yet well-groomed. Alice didn't feel one way or another about it; there were no memories of her mother cradled within those walls. Alice supposed it was bravado of some sort that her father hadn't transplanted them to another area after her mother's disappearance. Perhaps just a desperate attempt to keep things normal. But after he had met and married Denise, he'd unbent enough to sell the original house and move to a different suburb.

Denise couldn't crack an egg into a pan without making a mess, but she loved gardening, and a huge yard ripe for planting had been the new house's selling point for her. At the time, Alice had thought it very odd that her staid father would listen to an impractical reason like that. Later on, she realized it was because Denise had saved him in many ways.

Her mother's disappearance had left a deep wound, and Denise had been something normal, something good. It was really no surprise that Magdalene insulting her during the one and only time they'd all gone to dinner together had led to her father's polite ultimatum. Alice had never found out what Denise thought about it, or how much of that decision had come from her. It left her nervous as she rang the doorbell and waited, fingers twisting against the handles of the grocery bags.

But as soon as Denise opened the door, she smiled, eyes crinkling at the corners in genuine warmth. "Alice. I'm so glad you could come over."

Alice nodded, feeling a pleasant expression snap into place while Denise led her inside, still talking. "Fleur isn't here. She's busy at a leadership meeting. I told her not to wait until the last minute when she volunteers for something like this, but you know how girls that age are. Although you were never like that. You always seemed so much older. Responsible."

Alice just murmured something trivial, feeling dead inside.

The recipe was straightforward to an experienced home baker like Alice, and she quickly took charge of the pretty, aqua-colored stand mixer that looked as though it had never been used. Denise added paper liners to the muffin tins and then leaned on the counter and chattered while Alice measured ingredients and added them to the batter.

"Shannon has been asking after you. She spent a year in France and brought back a boyfriend. He's in training to become a pastry chef and makes the best croissants you can imagine."

Alice nodded while adding some sour cream. The bandage on her arm itched, but she knew better than to scratch it.

"Oh, and Felicia has two children now, can you believe it? A boy and a girl named Jack and Jill. She missed our anniversary party to stay home and watch them, but I know she's very interested in getting back in touch, too."

When Alice only made a neutral noise while scraping the sides of the bowl with a spatula, Denise's voice changed. "Sweetheart, it would be a good idea to get out more. None of your old friends have seen you even though you've been back for two months, and we never hear you talk about new ones."

"I left them back in the city. We didn't have much in common besides Magdalene." If she could have felt anything, it would have been shock over her casual mention of a very forbidden subject. How strange, that her life crumbling apart would leave her less fearful.

Awkward silence lingered between them before Denise said, "Well... That part of your life is over, and it's okay to let it go."

Her stepmother's hand felt like a stranger's as it squeezed hers, but Alice recognized the attempt at comfort, and made herself look up from the mindless movements of the mixer to smile at the other woman.

Encouraged, Denise added, "What happened to her sounded awful, but we're still here and we have no problem at all helping you back on your feet."

And Alice learned just how that would happen while portioning batter into the waiting cupcake liners. Surely she remembered Melanie Stiles? The daughter of a family friend. Well, she had a baby shower planned in the beginning of December and would love it if Alice went. Oh, and June Townsend? An associate of Alice's father. She *must* have remembered June. She now ran a sanctuary for golden retrievers and was always happy to take on volunteers to help with the dogs.

Alice pretended to pay attention as plans were made for her, but inwardly she questioned the neat trappings of suburban life. Was this really what she wanted? Was this why Darby and Rob's threats had frightened her so? True, the life of her parents was safe and good, as solid as cement poured into carefully measured wooden frames and left to harden into a foundation.

If she started down this path, then what? How soon before Denise's talk turned toward that of friends with bachelor sons? Alice could see it all mapped out before her, careful notches made in the measuring stick every time she stepped a bit closer to this comfortable, established life. A husband with a high salary and solid connections, a career under her belt that she could either juggle or give up when children came along, a house with neat hedges and bright, spacious rooms... It was their peace offering, she knew, their willingness to help her reach these things even though she had mired herself in mud by going off with Magdalene.

What would more scandal do? If she kept quiet and showed the cabin to Darby to prevent the past from crawling out into the open, *this* was what she would save. Not her life with Colton—she had tried protecting that, and look how it had already crumbled.

You chased him off, whispered that vicious part of her mind. *Sent him away like a dog.*

The thought hurt, but the next words were even worse, slithering up from the deepest well of her fears. *He would have left soon anyway. No one keeps company with a madwoman unless they're mad themselves.*

It got harder and harder to look happy as Denise continued talking. When her stepmother's phone rang, Alice felt her shoulders sag in relief, and quickly made the frosting while the cupcakes baked. Once they were out of the oven, a fifteen-minute rest in the freezer would leave them cool enough to be decorated, and then she could go home to the forest.

She was piping frosting on the final row of cupcakes when Denise appeared in the kitchen doorway, the phone angled away from her face so that she could whisper at Alice. "Remember Rachel? One of my oldest friends?"

Vaguely. As soon as she nodded, Denise added, "We're having a late lunch today to go over things for the Halloween charity auction we're all running. I asked if she'd mind you coming along, and she's so eager to see you. I'm sure the others will be, too. Can you make it?"

"I..." Something in Alice's expression must have indicated that her stammer could have been taken as a "yes," because her stepmother flashed a smile at her.

"Great," she whispered, and then her voice rose to its usual strength. "Rachel, that sounds fantastic. Alice is excited to see everyone. I *know*, five years!"

Later, as Denise drove her to the bistro, her stepmother sounded more sober. "Things might be a little awkward at first, but it's not your fault. Nicole is going through a rough period in her life but insisted on coming to help out with the auction details. She just signed her divorce papers today, so don't breathe a word about her ex-husband unless she brings him up. In fact, probably not even then."

Alice hardly listened, every muscle in her body tight with tension at having to pretend everything was good and normal for awhile longer. Time didn't move quite right, but she remained aware enough to recognize the bistro as that of a family friend's, and to follow her stepmother inside and murmur greetings to the three women waiting for them.

Her blood froze as she was introduced in return. More people to remember her. More people to feel a jolt of recognition if rumors ever surfaced about Tom Corrigan's daughter being involved in drugs and sex parties. Her heart knotted in fear even as she sat down and took the offered menu.

She was the youngest at the table by at least ten years, and bore their sighs and teasing remarks over her youth with patience, already remembering how she always felt at this sort of thing—a quiet outsider who said little to avoid showing just how baffled she felt by others.

Nerves twisted her stomach as she ordered the first thing on the menu. "The sea bass, please."

"Fish for lunch? Honey, you're not old enough to worry about your weight." That was from Rachel, who was thinner than Alice and had a face bearing the tight perfection of a scalpel's touch. Her red hair gleamed in thick waves, framing the diamonds glittering at her neck.

"It's so depressing when clothes no longer fit," said Brianne, who Alice now remembered. She'd been a source of gossip herself, back when Alice had been in grade school. The very young wife of one of her father's associates. Twenty-three to her husband's forty-one. The whispers had included turns of phrase like *gold digger* and *mid-life crisis*.

Looking at her now, Alice could see why Brianne would have stunned anyone into ignoring social tittering. Her heart-shaped face and bronze skin glowed even as she groaned, "Yesterday, I found some old jeans from before Logan was born. I almost cried when I couldn't get them up past my thighs."

"What does it matter?" said Nicole, her pink-painted nails looking more like claws as they curled around her wine. She had a beauty that would have been delicate as a girl but now came off as brittle. Alice watched her fingers flex and wondered if they would break before the glass did.

Undaunted by the lack of response, Nicole added, "Even when you starve yourself, exercise until you drop, and spend a fortune on erasing wrinkles and sagging skin, he *still* loses interest in you."

There was a brief pause before Alice's stepmother said in a bright voice, "Ladies, since we're waiting for our salads, how about we discuss the list for the silent part of the auction? I was thinking—"

"*I* was thinking about Irv," said Nicole, and then glared around the table as if daring anyone else to brush off her rage for a second time. All the others, even Denise, glanced away, but Alice found herself staring back at this woman she hardly knew, finding an echo of her own possible future in that heavily made-up face.

"Tom's daughter," said Nicole, slowly.

Alice heard Denise hiss in a breath, but it was as if Nicole's outburst had rendered everyone else speechless, and her words, ever so slightly slurred with the warmth of alcohol, continued unabated. "I remember you. Always so quiet. What happened to you? No, that doesn't matter. Here's the important thing: are you in love with someone?"

"Nicole—" said Denise, her tone losing its friendliness, and Alice realized that for all her stepmother's warmth, she would side with Alice's father in keeping their family safe from whispers and raised eyebrows. Magdalene was to be scrubbed away. Those entire five years were.

Alice knew her role to play: keep quiet and let others explain. She knew it and therefore was as surprised as anyone to hear herself respond, and worse, respond with the truth. "Yes. He's wonderful."

Such a foolish, vulnerable answer, but there was no hint of mockery in Nicole's face. "Of course he is. And you want to keep him. Well, then, talk to him. Don't *lie*, even if you think it'll make you look perfect. Look at me. I did nothing but lie to keep mine smiling, and *look* at what I've become."

"Nicole, honey, people are beginning to watch," murmured Rachel, quickly fluffing at her hair as if to make sure she would look put-together for any curious glances.

The other woman ignored her, gaze now dropping from Alice's as she continued. "I didn't like Guillaume. I didn't even understand half of what he said! But I was so tired of being alone in that house day after day, year after year, not knowing how to talk to Irv about anything during the rare times he was home. I told so many lies about myself that I forgot what the truth even was."

She slammed her wineglass down with that last word, and the stem shattered, spilling wine everywhere. Brianne, the nearest to her, yelped and jumped up to avoid the mess. Rachel and Denise both hissed words to Nicole, but the woman had broken with her glass, sobbing into the soiled tablecloth.

As her stepmother sighed and motioned at a waiter discreetly waiting nearby, Alice found herself reaching for Nicole's hand. When her fingers wrapped around heavy rings and paper-thin skin, the other woman hiccuped and looked up again.

"You always were a sweet little thing. Don't end up like me. Go tell your wonderful man everything. *Everything*. You'll never hurt him more than when you lie."

At that point, Denise walked around the table and tried coaxing Nicole upright with a hand against either shoulder. "Come on, sweetheart. We're all know you're having a hard time. Let's just schedule this meeting for another day."

All the fight seemed to have left Nicole, and the woman stood without resistance, clumsily reaching for her purse. She alone seemed unaware of the stares following her out, while the other women only pretended that they didn't notice.

Alice drifted after them. Nicole's words rang in her head like bells, stirring the part of her that still remembered the cool touch of moonlight on fur and the excitement of freshly spilled blood, and she remained lost in thought until her stepmother called her over to the car.

As Denise began driving back to the house, she said, "I'm so sorry about that. I didn't think she would completely fall apart."

When Alice shrugged it off, her voice turned curious. "He's wonderful?"

Alice already regretted having said that, but there was no taking it back. "I've been seeing someone for a few months. Quietly."

Her stepmother didn't seem to know what to say. "Is it serious?"

"I'm about to find out." Fresh panic rippled through her, but so did something else: determination.

Her attempts at ignoring the strange things that had been happening to her, at pushing away her crippling fear of becoming like her mother... None of them had worked. Why was she even here? To put on a brave face and convince people she was all right? She wasn't. Nicole's words had lit a seething need within her, one that wouldn't be satisfied until she found Colton and revealed everything. If she had driven him away, then he should know why it had really happened. And if she was going mad, then she could at least say how much she loved him before she finished the spiral down into becoming a paranoid shell like her mother.

She left for home as soon as possible, impatience pushing her to drive faster than usual while she tried calling the sawmill, wanting to hear his voice, wanting to finally *explain*. Fear choked her when the man who took her call admitted that Colton had never shown up for his shift.

Tears blurred her eyes after she hung up, and she blinked rapidly, trying to clear her sight. Had he left for the forest? Even if he had, she still wouldn't give up, not now. She had to find him. She had to—

A form flashed in front of the car, a blur of movement more than an actual shape. Alice gasped, stomping on the brakes as her mind scrambled to take in what was happening. Something on the road... God, she would kill it...

Even as she wrenched the wheel, the car swerved close enough to see the figure in full, feet now planted on the asphalt. She had only a heartbeat to take in that familiar, wicked smile before the guard rail loomed. Then tires squealed, metal crunched. Alice felt the sickening sensation of airlessness for one breathless moment before the world jolted around her and closed in.

Slowly, she grew aware of herself breathing, and of how the sun glittered through the fractured windshield like dew on spiderwebs. Footsteps crunched in the leaves, slow and steady as they drew near. When she whimpered, mouth refusing to shriek for help, someone leaned in through the driver's window, heedless of the broken glass. Despite the crumpled metal all around, Alice managed to turn her head, blinking as blood dripped down her face.

Magdalene smiled, a cigarette hanging loosely from the hand that braced itself against the window frame. "You never could understand subtext, could you?"

More wetness trickled down Alice's cheeks. She wasn't sure if it was blood or tears.

In the brilliant light, Magdalene's eyes looked amber. A dip of her head that left them in shadow, and they turned black. Just like when she had been alive. "It's not that mangy fucking wolf I'm after. What I want, dear Alice, is you."

Alice's breath scraped against her throat as she choked out syllables. "But... Indigo?"

The smile faded from Magdalene's face. "She's been gone for years. You're all I have, and I'm not leaving this world alone."

Then her free hand reached for the broken glass of the window. Most of the pane had fractured into glittering chips, but one piece was big enough to hold like a razor blade, and its edge gleamed just as wickedly.

Alice still couldn't move, but now a shriek flew out of her, terror driving it on as Magdalene angled the piece for her neck, smiling again.

Then a sound rose above her ragged voice. The rumbling of a truck slowing down. Magdalene recoiled, the piece of glass gleaming as it dropped from her hand. Even when she disappeared, as silent and sudden as a snuffed candle flame, Alice continued to scream, thrashing against the metal trapping her still.

A man slid down the muddy walls of the ditch, his words drowned out until her voice faded into wracking sobs that made her entire body flare in pain.

"You'll be all right. Ma'am? You'll be fine. I already called 9-1-1. Everything's fine."

"No," she managed, but the word was too mangled by her hiccups of breath to be understood. Fine? It was all very far from being fine.

CHAPTER SEVEN

TWO HUNTERS

Alice had never been admitted to a hospital before but there she was, dressed in a medical gown and tucked into bed. Needles were attached to both arms; she didn't ask why, or bother reading the fluid bags that they led to. Denise sat in a chair by the bed, eyes averted from Alice as if hospitalization was somehow catching. Her father stood stiff and grim-faced, still in his suit from work.

Alice glanced at the clock, wishing time slid by faster. Wishing the doctor hadn't ordered her to stay a few hours for observation.

"I don't see why I can't go home," she said, timidly. "The x-rays and MRI came back fine."

Her father sighed. "Ally, I saw your car. It looked like a crushed tin can. If they want to watch you for signs of a concussion, then that's that."

"And we can take care of anything that needs to be done at the house," added Denise. "Feed a pet, or drag out the garbage cans, or... Well, anything."

The next words that came out of her hurt and not because of her scraped, battered body. "Did you try the sawmill again?"

Her father answered. "Yes, just before I came back in here. He still hasn't shown up. Doesn't he have his own phone?"

Alice shook her head. She had once asked Colton something similar and had gotten the reasonable answer that the more he carried with him, the more he was likely to lose in a sudden switch to his wolf form. So simple and yet so impossible to reveal to others.

She didn't miss the gleam of curiosity in Denise's eyes, or her father's dubious expression. Her first rambling words to them in the hospital had been to call him; outside of her brief answer to Nicole's question, it was also the first time she'd revealed that he even existed in her life, and she half-wondered whether they thought she'd made him up under the stupor of pain medication.

After a short silence, Denise said, "Your father also called Phil. It's obvious you'll need a new car, and you know how he loves to battle with car dealers."

Phil Harris, her father's financial adviser. "That's really not something that—"

"You need a car," said her father. The undercurrent to the words warned her not to argue. "An SUV for those mountain roads."

Her stepmother's voice brightened. "How about a Subaru? Terry loves hers."

Alice said nothing, realizing that giving them something to talk about would be better than waiting in suffocating silence. Looking at the needles taped to the backs of her hands made her feel sick, so her gaze drifted out through the doorway. The nurses' station was within her line of view, men and women in their scrubs hurrying in and out like bees at a hive. For one heartbeat, she thought she glimpsed a flash of black among the dull blues and greens of weaving bodies, and thought she heard the rap of a heel among the squeaking of rubber soles. Fingers digging into the blankets, she closed her eyes. If she saw Magdalene's face again, saw that smile, she might scream before she could stop herself.

"Honey, was it really a deer?" Denise sounded hesitant. "It's just that you were acting a little odd this morning..."

"Denise." Her father's voice sounded low and curt, the tone that Alice recognized as a warning to change the subject.

She kept her eyes closed, panic starting to itch at her. "Is that how you really want to put it? Or do you actually mean that I was acting crazy like my mother?"

"Alice." Nearly a growl, that.

"I'm sorry." She opened her eyes again, but kept them fixed on her fingers, which were still white-knuckled against the blankets.

Fortunately, a doctor appeared soon after that, announcing his presence with a crisp knock on the doorway. Alice remained quiet as he checked her over, heart pounding in her throat while waiting for his pronouncement.

"You can go home," he said, finally, and she sagged in relief until he added, "But someone needs to watch over you for the next twenty-four hours."

"We will," said her father, and Denise quickly added, "It'll take no time at all to set up the guest bedroom."

Alice didn't have it in her to argue.

The discharge process from the hospital was both stressful and tedious, dragging on until Alice finally found herself blinking outside the entrance doors, the late afternoon sun casting the parking lot in hues of orange. Beyond the busy street, hills rolled toward the horizon, leading up to the dim shapes of the mountains. Her thoughts drifted back to Colton. Where was he?

"Sweetheart?" said Denise, the word pulling at her attention, and Alice felt nine years old again while being led to the car.

Her body hurt with each jostle in the road on the way to her father and stepmother's house, and the lingering smell of antiseptic on her skin began to make her feel ill. Alice kept her gaze fixed outside the window, trying not to think about anything.

The guest bedroom was decorated in soothing shades of lilac and grey. Unable to face the thought of talking to her father or stepmother for the rest of the evening, she pointed out that the doctor had said she could sleep if she felt tired. It got them to leave her in peace, and she closed the door for extra privacy before dropping onto the plush bed.

She had just curled up into a fetal position when her phone vibrated. Darby's name flashed across the screen. Alice denied the call without a second thought. What a delicious twist to add to the book: a car crash that further questioned her sanity. Tears burned in Alice's eyes even when she tried closing them.

The sky visible through the windows darkened. Occasionally, Alice heard the murmur of her father's voice. Denise checked on her twice, apologetic about the fact that she had to be woken up every three hours to make sure she hadn't slipped into anything deeper than sleep.

Finally, when the moon hung high in the sky, she drifted off, feeling as if she fell into a darkness that soaked into every limb. Her dreams were wild, thrashing things, feverish in their intensity. Hands clawed at her. Glass chips stung against her skin. She howled like a wolf, but the call went unanswered. Eventually, the suffocating darkness solidified into leaf litter beneath her feet and stars above her head. Trees surrounded her, scarcely more than shadows, but Magdalene stood before her clear and bright. The smell of her cigarette wrapped around Alice's senses like a rope.

"Alice." She held out a hand.

Alice didn't move, skin breaking out into shivers as she said, "What do you want?"

"To talk with you."

"After you tried cutting my throat on glass?"

"Do I have any with me right now? Anything dangerous at all?" There was that sardonic humor, rippling through her voice like an electric current as she spread her empty hands wide. "I've hurt you before and you're still alive. Don't tell me you're scared."

"I was always a little afraid." The words slipped out before she could stop them. Alice glanced around the clearing again, embarrassed that her heart was already so open.

"You shouldn't have been. You made me bleed just as much." Such words should have been harsh, but instead they felt as gentle as a caress, drawing Alice's gaze back to the woman she had never truly understood. She looked free of injury, slender throat whole and pale against her dark hair, and her mouth smiled knowingly, free of the bitterness that had been constant in their final years together.

When Alice remained quiet, Magdalene tilted her head. "Don't *you* wish to talk? To find out what this is all about?"

"What if it's a trick?"

"Tricks are only dangerous if you have something left to lose. Do you?" Then Magdalene's fingers stretched toward her once more.

Alice hesitated, doubt and fear and weariness all clamoring within her as the question sank into her heart like a stone dropped into water. But slowly, she reached out and placed her hand in Magdalene's, watching her eyes glint gold in response.

"Finally," breathed Magdalene, and led her further into the clearing.

The hunt had been an easy one, quicker than many others of his past. The black wolf shifted in his seat, always aware of his surroundings even while in human form, and turned to the next page of the manuscript. He was nearly through it all.

The neck pinned beneath his shoe spasmed and choked out froth-filled words. "I'm telling you, it's exactly the same. The copy she made for Alice isn't any fucking different."

The wolf gave the human his full stare until his voice died away. Perhaps it was the same; perhaps it wasn't. He wanted to be sure either way.

At the flick of another page, the man groaned. "Just take it. Please. You already have the photos. Why are you even still—"

The wolf moved his foot, choking off the windpipe until man's face changed color. "You gave me a handful. How many are still hidden?"

"None, I swear. She didn't like doing it, so I don't have many shots of her."

"You forced her."

"No!" Now there was an actual whine in the man's voice. His eyes looked as wild as a trapped rabbit's while the tip of the wolf's shoe dug into the softness beneath his chin. "It was Magdalene. She liked seeing what Alice would do for her. I never pushed her into anything. I swear to God."

The wolf closed the manuscript to study the man. He had let the human speak and squirm to see what he would do. Fight back? Threaten him? It turned out that he hadn't the balls for either action, not when he was the one caught in a trap. Even now, bleeding on the floor, the human could have snapped at him. Maybe not with those blunt little teeth, but surely with details about the photos. Some that thought they were about to die turned vicious.

But this one... This one was like a coyote, ready to pounce on an opportunity to feed himself. Always screaming when he was caught with a mouthful of stolen meat. Above all else, he served himself, and that meant doing whatever he could to stay alive.

As much as the wolf hated to admit it, Alice might be safer if this human lived and fought against his wife's obsession... For now.

When the man's sniveling dwindled away, the wolf resumed thumbing through the last pages of the manuscript. He had come across the one given to Alice after returning home to find her gone, the note left on a casserole being her only explanation. Fear had drowned out every other hint of her lingering scent, and yet she'd still tried to make sure he wouldn't go hungry.

If the wolf hadn't had years of control to guide him, he would have growled then and there over her being out of his reach. Why wouldn't she talk? Before that pink-haired human had visited, she had licked at his teeth. Now she couldn't even look at him. Guilt. That was always in her scent, too. But over *what*?

Then the mail for the day had arrived. Traces of that cunt's scent had lingered on one of the envelopes, and the wolf had ripped it open without another thought. And with that, the guilt had made complete sense.

Now finished with reading, the black wolf set the manuscript aside. Beneath his foot, the human twitched, realizing his last moments of limbo had drawn to an end.

The wolf leaned down, putting pressure on the man's throat. "What else does your wife have?"

"Nothing! Just the cheesecake ones I gave you."

"There was a note with the photos that came in today's mail. She said there were worse ones. Penetration shots with a man."

Profanity hissed out of the human's mouth. Fresh panic flooded his scent.

It was all the wolf needed to confirm his suspicions, and a growl thundered in his chest. "You did more than take the photos. You're in the other ones."

"No! You *have* all the nudes and all the nega—"

The rage that had seethed through the wolf from the moment he'd seen the first photo now spilled over, and his kick to the human's ribs cracked bone. The man shriveled in on himself like a slug, but the wolf wasn't finished, hauling him up to throw him against the desk. Wood buckled. Papers flew in the air.

He knew how to maul, how to maim beyond recognition, and his teeth ached for it even as he restrained himself to fists, treating the human as an enemy too weak to even be a true rival. Harry it, threaten it, bruise it—but don't kill it. Let it survive long enough to understand terror.

When the human's scent turned hazy with shock, the wolf grabbed him again, ignoring a wheeze of words to slam him against a bookcase. "You think you're in pain now? Tell me where they are or I'll start bleeding you."

There was a breath of silence before the man crumpled. "She doesn't have them. I do. They're in another envelope in my desk. The second drawer on the right."

Still suspicious, the wolf went through them all without care, wrenching wood and spilling papers. The human coughed, limp on the floor and clutching at his ribs. Soon, the wolf found the envelope and ripped it open. With his foot back on the man's throat, he looked through each photo as carefully as he had with the manuscript. Alice's face was visible in most of them, clearly so, and if it wasn't a question of what kept her safest, he would have torn into the man's belly then and there.

He waited to speak until he knew the words would come out flat. "I'll kill you. Not now. Not tomorrow. The moment any other photos of her are released. Either through you or through your wife."

As expected, the human whined and cringed, and the wolf nearly snarled in disgust that this whimpering thing had ever had touched Alice. *This* wretch was what had tried to leash her?

He ignored the panicked wheezing while sliding the photos back into the envelope, but just as he tucked it all into the inside pocket of his jacket, the human coughed and managed, "Darby will do what she wants. I can't stop her. She's fucking obsessed. Thinks Magdalene is talking to her in dreams and showing her how to avenge her death or some shit. She doesn't even make sense anymore. Please. I can't stop her."

The wolf fell still. He never trusted words, but these ones revealed glimpses of a pattern all too familiar. "She appears just in the dreams or during the day, too?"

The man coughed again, hope filling his expression. "Yeah, in the day. Flickers in the corners of her eye. Seeing her at the other end of the street. Things moved around the house. That's why she's obsessed with Halloween. Samhain. She wants to do a fucking—"

"Seance." The wolf licked his teeth as they grew out. It had been years since he'd lost enough control to let his features twist like that. He forced them back into blunt human shape, but his fury remained. More things now made sense. The cunt was haunting Alice. Haunting her and using the female human like a puppet to hunt her. Those cigarette burns on her arm. The way he'd caught Alice jumping at nothing, fear flooding her scent. At *him*, he'd thought, even... And Alice had gone through it for weeks in silence, unaware she was being driven into believing she was going mad.

A snarl burst out of him and the human flinched, mistaking the reason for it. "I'm telling you, I can't do anything."

Hands scrabbled at his shoe, silently begging him to believe the words.

The wolf kicked them away. "Stop your wife or I'll kill you. It's that simple."

Then he pulled away, the hunting drive already hot in his bones. He needed to find Alice *now*. She wasn't mad like she feared, but with her witch blood it wouldn't take much to send her tumbling into the shadow world. She worried about losing her mind, but the bitch was trying to take her, soul and all.

CHAPTER EIGHT

A VIOLENT TRUTH

"Do you know why your mother left you?" Cruel words, but Magdalene's voice sounded gentle, even sad.

They sat facing each other, Magdalene serene among the creeping ferns and Alice shivering, bare feet tucked beneath her and shoulders hunched under the thin sleep shirt. Thick moss gleamed green between them. Firs loomed all around. The sky looked jet-black—not a single star in sight to suggest with its wheeling path where they were or how long they'd been there.

The question stung at Alice's thoughts, but instead of answering, she glanced out at the dark water of a stream that burbled mere feet away. Fresh shivers ran through her at the lack of frogs croaking on its muddy banks, at the lack of rustling in nearby undergrowth where water rats or raccoons would have foraged. And the trees—they didn't shift in the wind that tugged at her hair like cold fingers, and their shadowy trunks absorbed none of the light from the moon that hung overlarge in the sky. No, this wasn't the throbbing, heedless nature that she knew.

"Where are we?" she said, aware of Magdalene's unwavering attention.

"In a place where we can talk in peace." There was a silkiness to the words that suggested no firmer explanation would be given. "I've answered your question. Are you going to answer mine?"

Without looking in her direction, Alice quietly said, "My mother left me because she was crazy."

"She *was*, but that's no reason to do what she did. Many people are crazy and yet never abandon their children. The bond between mother and child is supposed to be the most sacred."

Reluctantly, Alice's gaze returned to the other woman. "Why, then?"

In the strange stillness surrounding them, Magdalene's eyes were the only thing that seemed real, vivid, alive. "It's because she didn't love you enough to stay."

Alice felt her mouth tremble. "How can you say that?"

"What, the truth?" Magdalene leaned closer, her expression still gentle. "Where's the wolf?"

She didn't want to answer, but when Magdalene raised an eyebrow, her voice came out as an ashamed whisper. "I... I chased him away."

"No, he *left*. He found you to be too much trouble." Then Magdalene reached out and caught Alice's chin, fingers soft as they stroked her chilled skin. "Remember, I study people for a living, absorbing everything they do to uncover the truth behind all their lies and posturing. I find their hearts. I see what they try to hide."

Alice didn't trust herself to speak, not when tears threatened to spill down her cheeks. But she didn't pull away, either, and her gaze now met those inscrutable eyes in full, asking the question that refused to come to her tongue.

Magdalene saw it and answered. "People look at you and like you, Alice, but that's it. They leave because all of them eventually realize you're not worth fighting for."

Alice broke, face crumpling into tears and body sinking like a puppet cut from its strings. Cries wrenched from her throat, echoing raggedly through the trees.

Then Magdalene's arms folded around her, still painfully familiar, and that velvet voice whispered in her ear, "All of them except me."

Alice gave her something that was half-sob, half-growl, and tried to shove her away. Magdalene held on. "Have I ever abandoned you?"

"No." Her lungs hurt with each word. "You just fed off me."

Magdalene laughed, the quiet, reluctant one that was the closest she ever came to revealing a vulnerable point of her being. The sound of it made Alice fall still and unresisting even when Magdalene wiped the wet tracks from her cheeks. "True, but I couldn't help it. You were always so pure. So sweet. I took it for granted that I could turn to you whenever I felt too miserable with myself."

"Your second heart," said Alice, her voice still thick with tears. She felt as cold as ash, nothing more than the remnants of something long burned away.

Magdalene nodded, eyes glittering despite the surrounding darkness. "Why do you think I haven't left?"

"Revenge."

Another laugh, and now Magdalene brushed hair back from her face. "Who cares about that fucking animal? Did he ever even say he loved you?"

"He doesn't like words," murmured Alice, but uncertainty hitched in her voice.

"No, what he likes is comfort. A full belly. A warm, dry place to sleep at night. And now that you're having trouble providing that for him..."

Oh, it stung, seeing the pieces laid out so neatly before her, but Alice still tried to refute Magdalene's points, still tried to rattle her calmness. "I love him."

"Of course you do, poor Alice. You're really too good for the world." Magdalene caressed her face again. "You'll never be recognized, you know. So many people will pass you by without understanding your worth. I'm the only one who can truly see you and love you for it."

Alice opened her mouth, groping for a response that could deny what sounded more and more like a terrible truth. But then Magdalene's lips caught her own, soft and coaxing and clever.

"Leave it all and join me," she breathed, soft fingertips tracing the pulse in Alice's throat before slipping further down. As she eased the sleeves of Alice's over-large shirt from her shoulders, she added, "What do you have to look forward to? What's the point of squirming blind through the world and always being disappointed? Always finding yourself left behind?"

The chill in the air hardened Alice's nipples immediately, and she shuddered when the heat of Magdalene's mouth followed. It had always stunned her, receiving such tenderness when she knew full well the venom that could hide behind those crimson lips. She shivered again, back arching. The crust of salt from tears itched at her cheeks, but already she felt flushed and even dizzy.

The world slipped and slid as clever hands eased off the shirt in full. Then they flexed against her shoulders, pushing her down until the skin of her back prickled against damp leaves and earth. She felt her hair spill out around her and heard the lapping of water, but Magdalene's kisses coaxed her full attention, each one honey-sweet and numbing.

It was almost enough to lull her, to let that final spark of doubt burn out so that velvet darkness could rush into its place unhampered. But then she felt a hand slide over the sensitive skin between her breasts, palm pressing right where her heart beat hard and fast.

Alice twitched in response, and even as the lips against her smiled, ghostly words flashed into her mind like lightning piercing the suffocating murk of a storm.

My second heart...

A promise. A damnation.

"No!" Her hand shoved at the one on her chest, skin burning as if the very touch had been poisonous. Then she twisted from that treacherous mouth, fumbling for her shirt.

Magdalene seemed stunned, even letting Alice push her away and sit back up.

"I'm no longer that stupid little girl," hissed Alice, covering her chest with the fabric. "You took five years of my life, but you're not taking the rest."

At that, Magdalene managed a scoff, but her eyes were still wide with shock. "What life do you have left?"

Something rose up within her, something desperate and savage. "I don't know. But it's still *mine*."

Magdalene had already found her smile, the amused one that suggested she always knew better. "You'll see differently once you cross the veil. I did."

Then the other woman was on her, her wiry strength flattening Alice against the ground. Alice snarled, scratching at whatever she could reach even as a hand slid up to her throat and tightened. Before Alice realized pain was pain, her head was being pushed backwards. Her whole body was, she and Magdalene both slithering down through moss and mud while they fought. Water caught the tips of Alice's hair, and her movements turned panicked. They were at the stream and still sliding.

Sedge and reedgrass lashed at Alice's cheeks before air plunged into water. She flailed, neck feeling like it was about to snap in Magdalene's grip as currents rushed to fill her mouth and nose. The other woman now straddled her, pinning her down, pinning her still beneath the surface of the stream. Alice's heart raced as she ripped at the arms holding her under, bubbles of air already escaping from her mouth.

A scream choked in her throat as her lungs started burning. The murky water stung at her eyes as her hands scratched with fresh desperation. She couldn't die like this. Lost to the world with only Magdalene as a guide to whatever waited beyond? Hell itself would be kinder.

But Magdalene's fingers felt like bands of iron, unflinching and inescapable. Alice kept fighting, but as her lungs tightened to knots, her strength dwindled from attacking Magdalene to begging her. Please... *Please.*

Just as the blackness around her began to spin, Magdalene's grip flinched. Then it was gone.

Alice no longer knew up from down, but she flailed anyway, fighting until suffocating water broke into lapping waves and sweet, chilled air. As she gasped and clawed at nothing, screams reached her. Not her own—her lungs spasmed in her chest. Helpless, coughing, she scrabbled until her fingers found mud leading up. With the last of her energy, she grabbed handfuls of wild grass and pulled herself onto the bank. Even as the shrieking reached a new pitch, she raked at the wet mass of her hair with a shaking hand, clearing her vision enough to see.

The black wolf's fur bristled as he ripped at Magdalene. Savage teeth lacerated her arms as she covered her face and throat. Screams echoed throughout the trees. The wolf moved like a shadow, quick and silent in his hunt, intent on the slightest opening. Nothing would satisfy him except a killing bite.

When Magdalene tried to roll away, he caught her nearest elbow and jerked at it in the vicious way Alice had seen him use to disembowel prey. Bone snapped and Magdalene's voice turned ragged as her arm went limp, revealing her face.

The wolf let go to lunge for her throat, but she was already gone, vanished like smoke. Alice, still struggling to see with watery eyes, thought she caught a ripple of darkness among the stark trees as Magdalene's final scream rang through the air. Within a heartbeat, it eeled away into the larger gloom, disappearing like a shark's fin sinking back into the water.

Then it was only her and the black wolf. He loped over, tongue lolling and eyes glowing like fire.

Teeth chattering, Alice forced herself up, both hands reaching for him even though she well knew he could—might —tear into her just as viciously. A cold nose sniffed at her throbbing throat; bloodstained jaws nuzzled at her sodden hair. Alice's breath dipped into a sob as she buried her face into thick, coarse fur. "Colton."

He twined around her restlessly, panting as his ears twitched this way and that to catch any hints of lingering danger. With every cough that wracked her body, though, he pressed close to let her cling against him. Blood covered his fur, filling her senses and slicking her skin, and she started shaking as the enormity of it all hit her.

"R-real," she managed, despite how her lungs still choked on air. "She's *real*."

He growled briefly, nosing at her as if to urge her up. It was a clear enough message; they needed to leave wherever they were and reach true safety. Alice rose on shaking legs, one hand buried in the thick fur between his shoulders as he led her through billowing mist that shined strangely. Her hair still clung to her face and neck, proving there had been water at one point, and fallen fir needles stuck to the swathes of mud on her chest and belly from where she'd crawled up the bank, but their surroundings had shifted into a vague landscape of grey and the ground felt as insubstantial as the air.

Lights glimmered in the distance. Colton guided her toward them, silent and sure. Alice didn't know how long they walked before the cloying fog receded, taking its glow with it. Stars began to glitter in the sky once more, and an owl screeched as they crossed swells of grass damp with dew. The rhododendrons looming on either side were the last clue she needed to recognize where they were—on the slope of earth that separated a manmade pond from the cul-de-sac that held her parents' house.

She nearly stopped to look behind her, wondering if glimpses of that strange forest yet remained, but Colton pressed close to hurry her steps. And with good reason; they were now in full view of houses. Alice knew what a sight she'd be for anyone who happened to glance out a window. Naked and covered in mud, one trusting hand buried in the thick pelt of a rangy wolf that looked ready to attack anything that drew too close... They must have appeared as though they were figures slipping in from another world. A hysterical laugh bubbled in her throat over how true that was.

All the windows were dark as they pushed through the neatly clipped shrubbery that bordered her parents' backyard. Alice ignored the stinging of branches jabbing at her legs, all her focus instead on the small patio that led into the guest room. The sliding glass doors had been left open and the room appeared as unlit as the rest of the house. She might just make it inside without being caught.

Metal railing fenced in the patio, thin yet sturdy. She didn't see how she would get back over it; her legs trembled as hard as the rest of her body, and her lungs still hitched whenever she breathed in too deeply.

But as soon as she paused, the wolf beneath her fingers flickered like a shadow, and hot skin replaced fur. Hands caught her by the waist, easily lifting her up and over the railing. Then Colton jumped it himself, the movement smooth and deadly like the hunter he was. Moonlight picked out the blood trailing down his jaw and chest, but his eyes remained in shadow, unreadable.

Alice reached for him anyway, needing to touch him again, needing to feel that he was real. Rough hands pulled her close to tense muscle, the mud on her skin smearing with the blood on his. His touch felt nothing like Magdalene's. It was thrilling instead of numbing, demanding instead of enticing. It reminded her of blood beating through veins and the tender danger of teeth *just* pressed against skin.

As he pushed tendrils of hair from her face, she whispered, "You found me."

"Always, Alice."

Then he was kissing her, and iron filled her mouth. Yet she didn't flinch from the taste, nor from those savage teeth as his arms tightened around her. Now she welcomed the dizziness of being breathless and delighted in the possessiveness of fingers running over her in the same way that hers ran over him. Yes, let them devour each other, simple and clean in their hunger. Let the sweetness of tongue meet with the honesty of fang.

Then one of his hands slid up the curve of her neck, intent on grabbing a fistful of hair. But the rasp of calluses against battered flesh made her wince, made her flinch. He noticed and broke off to examine her. She panted through a sudden spike of nerves, waiting for his reaction, and when he growled, she knew it must have looked as bad as it felt. His touch turned feather-light while tracing the nearest marks, but his eyes had gone as hot as molten metal.

"It doesn't matter," she said, and meant it.

He just growled again, leaning in until his mouth replaced his fingers. Heat rushed through her as his tongue began soothing the throbbing skin there, tender and unhurried. As he nuzzled along her neck, finding each mark and easing away its pain, she fell boneless in his arms. Words slipped out of her, unburdened by fear. "I'm sorry for everything."

"Fuck apologies." He licked at the part of her throat where Magdalene's nails had scraped the skin.

"I should have told you," she insisted. "I should have explained why I thought I was going crazy. I didn't realize it was real. That she wants me *dead*."

Then she shivered, understanding just how close she had come to being found floating in the pond, lifeless and caught in the cattails. Poor Alice Corrigan, driven by the same tendencies as her mother. At least this time the body had been found...

She didn't realize she had gone stiff with tension until Colton kissed the point of her neck where her pulse beat hard and fast. "The fear's hitting you."

A new type of it, yes, one more numbing than the sharp anguish she had felt in the past weeks. The raw awareness that all her hiding still hadn't kept the past at bay. "A little. I never thought she could come back."

The moon had crossed enough of the sky for its light to shine into the room, and Colton's eyes gleamed at her as he said, "You're safe. The bitch is gone for the night. If she comes back, I'll snap her neck instead of her arm."

It coaxed a laugh out of her, but she quickly fell serious again. There were a million questions left to ask. What was Magdalene, now—a ghost? Something more? And what was that strange forest? How much did Colton know? How much of this related to Darby, for that matter, who had grown obsessive over Magdalene? Two worlds now slipped around Alice, and the one of ghosts in dead forests was too furtive to explain in the mundane light of day. What would her parents think, should she try to tell them about it? They already worried she was mad.

So many questions, but all that filled her mind as the fear receded was a need to touch the body warm and sure against hers, to bask in the solid presence of at least one other creature who would never question her own strangeness. She dropped her head against his as another shiver broke over her.

He noticed that as well. "You need to get dry. Warm up."

"We both do," she said, rasping fingers against the blood that had dried thick and sticky on the scruff of his jaw.

In the shower, he tasted every part of her body while the water sluiced over them both. Her skin was a mass of bruises and scrapes from the car accident and Magdalene's attack, but his mouth made her feel like the sweetest thing alive even as his expression changed now that she was clean and exposed, her near-death experiences mapped out in front of him in ugly red and purple.

He grew more insistent in the bedroom, as restless against her as when he'd been a wolf. His hands ran along her arms while she locked the door, no longer caring if her parents grew upset at being kept out, and his gaze kept jumping to the large bruise on her sternum, the exact place where Magdalene had placed her palm.

When she turned to him to ask if he was willing to risk being found with her, a hard kiss caught her question and swallowed it unsaid. She hummed as he pinned her to the bed, hot skin and hard muscle managing to avoid the worst of her bruises even while agitated energy seethed in his every movement.

His voice was as rough as his mouth as it rumbled against her neck. "Thinking she could fucking take you. Her smell's still everywhere on your skin."

If she didn't know him better, she might have taken the words as ones of disgust or suspicion. A questioning of how much of her had wished to leave with Magdalene after all. But she *did* know him, this wolf. He had nearly lost her. Had nearly seen her die. He needed to feel that she was real as surely as she did with him.

Even beasts of the night seek reassurance. A howl in the dark is a howl wishing it will be answered.

But what were words to such a creature? Meaningless huffs of breath. Carriers of confusion and lies. No, she had hurt them both by hiding, and now she would reveal herself in full. She would give herself over as soft, willing flesh and let the predator taste how sweet she really found it, sating his hunger.

Ignoring the flare of bruises, she wrapped her legs around him and watched his expression change. His cock was already hardening against her thigh when she murmured, "Then replace her scent with yours."

"I can't go easy while I fucking smell her on you. Understand?" A warning from him, a last chance to back away from his hunger even while desperation gleamed in his eyes.

She felt like laughing. Was she supposed to feel fear or mistrust? Let him savage her. She would treasure every hint of his teeth.

"Perfectly," she whispered against his mouth. Then she licked at it.

In a mere heartbeat, she found herself with her head over the edge of the bed, a hand cradling the back of her skull. She knew what was coming, and grinned in anticipation as the head of his cock nudged at her mouth. She took him eagerly, tongue sliding against the thick length while he pushed in, hand tender against her chin even as he growled.

His first thrust was hard and deep, slapping his heavy sack against her face, and her laughter hummed around him. Yes, this what she wanted, always—this was what she had been so afraid of losing. The filth and abandon of keeping company with a monster. A hunter's devotion, always intent on her as something to catch and savor.

Salt and musk filled her senses as she sucked, each flick of her tongue drawing shudders from him. He braced himself against the bedpost with one hand, still grinding his hips against her face while his other hand slid over her feverish skin, squeezing at vulnerable flesh. He was rough where there weren't bruises, merciless at drawing out her need, and soon she was panting against him quick and soft, clenching her thighs together.

Then she felt his weight shift even while his hips continued thrusting, felt the hardness of his body press against her own shaking one. He sucked at the tender skin of her lower belly, teasing a path ever closer to her already aching cunt. Then he nipped at one fattened fold, and the feel of his teeth left her hips arching.

The rumble from him sounded amused as he pinned her still and spread her legs. As air rushed against her exposed cunt, she moaned against him, already close. He took her even further, rasping his chin against the sensitive flesh as his tongue tasted every part of her it could find. Teeth finding that exquisite point between tenderness and agony, breath teasing in its very softness... He had a predator's patience, savoring every moment it took for her to lose all sense and howl as if she were a beast herself.

Her first climax left her shrieking against his cock, but he didn't stop, stoking her into another when he sucked instead of licked. Her hips writhed, trying to lessen the delicious torment of that wicked mouth, but he only held them still and kept going. Her third time was body-wracking, bone-melting, and after that she fell limp, dazed as hot aftershocks shivered through her.

Dimly, she felt his thrusts turn sharp and fast, and grew aware enough to suck at his cock as it bucked deep in her mouth. Colton's teeth bit into her thigh, growl rising into a snarl as hot seed flooded her full. She sighed around him, managing to suck him clean before falling completely limp.

A few heartbeats passed as they panted and shook against each other, and then Colton pulled out. In another moment he stretched over her again, this time face-to-face, and pulled her into a lingering kiss. As the taste of her excitement mingled with the musk of his, he shifted just enough to catch one of her thighs and push it up. The head of his cock nudged at her swollen folds, drawing a gasp out of her.

"Already?" she breathed, fingers digging into his shoulders.

He licked at a bead of sweat trailing down the hollow of her throat, still hungry, still intent on devouring her alive. "It's been days. They're still full."

"I can tell." Despite her exhaustion, she slid a hand down to cup his balls, finding them heavy and swollen. "Is that from being a wolf?"

"Questions, always questions." He swallowed her laugh with an impatient kiss.

In response, she hooked her legs around him, the only invitation he needed to thrust all the way in. He was too intent to pace himself like usual, the frenzy of his hips jolting her entire body. Drops of sweat fell on her skin as his eyes stared into hers, their green dark, ravenous. When his teeth caught the damp skin of her shoulder, she shook in bliss even without the waves of a climax to pull her along. Oh, yes, she bore fresh marks now, love bites that would later be soothed by a devoted tongue into light bruises. In the morning, all would look the same, but these ones would remain precious. A chase ended so that a new one might begin.

In those final hours of darkness, she slept deeply, mind quiet and dreamless. A hand tracing the curve of her cheek woke her, and she opened her eyes to find Colton sitting beside her, comfortable in his skin and watching her intently. "It's nearly dawn. You're safe."

She glanced at the sheets around her, taking in their less than pristine condition. "I better start a load of laundry. If I don't wash these, then I'll have to try explaining things to my parents that they'd never believe. Sleepwalking to the pond. Magdalene. You."

"I'll explain myself."

She blinked, her fuzzy thoughts trying to grasp what he was implying, when he made it clear. "When do they get up?"

"Around seven." Then she pushed herself upright, catching the hand still against her cheek. "You don't have to do this."

He looked amused. "It's time I stop living in the shadows."

She hesitated, still trying to understand. "You mean, with my parents?"

He seemed to consider his next words, but they came out steady and sure. "With you, too. We've both hidden from each other, Alice."

His thumb traced along her palm as she thought about it all. There were fights ahead with her parents anyway, after the car accident. And if nothing else, the handprints around her neck proved how keeping quiet, docile, and obedient hadn't helped at all. Perhaps it was time to learn how to do more than endure.

When she looked back up at him, her smile was nervous yet true. "I'll see if I can make anything for breakfast while we're all here. Sometimes food helps smooth over conversations."

"Don't have to."

She felt her smile warm into the one that always left him pulling down her clothes and bending her over. "I know your appetite."

He tilted his head, a lazy smolder appearing in his eyes while his hand slid between her legs quick and smooth, thumb pressing in on a clit still swollen from his attention. "And I know yours."

Then his hand pulled away, and he kissed her instead. "I'll see you in a bit. Don't worry about the bitch sneaking in. I wouldn't leave if she lingered on this side."

As he drew away, she couldn't resist saying, "How do you know that? What *are* you, you infuriating man?"

He gave her a final, sly glance. "I'll tell you."

"When?"

"After your parents find out I exist."

CHAPTER NINE

BARING HEARTS

All things considered, Alice felt surprised at how refreshed she appeared in the mirror. True, some of it was an illusion from a turtleneck covering her neck and concealer masking the small scrapes and bruises, yet her face glowed and her shoulders no longer hunched like a beaten dog's.

Each breath sent a dull ache throughout her throat, but it also left her deliciously sore nipples rubbing against the fabric of her bra, and while her body ached from being jolted by a car, it had also held onto the shivering awareness that came from spending hours entwined with someone else. If she had woken up alone, still convinced of having her mother's madness, she would have turned away from the sun and burrowed back beneath the blankets. Instead, she felt ready to at least *try* facing the world.

She remembered the layout of the kitchen well enough to start a pot of coffee without trouble, hoping the smell would wake up the rest of the house. At the moment, that meant only her parents. In those first, blurry hours after the car accident, Denise had explained that they'd sent Alice's sister to a friend's house in case they needed to spend the night at the hospital. Alice probably wouldn't even see Fleur before she left with Colton.

The realization didn't give her as sharp a pang as she'd expected. But then, she'd never had a close relationship with Fleur—too many years between them, and Alice had frankly enjoyed her baby sister taking all her parents' attention. Cooing over Fleur meant less worrying over Alice, and she'd appreciated that. Yet seething jealousy was a strange sort of bond itself, and the lack of it or any other connection left Alice viewing her sister with the same distance as she often experienced with her parents. That feeling of somehow being different. Separate from them.

Witch girl.

Even as a swirl of steam rose into her face from pouring the coffee, Alice shivered. Had that been the true cause of that sense of isolation? Had she unconsciously sensed herself to be so very different? She hoped Colton knew how many questions she'd pepper him with once they were alone.

Just as the sky brightened with true sunlight, the sound of footsteps drifted through the ceiling. From the soft tread, Alice guessed it was her stepmother, and took out the almond milk along with a second cup. Then she sipped at her own coffee, hip cocked against the honey-colored cabinets as she waited.

In a few minutes, Denise appeared in the kitchen, dressed in a fuzzy, pink robe and with her hair pulled back in a messy bun. "Alice? Are you all right?"

"Everything's fine. I just felt ready to get up."

Denise nodded while shuffling over to the coffee pot, but her expression remained troubled. "No one expects you to jump out of bed right away. It's not even seven, and the doctor told us over and over that you need a lot of rest for the next two weeks."

"I feel great. Really." Alice didn't even have to work to keep the words relaxed. She wondered what it said about her that being fucked senseless left her calm and cheerful in a way that nothing else ever had.

"Maybe, but you aren't. You almost *died* yesterday, sweetheart."

Twice over, in fact. Perhaps that was why she now felt so alive. The bitterness of the coffee tingled on the back of her tongue, and the heat lingered along her throat. The grass and bushes outside looked very green, every leaf defined and glittering, and the family of jays calling to each other sounded like raucous shouts to wake up the rest of the world. There was nothing dull to her senses, nothing too small to absorb.

"Why don't I make us some smoothies?" Denise's voice sounded overly cheerful, and Alice realized she'd never responded. "The doctor sent home a sheet of recommended food while you're healing up. I'm sure I can mix together a few of those."

Deciding it was better to pick her battles—and there would be a nasty one once Colton arrived—Alice smiled and nodded. She could make breakfast anytime.

Silence fell while Denise stuffed various berries and leafy, green things into the blender. Alice's hands clasped and unclasped her coffee cup as words snarled in her mind, words that no longer seemed safer to hide. They were old ones, polished smooth from years of tumbling together in the back of her mind, now tumbling onto her tongue from watching this woman who had always tried her best at being a stepmother, even during the times when she and Alice had been mutually baffled by each other. "I'm sorry, Denise. For how Magdalene insulted you, I mean. I should have asked her to apologize right away."

Her stepmother looked startled at the abrupt words. Then she laughed, a genuine one that crinkled the corners of her eyes. "That? Sweetheart, I forgot about it five seconds after she said... What was it? Something about being a boring housewife. There are plenty of people like her out there in the world, bitter and unhappy and attacking everyone else to feel a little bit better about what they aren't."

Then she fell serious. "You know how your father is. I argued with him about keeping distant while you were living with her, but he insisted that it was what he'd said, so it was what he'd have to do. He's so stubborn sometimes. I kept telling him you shouldn't be left alone with someone like that."

And then there it was, hanging between them like its own ghost. The question mark of the past five years. Did she want to reveal how wretched things had become? Would it even do anything, letting Denise see a glimpse?

Suddenly, Alice found it painful to look at her stepmother's face, bare of makeup and strangely vulnerable in the early morning light, and dropped her gaze to her coffee. Her distorted reflection blinked back at her as she said, "It was a relief when she died. That's all I really want to say at this point."

"Oh, Alice…" The words wavered, and in them she heard worry hardening into grief.

Before she could look over, Denise was there, sweeping her up into a fierce hug. "I'm sorry, sweetheart. Whatever she said or did to you, it's not true and you didn't deserve it. You've always been *wonderful*."

For a moment, Alice remained stiff, so unused to familial affection that she didn't know how to react. But then the softness of her stepmother's robe and the warmth of her arms sank into her senses, conveying something she hadn't felt since before she could even properly talk.

A mother's touch.

Slowly, Alice hugged her back. Her muscles shuddered as if they didn't remember how to be held so gently, but her heart ached just like when she flashed onto a rare, sweet memory of her mother brushing her hair, or humming to her, or showing her how to whistle back at the sparrows hopping around in the rosemary bushes.

Before her trembling could turn into true tears, the sound of the upstairs shower hissed through the ceiling. Her father had gotten up. Alice pulled away in a spike of nerves, embarrassed at the smallness of her voice as she said, "I don't want to tell him yet. I don't want him to know..."

To know what? That she was much more screwed up than he had expected? But even as she groped for words, Denise caught her hands and gave them a brief squeeze. "It's all right. Whenever you want to talk about it, you can. Until then, I won't."

Her hands squeezed back as relief swelled through her. "Thanks."

A minute later, Alice set placemats on the kitchen table while the blender whirred. When Denise paused to add a little more milk, a knock came at the door, short and hard against the wood.

Even as her stepmother cast a puzzled glance at the nearest clock, Alice felt herself light up. "It's Colton. I meant to say— we finally talked earlier, and he's here to take me home."

"What?" Denise's hand fluttered to her messy hair. "But I have no makeup on. And your father's still in the shower."

Alice had already left the kitchen, now raising her voice as she hurried for the door. "It's okay. We can talk outside until you're ready."

"No, bring him right in! Just tell him I don't always look like a hag."

"You look fantastic, Denise." By then, her hand grasped the doorknob. Even as she turned it, the uncertainty of the past few weeks flared back into life, wrapping a thin line of dread around her heart. What if Magdalene stood there before her with that crooked, sharp smile? A nightmare sliding back into reality...

The door opened without a creak, as well-heeled as the rest of the house, and then she saw nothing except Colton, hands easy in his pockets while he waited. His eyes had picked up the vivid green of the porch plants, and they warmed further at the sight of her.

As he stepped over the threshold, gaze never leaving her face, Alice felt a jolt of surprise over his appearance. Gone were the flannel shirt and shapeless coat. Instead, the white collar of a dress shirt peered out from beneath a dark leather jacket, and well-fitted slacks had replaced the rough jeans. Even his shoes looked nice, polished and well-cared for. With his dark scruff and sharp eyes, one couldn't say he seemed clean-cut and safe. But it was a new type of formidable from him—an indication that he could handle civilized threats as easily as the primal kind found in the forest.

"Infuriating man," she whispered, tugging at his jacket as he pulled her close. He smelled like fresh soap, as if he'd been careful to wash away any lingering traces of blood, but beneath that, she caught a hint of hot skin and the tang of iron. Even cleaned up, he exuded an earthiness that dared anyone to dismiss his presence.

He gave her that hungry look that always left her breathless, but his hand remained gentle as it traced the curve of her cheek, and concern rumbled in his voice as their mouths brushed. "Been prowling for a while. Smelled you growing upset."

"I'm fine. Especially now." Even as she reluctantly pulled back, her fingers twined with his.

It felt strange, having him there in her parents' house. Their own home always had a sense of the not-quite-normal out there in the forest, as if it existed separate from the rest of the world. As she led him to the kitchen, watching him walk on the shining, hardwood floor and cast a shadow against the spotless, cream wall, she felt nearly giddy at seeing how easily the supernatural could slip into the mundane. Even well-dressed and relaxed, without a hint of yellow in his eyes, she sensed how he could still shift into a wolf if he wished, how he could turn into a living shadow among the granite counters and gleaming pots of the kitchen.

When Alice introduced him to Denise, her stepmother had a ready smile on her face, but her eyes widened in surprise. The few boys who had come over to the house during high school years had been clean-cut and teenage-awkward, and the vague expectation formed from those memories obviously didn't fit Colton.

He waited to shake hands until Denise held out her own first. The surprise then filtered into her voice, turning delighted. "Old-fashioned manners. You don't usually find a man who knows them outside of my parents' generation. Sit down and get comfy. Alice and I were just about to have breakfast. I'll get some for you, too."

Before Alice could warn him of her stepmother's definition of a meal, Colton nodded. "Thanks."

He took in the kitchen with a sharp glance, and Alice's mouth twitched toward a smile as his forehead furrowed in confusion over the cold stove and empty oven. They still held hands underneath the table, and she squeezed his to get him to look over.

"You'll only have to take a sip," she murmured. "I'll drink the rest."

Before he could respond, Denise set the smoothies before them. Colton blinked at the olive-green concoction, expressionless, but Alice understood the flicker in his eyes as clearly as if he'd spoken aloud. *It's fucking rabbit food.*

He kept a stoic face during the first swallow. On the second, he made a muffled noise that might have been a repressed cough. Alice rubbed her bare foot against his leg, trying not to laugh into her own glass.

"Very healthy," he said, at last.

Denise beamed in response while sipping from hers. "It's one of my favorites. Kale, flaxseed, Goji berry, and a little apple for sweetness."

"I taste strawberry, too," said Alice, drinking more of hers.

"That's from the homemade almond milk. I wanted to make something special while trying out my new nut milk bag."

Alice nodded, most of her focus still on Colton and the way he eyed his glass. He probably would have looked happier if he'd been told it was poison.

He managed another swallow before Denise returned to the counter to clean up. Alice, who had already finished her smoothie, quietly switched their glasses, and received a glance that had her biting back another laugh. Her foot rubbed against him again just as Denise spoke up.

"I'm glad you found out what happened with Alice. We tried calling the sawmill yesterday after her accident but couldn't reach you." Such words could have been an accusation, but Denise had a knack at making any observation sound pleasant.

Colton pushed his glass away as if even the dregs were too repulsive to be within sniffing distance. "Bad timing all around. I took off work to take care of a few things in the city. When I got back, I knew something was wrong with Alice not being there. Called someone from the mill to see if she'd left a message, and he told me about the accident. The hospital told me a little more, but by then it was too late in the night to come here and pound on the door until I saw her."

No outright lie, just a vague circling around the truth. Alice listened carefully, aware that she'd likely need to learn how to do this herself. She was so intent on the words that the feeling of his hand sliding up over her knee startled her. She looked over and found his gaze warm on her. When he gave her leg a light squeeze, she smiled back, aware of how her face must have glowed.

If Denise caught the change in her expression, it didn't show up in her voice as she rejoined them at the table. "How did you two meet?"

"Unexpectedly," said Alice, aware of how it would look if she kept quiet and let Colton do all the talking.

He elaborated. "I knew Franny Harford from doing work on the cabin."

When Denise only looked puzzled at the name, he added, "Alice's grandmother."

Alice knew what sort of reaction that would have garnered from her father. Denise's eyes only lit in realization. "Oh, of course! The place Alice inherited. Did you know her grandmother well?"

"No. I was just a handyman that came by every so often."

Denise nodded, her smile growing. "And then what? You once stopped by to see if the cabin needed any repairs and found Alice instead of her grandmother?"

Colton gave an easy tilt of his head that could have been taken for a nod.

"And it did," said Alice, voice wry as she thought of the poor shape it had been in. "Romance in the shape of hammers and nails."

"I think that's sweet," said Denise, her face now in her hands. "Not everyone wants flowers."

Cautious hope bloomed in Alice's thoughts at the idea that things might turn out well. It withered just as quickly when her father's footsteps sounded on the stairs, and she felt herself stiffen up even as Colton's hand slid along her leg in reassurance.

Denise called out as she rose from the table. "Tom? We've got company. Alice's boyfriend came over."

There was a quiet growl of a laugh from Colton over being called anything close to "boy." Alice just clutched at his hand, the lightness of the earlier conversation evaporating beneath the heavy lump of apprehension that her heart had turned into.

Her father didn't reply to Denise, but in the next breath, he appeared in the kitchen. He'd already dressed for work, shirt ironed and tie straight, but hadn't yet shrugged on the jacket of his suit. It hinted to Alice that he expected to have a long talk before he left for the day. Her muscles tightened into knots, and this time, Colton's hand eased free of her grip until one thumb could stroke along the area of her wrist where her pulse beat like a frantic bird.

When her father's gaze fell upon Alice, she smiled, hoping it didn't seem too strained. "Morning, Dad."

"You shouldn't even be out of bed." His voice sounded tired, not harsh, but Alice still glanced away.

"I wanted to make sure I was ready when Colton came to take me home."

"We already agreed you'd stay here." Then he sat across from her, absently smoothing his tie. The sunlight picked out the grey in his hair. There was more of it than she remembered seeing before, and guilt slid through her while she wondered how many of those grey hairs had come from her.

She wasn't used to arguing, not really, but took a deep breath and tried. "I know we did for last night, but that's only because Colton wasn't there to drive me home."

Her father finally glanced over at Colton, who remained easy in his seat. The men stared at each other for a moment, neither seeming very impressed. Her father was the first to look away, distracted by Denise setting a final smoothie before him. "You're a hard man to reach. We tried all day yesterday."

"He already explained that." Denise's voice remained airy while she sat beside him. "He was away in the city."

Before her father could question why, Alice quickly spoke up. "There's no reason why I can't go home. The instructions from the doctor are right here, and Colton can look after me until I'm recovered."

Denise acknowledged the point with a nod, but it was as if her father hadn't even heard. Instead, he rubbed at the dark circles beneath his eyes, actually slouching enough for his elbows to rest on the table. "Let's set that aside for now. There's something more important to talk about."

Colton shifted in his seat, a movement small enough to go unnoticed by all except Alice. She took in the set of his shoulders and the tightness in his jaw, realizing he hadn't liked something he'd heard in the words.

She was more struck by the rare glimpse of vulnerability in her father. He had a busy life, even a harried one, but the only time he had ever appeared so tired was the day the official search party had been called off for her mother. That evening, he had slumped like a broken puppet while carefully explaining to Alice that her mother might not come back for awhile, and that they would have to go on and learn how to do things without her. Gut-deep, Alice knew this conversation would somehow be related to her.

She waited in silence while her father straightened up in his seat and looked at her. "You need help."

"Help...?" she repeated, her focus now jumping between him and her stepmother.

Denise nodded. "Just for a little while, until we're sure you have your feet under you. Go back to school, maybe start seeing a therapist over everything. It's okay to get support from others."

Alice understood that. And looking at their faces, she saw true concern. Instinctively, though, she sensed the danger of agreeing to any such plan. Following someone's words yet again. Lying to whatever therapist she ended up with because the truth was too strange, too fantastic. Picking up school when she barely knew who she was, let alone what she wished to do with herself.

What she *did* know was that no part of her heart ached for a perfect life protected inside a bubble. Not for her was the tried and true, the velvet green lawns and the stonework borders. She had sensed that even in those confusing teenage years, and had been sure enough of it to go off with Magdalene when the time had come to decide. Yes, it had turned out badly, horribly, and yet... The urge remained. And at this point, not one bit of doubt lingered. Not while Colton sat there beside her.

When she said nothing, Denise added, "Sweetheart, you haven't been the same since you came back from the city. You don't go out to see anybody, and you're always so pale and worried-looking. You don't seem to be, well... Thriving."

Her eyes said more, said that she now knew why, but Alice's father remained unreadable but for the lines of weariness etched on his face.

Alice's fingers pressed tight against Colton's as she admitted, "Magdalene's death hit hard in a lot of ways. I'm still working through it."

The smooth skin between her stepmother's eyebrows pinched together in sympathy. Her father just sighed. "What about yesterday's car accident? You never said what you swerved to avoid."

"It happened too fast," she murmured, aware of how feeble her explanation sounded.

So feeble, in fact, that her father finally snapped. "Alice, enough. You're making the same faint excuses that your mother used to."

"No." Colton's voice landed in the conversation like a chunk of granite, solid and uncompromising.

It was as if her father hadn't expected him to even speak. In the brief silence that followed, Colton fixed his eyes on him and added, "There's nothing wrong with Alice."

Frustration showed on her father's face, but his next words came out calmly enough. "I appreciate the loyalty toward my daughter, but you don't know what you're talking about."

"I know enough."

It was always the indifference in Colton's words that stumped people. His full attention could be unnerving, like finding gleaming eyes in between the shadowy shapes of trees, but once he had made up his mind, his disregard proved even harder to grapple with. Alice had figured out a few ways to crack that enigmatic shell, but suspected it was more him indulging her than anything else.

Her father wasn't about to be indulged.

When her father drew in a breath, obviously wanting to approach things from a different angle, Alice took the chance, surprised at her own boldness. "What my dad means is that they're worried I'm going crazy like my mom."

"You're not crazy." Colton's voice didn't change, but something flickered in his eyes. "And there's nothing wrong with you."

"Giving my daughter false reassurances won't help anything."

"They're not false. Thinking she's her mother—that's false."

Alice felt torn between avoiding her father's eyes to help soften the arguing and looking up to catch his expression. She couldn't remember the last time someone had so openly challenged him. And over a subject that people always avoided! From her father's silence, he was just as shocked.

Colton didn't give him a chance to respond. "I know the family. Franny Harford wasn't a nice woman. Whatever she did to Alice's mother would have lingered. She never met Alice, though. Couldn't do it to her. Everyone has problems, but Alice has her own, not her mother's."

It felt like her heart jumped into her throat as she watched her father finally crack. "Who the hell are you?"

"Tom," said Denise, resting a hand on his arm, but he ignored her.

"How long have you known my daughter? A few months? You have no idea what needs to be done to look after her."

"No, Dad." The words came out of Alice before she could stop them, and in the ensuing silence, she added, "I know you just want to help, but I think I'd do better working through things on my own. I need to make some changes, you're right. But seeing a therapist or going back to school—that won't help me right now. It'll just *look* like I'm doing better whenever anyone asks."

From the flash of confusion in her father's eyes, it was one and the same. Denise, though, studied both her and Colton, the line of concern between her eyebrows now smoothing out.

"Then what's your plan?" Her father still sounded irritated. "To go hide in the forest with him?"

Colton shrugged. "You can find us easy enough."

Her father's face grew red just as Denise turned to him and murmured, "Tom, don't grill her about this. She's tired and wants to go home. Let's wait for a better time to talk about her future."

"I did that when she went off with that woman. What were the results?"

At that, Colton's eyes glinted with a dangerous light, but Alice squeezed his hand in a silent signal to let her respond. A sick pit opened up in her stomach as she said, "Do you want to talk about her, Dad? Are we finally going to talk about things that happened instead of just how to cover them up?"

She had never been so frank with her words, and it terrified her to wait for him to respond. Her father drew in a deep breath, a vein now visible in his neck. Denise watched him carefully, her hand still light on his arm, and Colton had fallen very still, leaning forward in his seat as if ready to lunge.

Finally, her father said, "There are only so many times you can step out of this life, Alice."

That drew a smothered sigh from Denise, but Alice only nodded, skin prickling as she waited for an ultimatum she'd already once heard.

"We've both discussed it and decided that if you don't want to get help, we have no choice but to—"

"We'll keep supporting you," interrupted Denise, her voice unusually firm. As everyone else looked over, she added, "We won't cut you off like last time."

"What?" Alice's father stared at her in disbelief.

Denise remained serene while rubbing at his arm. "We *all* made mistakes back then."

"She's still making them."

Alice heard a soft growl from Colton, but when Denise's gaze landed on them, her expression seemed thoughtful, not startled. "I don't think so. He adores her, Tom. Can't you see that?"

"And I'm sure that Magdalene Bishop looked exactly the same."

"No," said Alice and her stepmother, voices matching in tone, and Alice realized they both remembered the faint amusement that had always imbued Magdalene's expression.

Anger and fear scratched at her words as she added, "Magdalene *was* a mistake. I left with her because I didn't want the life set up for me and didn't know how to explain that. I should've stayed and told you. And that's what I'm trying to do now."

There was a brief silence. The air felt sharp, uncertain. Finally, her father said, "I want you to be happy. That's all this is."

"Then let me figure out how to be." She studied them, trying to see if they understood. Her heart shivered between her ribs at her audacity.

There was a final sigh from her father before he stood up from the table, face closed off. "Then there's nothing more to say."

It hurt, but it was also an old pain, and Alice only blinked a few times to keep tears at bay. Colton's thumb stroked over her white-knuckled hand.

"Tom," said Denise, voice quiet.

He glanced at her. "I'm late for work. If you want to entertain them, then go ahead. But I don't want them here when I get back."

Alice tried to keep her breathing steady as the front door opened and slammed, taking her father with it.

Now Denise sighed. "He doesn't mean it. You should have seen him at the hospital's front desk while the receptionist was searching for your room number. He's just being stiff-necked over his plans."

Alice tried a smile, feeling tired. "We do need to go."

Her stepmother smiled back, her natural sunniness already returning to her face. "He'll cool down in a few days. You'll see."

Alice's head throbbed as they hugged goodbye, Colton lingering near the door. Once they were in his truck and pulling out of the driveway, she relaxed enough to rub at her temples, trying to ease the aching there. "Well, those were my parents. I don't know if you'll see them again, but I'm glad they didn't scare you off."

He sounded as unshakeable as ever. "Your father's a father. Stepmother's nice, even if she likes drinking things that taste like dirt."

The sound of her laugh surprised her. "That's the kale."

When his shoulders twitched in disgust, she ran a hand along the nearest one, drawing a warm glance from him.

They traveled a few more miles before she said, "You didn't even have to lie about what really happened last night."

"Usually, you don't."

She looked at him as he drove, calm and easy and appearing as nothing more than a normal man. "You're used to it, aren't you?"

At that, his nearest hand left the steering wheel and found hers. "It's something you'll learn, too."

There were more words waiting, ones that would take the events of the night before—of the weeks before—and reveal their true shapes. The glimpses of Magdalene; how easily dreams had twisted in her mind. How she had slipped to another world without realizing it.

Alice sighed. "I *am* a witch."

Colton's silence was answer enough.

"But I won't end up my like mother or grandmother."

"No." His hand squeezed hers.

She thought about it for awhile, watching the land around her shift into oaks brilliant with red leaves. The gentle hillsides roughened into dips and rises around the road as they began the slow ascent into the foothills. Into the wilderness. The tension bled from her mind, and the guilt over her father eased into an ache that disappeared among the many physical ones marking the more battered areas of her body.

When the view opened into the first swathes of forest bristling out to the horizon, she asked another question. "That wasn't the full story, was it? Going into the city on business."

He seemed to consider every angle of what she'd said, although his grip remained relaxed on the steering wheel, relaxed against her hand. "I did go into the city. The business was finding out what was happening with you."

The unease that had just faded from her thoughts now flared up once more. She bit at her lip. "You mean my silence about Magdalene? I'm sorry. I should have told you from the beginning, but I was scared. No one else saw her."

"She first appeared at the fucking party, didn't she? Your fear that night... And it's been with you ever since."

"Yes. And it was her that was in the road, not a deer. But I couldn't..."

"Tell the truth." His face was expressionless, but she caught the tightness in his jaw.

"I was scared, Colton. How my father looked at me back there... I didn't want to see that expression on your face, too. I thought I could handle hallucinating things. But you thinking I was crazy—that would have shattered me."

"I'm not your father."

"No, you're not. I just didn't want to ruin things." Then her hand pulled free of his, and she picked at her fingernails to avoid looking at him. "There's something else, too. Something related to Darby wanting to see the cabin. You see, her husband, Rob—"

"Had photos of you."

Her head snapped up just as he withdrew an envelope from his inside jacket pocket. It looked like the same one Rob had shown her. Alice felt her cheeks burn.

"Did you look at them?" she whispered, but already she knew the answer. He would have had to in order to make sure they were the right ones.

"I did, and I know why they exist." His tone revealed nothing of what he thought, and neither did his face.

When he offered the envelope to her, she shrank away, not wanting to touch it. He noticed, and the flatness in his eyes flared into something savage.

The envelope disappeared back into his jacket before she said, "I'm sorry. I didn't want you to know about the things I did with him."

The anger showed itself in his voice, too, roughening it into a growl. "He was lucky to have you. At the risk of sounding like a fucking poet, you graced him. He didn't lower you."

Her eyes blurred over, and her words wavered while she wiped at them. "I didn't know what would happen if you found out. I didn't know if you'd..."

"Leave? You think I'll do that at the first sign of trouble? The first time you don't smile bright enough? I won't. It was easy to guess the bitch had put you through things. Easy to smell your guilt. But I still tracked you down to find you."

Coming from Colton, it was as good as an impassioned speech, and Alice stared at him, at a loss for words.

He glanced over at her, a searing gaze that showed all his anger, frustration, and, yes, love. "Tell me you don't want to talk if that's what you want. Tell me you'll fight it yourself. But don't lie that it's fine when I can smell the salt from tears on your cheeks. How the fuck am I to take that? Just watch the wound rot because you won't lick at it?"

Alice knew she'd dissolve into ugly sobs as soon as she opened her mouth, so she only grabbed for his hand, trying to squeeze all her feelings into the act. The warm touch, sure and rough with calluses, coaxed her fingers into relaxing enough to twine with his.

In a quieter voice, he said, "You didn't smile at all when we met, but I couldn't keep away from you."

She nodded, still unable to speak, still clutching at his hand. Trees flickered by while she fought for steady breaths. The road narrowed and the surrounding land opened up into vast crags and crevices. They were almost home.

"Then I won't lie," she said, at last, and now she was able to look at him without shame. "And I'll only smile when I want to."

Their fingers flexed against each other before she sighed, her voice growing steadier with each word. "Thank you for getting the photos. Whatever you did with Rob, I'm sure he's out of the way. And considering how things went with my father, Darby's no longer a concern either. That just leaves Magdalene."

"We'll wait to see what the bitch does. She probably went off to heal. I got some good bites in. She didn't expect me to be able to reach her and hurt her."

As tired and emotionally spent as she was, Alice had to laugh. "Even ghosts don't know what you are."

He took in her expression, eyes warming. "I remember what I said. Once we're back and know the house is safe, I'll tell you about myself. If you still want to hear it."

"I do," said Alice. And then she smiled at him.

CHAPTER TEN

THE WITCH AND THE WOLF

In the brief time Alice had been away, the house had fallen into disorder. As soon as she stepped through the doorway, mail crinkled beneath her feet like dead leaves—advertisements spilling their inner pages, catalogs sliding against each other, envelopes ripped open and gutted. When she stooped to pick it all up, Colton shook his head and kicked enough to the side to clear a space to walk through. He did the same for the clothes scattered on the floor in a path to the bedroom. They looked like the ones he usually wore to work, as if he had let them fall forgotten while stripping down.

"Things got away from me," he admitted, sounding perplexed more than apologetic as they stepped into the bedroom. Muddy pawprints marked the hardwood floor, and black fur dusted whatever furniture he had brushed up against.

Alice shook her head, smiling as she sat on the bed. "So, that's your weak spot. Cleaning up after yourself."

Her voice turned it into innuendo even before she reached out and traced the fly of his slacks as he lingered nearby, eyeing every corner of the room as if making sure nothing had changed while they'd been gone. He gave her that hot look that always ignited an ache between her legs, but only caught her hand and squeezed it before pulling away.

He continued to prowl throughout the rooms while she dropped the hospital paperwork onto the nightstand. She also put her purse there and then rummaged through it to find her phone. Her fingers brushed the white pharmacy bag Denise had given her on the way out, and she pulled it out to check the contents. Nothing there beyond the pain medication prescribed if she started hurting too much, and she set it aside without interest even though she *had* began to hurt, much more than the night before.

The turtleneck felt uncomfortable against her neck, scratching at the swollen skin until she tugged at it for relief. Each movement, even a single breath, angered her bruises and strained her muscles, and the simple act of taking off her shoes and socks knocked her bones about. Every inch of her body felt rattled and sluggish, as if it had only now absorbed the impact of being thrown through the air and back to the ground with the same force that had crumpled her car like tin foil.

Dimly, she remembered the doctor explaining the phenomenon—something about pain receptors remaining dulled for awhile after the first shock of the accident. It likely didn't help that she had almost drowned the other night, or that she still felt drained from the conversation with her parents. But she was safe now, and at home. Free to hurt instead of having to hide it.

Finally, she found her phone and plugged it into the charger before checking to see what she'd missed in the past day. She wasn't surprised by the calls from Darby and ignored her texts outright, but did pause at the handful of emails from Rob. She opened the latest one and started reading.

I called the medium to make sure everything's cancelled. Don't believe whatever Darby says. It's cancelled. Here's her number if you want to call for yourself.

She scanned over the number but decided to read the next-newest email to see if it revealed more.

Darby's lying. There aren't any other photos. The ones she sent you through the mail are all she has. Don't send your fucking boyfriend over here again because he already took the ones she's talking about.

I'm still trying to find out who's doing the seance. Just give me a day or two. Halloween isn't for a few weeks, so there's a lot of time to cancel it. Don't fucking send him over.

The first email from him made everything all the more clear, including his very un-Rob-like helpfulness.

After yesterday's visitor, I changed my mind about things. Christ, where did you find him, the fucking mafia? I had to tell Darby there was a robbery while we were both out.

I went through her files and found out what she's planning: a seance for Magdalene on Halloween night. Supposed to take place at your cabin. She found a few mediums, so I have to call them all to find out which one she picked to do it. Give me a few days, all right? Shouldn't be that hard to cancel it.

At any other time, Rob's panic might have been laughable, but Alice was too struck by what she had learned to pay it any attention.

"A seance," she muttered, thoughts flashing together from that single word. Then she remembered the number 31 circled and pinned by the address of the cabin on Darby's corkboard. The date of Halloween, yes, but also of something older, stranger, deeper: Samhain, one of the pagan roots for that night of jack o'lanterns and candy.

Alice, a fan of mythology and legends from childhood, knew a little about that ancient holiday. It had been a seasonal festival marking the end of fruitful crops and the beginning of winter starvation—and the play of life and death didn't stop there. It had also been seen as a day when the dead could slip in among the living. A day when the boundaries between life and death thinned to nothing.

Suddenly, Darby's desperate drive to get into the cabin made perfect sense, and Alice found herself laughing despite the pain it caused her ribs. "A seance to guide Magdalene back on the night she can fully *be* back."

Her shoulders were still shaking when the bed shifted with new weight. As Colton settled beside her, tilting his head at her phone, she looked up at him, still filled with a strange glee. "That's the perfect ending for her book—her getting to see Magdalene again, if only for a night. And the cabin would be just the place for the seance. Like she said, it's where Magdalene spent her final days. No one but you knows exactly *where* in the woods she died, so the cabin is the next best thing. And that's why she's pushing so hard *now*, because it all revolves around Samhain."

Then she tapped back to Rob's most recent email, skimming through it again. "And Rob said he didn't know anything."

"He lies a lot. Told me the truth only to save the rest of his ribs."

"You beat him up?" She was honest enough to admit feeling a brutal satisfaction over the idea. "Before or after you saw the photos?"

"Before. After I saw the photos, I knew that I'd go back and kill him. Later, though, when it won't come back to you. When he's spent time squirming over it." Colton's voice sounded as steady as ever, but something flickered in his eyes, there and gone again before she could understand it.

He had shrugged off his jacket somewhere else in the house, and now that crisp dress shirt looked a little disheveled—sleeves rolled up and the first buttons of his collar undone, exposing hard muscle dusted with hair. The veneer of civility worn down. The wild animal, restless and ready to escape.

He seemed to be waiting for a response, eyes intent and tension growing in his shoulders with every passing moment of silence. In truth, she didn't know what to say. Arguing for Rob's life—no, she couldn't bring herself to do that, not while remembering how she had once broken down crying during a session and how he had only continued taking photos in response, angling himself to better capture her face. Had any of those ended up among the ones Colton had seen? From his rage, it was likely.

And yet... Killing him? Would that help at all? Would it be sweet to her, blood gushing from his ruined throat? She needed more time to think about it, and reached up to trace the side of Colton's jaw, hoping to distract him from a straight answer. "You've got a definite bloodthirsty streak."

There was a growl from him before he said, "He hurt you."

That was true, and she didn't see a reason to deny it. "But he's not the big problem. Even Darby isn't. It's Magdalene. She's somehow driving Darby to do this, isn't she?"

"The slug of a husband admitted as much. The bitch is haunting her like she did with you. Saying things in dreams, appearing in flashes. But she's human. Can't be pulled away like you."

"Pulled away," repeated Alice, and watched fresh tension fill him. "I don't understand. Do you mean last night? Or is it something to do with the seance?"

Her gaze dropped to her phone as she considered going through Darby's texts in search of more clues, but then Colton

caught the back of her head, careful but firm while easing her
into looking up at him again. The line of his mouth had gone
grim. "You're a witch. Boundaries mean nothing to you. You
were right there on the edge of the shadow world, Alice.
Fucking walked there from a dream. You can live among
humans and be seen as one of them, but you're not. No
human can slip over to that world and join the spirits and other
creatures there. Not while alive. And if she'd fucking drowned
you... You would've been trapped."

"I would have died," she said, voice flat. Something rippled
through her; she supposed it was shock from how close she had
come to losing herself. When she shivered, skin prickling from
the memory of cold water filling her lungs, his face nuzzled at
hers, so wolf-like that she had to smile.

Their lips brushed as she murmured, "But you found me."

His soft growl turned into a kiss, and she sank into the slide
of his tongue against hers and the tenderness of his fingers as
they stroked the back of her head before catching a fistful of
her hair. She still felt tension simmering in the muscles pressed
against her, but unlike the night before, there was no fury in
his attention and no desperation in hers.

The various aches throughout her body flared as he pulled
her onto his lap, and then evaporated just as quickly when she
straddled him, pressing close as his cock twitched against his
pants. When his mouth moved down past her jaw, she sighed,
feeling drugged as he pulled down her turtleneck to taste at her

throat. The sweetness of his tongue against her throbbing skin left her dazed as she asked, "How does it look?"

"Fucking bruises everywhere. Does it hurt to talk?"

"A little. But I have a lot of questions."

He sighed before kissing at the tender hollow beneath her ear. "Of course you do. I'm listening."

"You made her bleed even though she's dead."

They both understood the significance of the words. They were a tentative query into what he was, a feeling out of how easy or how hard this subject would be for him.

He kissed her again before pulling away, eyes more yellow than green. "Yes. I can hunt anything I want."

She bit her lip, worried about this next answer. "If you can hurt her, can she hurt you?"

Even as fear spiked through her, he laughed in a humorless huff of breath. "Not badly enough for it to matter."

The trace of bitterness in the words left her studying him. "Colton?"

She expected him to fall grim again. Or to grow frustrated or wary. Instead, he suddenly looked very, very tired. "Nothing can kill me. I already went into the grave and came back out of it."

As cryptic as the words were, a chill stole through her. "What are you saying?"

There was a rare hesitation from him. Then the strong bone and hard muscle against her seemed to slump, as if the great weight they'd carried for an eternity finally proved too much to bear. "You always ask what I am. I don't know enough to answer. I only know what I *was*—an outlaw who got caught and punished."

Such an old-fashioned word, outlaw; one that most people would have laughed at. And yet it rang through Alice's mind, calling at memories like church bells tolling for the prayers of the faithful. All those beloved mythology books she had read as child, thumbing through pages of woodcut-style illustrations, delicate and terrible in what their lines depicted, now flickered back to her in half-remembered sentences. One word rose above the rest, and she shivered again while sounding it out.

"*Vargr*," she said, slowly. "It means 'outlaw,' or 'miscreant.' Or 'wolf.'"

His eyes gleamed at her, and when he spoke, the words held the finality of a death sentence. "Thou art murderous like a wolf. Thou art hunted like a wolf. Now thou art become a wolf."

"Oh, Colton," she breathed, reaching up to trace that bleak mouth, but he caught her hand, fingers tense.

"Not a wolf. Not a man. Something of both. That was the point of the punishment, to wander without end, always between worlds."

Once more, images from those books flickered through her mind. Black-furred beasts haunting the lonely countryside, shadow creatures at the edges of graveyards. Her other hand slipped over his chest, finding a strong and steady heartbeat even as she said, "You're not a ghost."

"No. But you could well call me a demon. Some have."

She laced their fingers together, thoughts still reeling. A punishment... No wonder his ribs had shown as if he'd grown used to starving. No wonder he had always held such savagery toward humans, such suspicion. "When did this happen to you?"

"A long time ago."

Somehow, the words held more weight than an exact number, looming in the way of a tree so gnarled and notched with experience that one *knew* it had endured centuries of existence.

He waited for her to ask exactly what had happened—how he had ended up in that grave and who had covered him up with dirt, knowing he'd shake it off and rise again. She could see the expectation in his face, eyes skittish like a wild thing, muscles tense beneath her soft touch. After so many years of slipping here and there, it was as if he didn't know how to react to being *seen*, separate from the shadows.

In silence, her hand eased along his chest, pushing aside the collar of his shirt to find the familiar scar beneath his collar bone. There were more, she knew, having found all sorts from the many sessions of worshipping his body with her own. Some hadn't even come from human weapons; one on his left side looked like a gash from an antler. And there was a raking of claws on the hard muscles of his stomach, as if something had once tried to disembowel him.

A life of constant fight or flight, mapped out on his skin.

He tensed further at her quiet touch, the very gentleness seeming to give him only more misgivings. How strange, that he faced danger with slavering jaws but flinched at a caress. What did he have to fear, this immortal wolf? His teeth cracked bone and bled out bodies. He was a shadow in the dark, cruel like the rest of nature. He ran feral through the woods and starved when the hares were too fast and the deer too nimble. He knew how to endure like any other beast.

And yet... He wasn't fully wolf. He calculated like a man, and had a man's cold dominance.

He felt loneliness like a man.

As her thumb ran over that bullet scar, the one that had brought him to her those few months before, his voice rumbled against her. "No more questions?"

She shook her head at the terse words, not trusting herself to speak. Tears burned in her eyes as she wondered how he could remain so detached and steady about what he had just revealed.

When she kept quiet, he caught her chin and tilted it up. The flatness in his expression disappeared, and then his thumb brushed over her cheek. "Alice, it's all right. I'm the last fucking thing that should be cried over."

"Don't say that," she managed. "That's not true at all."

Hearing that seemed to baffle him, for he fell silent while wiping the tears from her other cheek. When she caught his hand and turned her face into it, willing him to sense just how much she meant what she'd said, the surprise slipped into his voice.

"You're still not scared of me."

"Of course not. I've always known you weren't human." Had known it and loved it.

"It's scared off more than a few," he muttered. "People like monsters until they see what our teeth do. And you didn't want me to kill again. Then the human visited, reminding you of her, and guilt never left your scent."

There was so much left unsaid, so much brimming behind those colorless words. Alice straightened up enough to look him full in the face, realization glimmering through her thoughts. "I felt guilty because I started lying to you. Did you think it was over something else?"

When he only grimaced and glanced away, she grew sure. "You thought I felt guilty over being with you because you murdered Magdalene."

More than that—that she'd regretted what had happened to Magdalene. He had thought she'd pulled away from him out of fear. The girl returning to the safe path that led out of the woods, cringing from the gloom of the shadows after too much time spent in them. Cringing from everything he was.

Despite the tears clogging up the back of her throat, her voice came out steady. "I'm not afraid of you or what you did. When I think about what life would be like if she were still here... I can't imagine it without shuddering. I'm *relieved*,

Colton, even knowing you could do the same thing to me if you ever felt like it."

Now his eyes were intent on her, his entire body unmoving. The hunter exposed. The terror in the shadows frozen over the possibility of being accepted for exactly what he was—a nightmare creature that needed tenderness like every other living thing.

Quickly and without leaving his lap, she pulled off her turtleneck to bare her battered body in full, daring him to dismiss her experiences of savage attention. She tossed the shirt aside like the useless guise it was and then leaned in close, running hands up the back of his head. Daring him to flinch from the tenderness.

Even as his eyes grew dark, she breathed her next words against his mouth. "I've always known you were a monster. And I've never been scared of you."

He kissed her then, rough and insistent as if she could disappear from his grasp at any moment and he would do anything to keep her there with him.

Her fingers tightened in his hair as she pressed close, hungry for his heat and eager to show how she reveled in him no matter how many bruises covered her body. His tongue flicked at the roof of her mouth while he snapped the clasp of her bra and eased the straps over her shoulders. Every touch sparked a rush of heat, and she shifted impatiently, wanting those rough fingers to find her breasts.

He broke off to let her breathe, eyes gleaming in amusement as she arched despite the strain in her back, all but begging for his attention. Instead, he teased, licking at the bruise over her heart and easing away the stinging of sweat on damaged skin. "Easy. The pain's growing in your scent."

She just sank back onto the bed, trying to pull him down with her.

He shook his head, eyeing the welts and bruises. "You can't take my weight."

Even though her body shook and strained to do what normally took no effort at all, she felt too desperate to agree. "It'll be fine. I read somewhere that orgasms release chemicals in the brain that act like pain relievers."

Then she yanked at the zipper of her jeans, trying to pull them off.

His hand caught both of hers, stilling them, and when she looked up, she found his mouth twitching into his version of a smile. "I admit to being something so horrible that death was too good for me, and now you want to fuck."

Her hands flexed against his as she smiled back. "You're a man who changes into a wolf and a wolf that changes into a man. That seems straightforward enough to me."

Would he remember how she'd said that to him before, one rainy day not so long ago? When her life had been hopeless, loveless, dead but for a spark of curiosity toward this terse creature and the hunger she saw in his eyes?

Those eyes now looked very green as he growled, giving her jeans a quick jerk that ripped open the fly. His gaze grew insatiable as he pulled down the denim and took in the state of her panties. The modest pink cotton was soaked through and clinging to her plump folds, and she was already gasping even before his fingers slid down and squeezed the swollen flesh.

Her hips arched, sending flares of pain throughout her spine, but in the next moment, he soothed them down, palm flat and easy against the soft skin of her lower stomach until she fell limp.

"Easy," he said once more, hand sliding under the thin fabric of her panties. "We'll go slow."

When the rasp of his calluses found her, she jerked again, clawing at the blankets beneath her. She was always desperate when caught up in arousal, begging with every twitch of her hips, panting and throbbing for release at the merest brush of fingers. Her lust was a shooting star, brief and glorious and white-hot. Easy? She didn't know what that meant.

He showed her, every flick of his fingers pacing her, slowing when she began to gasp, moving away to stroke her hip or thigh when she began to shudder. She was used to sharp teeth, to the roughness of a stubbled chin rasping at her throat, down her back, between the sensitive skin of her thighs. She was used to coiled tension simmering against her body, every muscle tense with power and pinning her still for an insistent cock. This was completely different and yet just as delicious, his expression relaxed while she clenched her thighs around him, moaning with every motion of his hand. All sense of time faded, and all thought as well. It was only them together, him drawing her to the edge but never letting her fall over it.

Finally, when her thighs were slick with her fluids, his thumb pressed in. As soon as it found her clit, she was lost in a climax, hips rocking to his slow rhythm. Even after her release had dwindled to hot aftershocks and the prickle of sweat, her legs continued to weakly rub against his arm. The blankets were bunched wrinkles in her grip.

Dimly, she grew aware of his hand sliding over her lower stomach and continuing up, leaving a wet trail in its wake. When his fingers reached her panting mouth, she sucked at them without hesitation, limbs still limp.

"You really love it, don't you?" he murmured.

She just hummed, sliding her tongue against his calluses.

Before the haze of lust cleared enough for her to attempt words, he pulled back and stood. Even in her dazed state she sensed him tugging her jeans and panties all the away off, lightly stroking the backs of her knees to send fresh shivers throughout her. Then came the sound of him unzipping his fly, and her next breath was a hiss of excitement as he eased her legs apart.

The delicious pressure of his cock pushing in gave her a rush of energy, and she reached out, wanting to touch more of him. His thrusts were slow but deep as he caught her hips, keeping her still whenever she tried to writhe. When one of his hands slid back to her clit, she jerked and caught his wrist, fingernails digging in.

He let her clutch at him, his breath occasionally dipping into a growl while his thumb continued to grind against her, driving her ever closer to another climax. A change in pressure left her nails scraping hard enough to draw blood, and she winced, expecting him to shake her off. He did, but only to catch her nearest hand in his, lacing their fingers together. That hint of tenderness—even as it felt like he was splitting her apart with every thrust—left her panting his name through a fresh wave of heat.

He looked down at her, a sheen of sweat on his muscles and hunger in his eyes as he shifted, bringing their hips together at a new angle. In the privacy of their home, she could howl without being heard, and did, voice rising above his snarl as his final thrusts grew rough and quick.

By the time he was through his release, her skin was as slick with sweat as his, but the sting of damp scrapes and bruises faded to nothing when he stretched over and caught her mouth with his, his tongue now slow as if he savored every hint of her. Somehow, she found enough energy to kiss him back, licking at his teeth to remind him how she loved his monstrousness as much as the rest of him.

From his rumble of a laugh, he understood.

CHAPTER ELEVEN

HEALING BRUISES

The doctor had prescribed two weeks' rest for a full recovery, and Alice dutifully followed those orders, well aware that Samhain drew ever closer and carried with it whatever Magdalene planned next. In the first few days at home, her body demanded sleep to the point where she hardly bothered getting out of bed, the chilly autumn hours sliding by while she curled up with Colton in a tangle of limbs.

His patience surprised her, that ravenous appetite for her flesh tempered into a hot mouth that only tasted at her bruised skin, coaxing sweet releases from her battered body if her tension over Magdalene's menace became too much to bear. Whenever she dozed, he would read, his free hand tracing along her body as the rustle of pages followed her into calm, dreamless sleep. Awake, she talked about whatever slipped into mind.

Ah, but it sounded so simple, didn't it? To murmur into the ear of a lover content to let her speak about anything and for however long she wished as long as it meant *he* didn't have to talk back. To admit both deepest vulnerability and silliest pettiness to a beast indifferent to huffs of breath. What monstrous thing could she pull from her thoughts that would be worse than the very monster beside her? What secret would he bother to use when he had his teeth to savage? His was the danger of jaws in the dark and bloodthirst beneath the moon. The day he decided to hurt her would be the day she died from a torn-out throat. Her mind would remain untouched.

Such a simple thing, yes, to speak without care, and yet the freedom still stunned her. To let the syllables fall from her mouth like stones cast into deep water, rough and heavy and forgotten as soon as they sank out of sight. To shine a light on the wretched, clammy-skinned things curled in their hiding places, exposing them in full. And the beast beside her still listened without concern, that hunter's passion never ebbing from a wrong word said or a wrong opinion given.

"It's like she trained me," she said one morning, while thick clouds drizzled rain outside the bedroom windows. She was naked, belly-down on the crumpled sheets and chin resting on her crossed arms, eyes closed against the delicious afterburn of teeth marks on her shoulder. The bruising on her neck was still too violent to take his intensity.

Colton lounged beside her, the dry flick of paper meeting paper telling her that he was reading. His free hand followed the curve of her spine as she considered the truth to her words. "It was never obvious. All of her was unusual, beautifully so. It would have felt strange if she had been normal about anything. What you saw of her—she didn't used to be so openly horrible like that. In fact, she was really good at making people feel special. She just didn't care by the end and knew I was in too deep to pull away."

Colton's hand squeezed at her nearest hip then, soothing away the knot of tension there and coaxing out more words. "Rob told me it was a pattern with her. That she did it to girls who reminded her of Indigo. I always wondered if Indigo was different. Those letters that Magdalene wrote to her... They seemed vulnerable in a way she never was with anyone else. But that night by the river, she told me Indigo hadn't waited for her. That she'd gone on."

"Who'd want an eternity with that fucking woman?"

The bluntness startled a laugh out of Alice, and she arched into the rough palm that ran over the dimples in the small of her back. "That's true. *I* wanted it once, but now I can't think of anything worse."

Then she fell serious, opening her eyes as the handful of days left until Samhain bore down on her thoughts. The look on Magdalene's face there at the river's edge, so wild with fury and desperation... If Colton was right about her disappearing to lick her own wounds, what would happen once she recovered enough to attack again?

Before fear could do more than prickle at her, Alice heard the pages of Colton's book flutter shut, the only hint that his attention had shifted before she found herself rolled onto her back and held there as he stretched over her. His hair was still damp with sweat from the last round of fucking, but his gaze had lost its laziness, now alert as he studied her face. Alice instinctively wrapped both legs around him, but her voice fell breathless with worry, not lust. "Only eleven days left until Samhain. She'll have the whole night to try to take me back with her."

"Won't happen." The rough edge in his voice turned soothing as he settled his weight against her, the pressure easy, calming.

Still, her body shivered against his as another laugh left her, this one short and bitter. "Once upon a time, her attention felt like being blessed by a higher being. The idea of being needed by her—forever—didn't scare me like it should have. I was *that* deluded. And she was that good with words."

Her cheeks burned over admitting such stupidity, especially when she could feel the bruises pulling at the flesh of her neck with every word.

Then Colton cupped her face, coaxing her to look at him. "Hard to understand what forever means until you get a taste of it. What was yours?"

It was so rare to hear a question from him that at first she only blinked, mind blank for a few breaths. Then the answer came to her. "The first time she slept with someone else. We'd gone to a party thrown by... I can't remember. Either her agent or her editor. Magdalene was drunk, and she found a fan of *The Chrysalis* and went home with her before we'd even hit the second hour of being there. I had to stand there and pretend nothing had happened. That it was *normal*. And then the next morning, when she came back to our apartment, I looked at her face and knew it really would become normal. She'd crossed a line, and I hadn't left, and so she'd keep crossing it. We both knew it."

Then Alice swallowed hard, realizing her voice had started to tremble. Not from grief, no—from sheer fury. At Magdalene, at herself, at the sad, twisted thing that had become their relationship. The rage seemed to sink down to her bones as she looked up at Colton again, their noses brushing. "I can't go back to that. I can't go back to *her*."

"You won't," he said, his voice savage and sure.

Then he kissed her, slow and intent, as if he liked the taste of her rage as much as everything else about her. In contrast, her mouth was desperate against his, her limbs tight and twining while every inch of her body declared the words that she still couldn't say. *I want to live.*

As his attention shifted, the rasp of his beard teasing a path down the hollow of her throat, she arched, already feeling his cock grow heavy and hard. But she was still angry at herself, and at his first thrust, her fingernails ripped at her thighs instead of the sheets. He growled at that, a brusque warning reverberating from his chest to hers, rumbling against the sensitive skin just over her heart. But she didn't stop, long-repressed feelings now seething to the surface as if her earlier words had smashed the cage that had kept them still and quiet.

Her nails bit into her flesh again, and within another breath she found her arms pinned above her head.

She met Colton's glare without flinching, met his lingering growl with a snarl in her own voice. "I was so stupid. How could I have fallen for her? Stayed with her? There were so many times I could have left or made a different choice. I could have avoided all of this."

"Anyone can say that about themselves. I could've gone down a different path and died like any other man." Colton's hands remained unyielding against her arms, but he leaned in until their mouths brushed. "We are what we are, Alice. You're vulnerable, caring. The wrong person noticed. That's all."

She released a shaky breath, feeling her fingers relax from where they had curled into her palms. "And what are you?"

Something softer than anger glittered in those feral eyes as he began to move against her again, grinding in a slow, hard rhythm that brought a sweet ache to her hips. "Uncontrollable. Hungry. A hunter who made the wrong people realize they were easy game."

The words left her clenching against him, and he gave her that short, quiet growl that was the closest he ever came to catching his breath. When he spoke again, his voice sounded rougher. "You're supposed to be scared by that."

She shook her head, breathless by that point, arching to change the angle of his cock driving into her until it hit even deeper with every thrust. "I like that about you."

"I can tell."

His hands still had her arms pinned to the bed, but she relaxed under the pressure, the coiled spring of her heart easing as she matched his rhythm. She was always so hot, so sudden with her need. Writhing against him out of desperation. More, more... He was never too much, not for her. And he—he savored her, thrusting hard and slow to feel her body jolt and shake, nuzzling his nose against hers so that their mouths panted together. Her release was wracking, white-hot, and her voice sounded close to a howl as it filled the room.

Later, as he licked the salt of drying sweat from her throat and breasts, she tightened her legs around him to keep him close.

"Thank you," she mumbled, still caught up in the afterglow. "That grounded me."

A rumble of a laugh against her. "Not like I got nothing out of it, myself."

With her hands free again, she managed to lift one enough to stroke at his thick, dark hair, the other remaining limp by her head. Thoughts slipped back into her mind, calmer now. One breath, two, and then an idea rose from her haze, sharp and dangerous with its very newness. "I still have the letters she wrote me. They're in a moving box now, but I kept them out of sight even before she died. At first they hurt too much to look at, and then later on I never wanted to learn whether they still held power over me."

"And now?" He tasted at the hollow of her throat, right where her pulse beat slow and steady despite the decision forming in her mind.

"I want to see them."

She pulled on his flannel shirt against the chill before dragging the cardboard box from its space in the closet. Colton remained easy in his skin, focused on lighting a fire to chase away the shadows in the room. She settled on the floor, sitting close to the hearth so that he could watch if he cared to, and began sorting through all that remained of her time spent with Magdalene. She moved cautiously, carefully, as if she handled poisoned gold or bloodstained diamonds. Precious things that had turned ghastly, preening things that had gone foul.

The notebooks and half-drafts were put into manila envelopes and then into the small safe where she kept all important papers; death often magnified an author's genius, and she didn't doubt that within a few years, people would come sniffing in hopes of releasing anything new that could be attached to Magdalene's name. The letters Magdalene had written to Indigo also went into the safe, sharing an envelope with the photo of the girl herself.

Then Alice picked up the letters written to her, rubbing the edges with fingertips damp from nerves. Colton remained silent, gaze intent on her face as she shuffled them like cards, keeping them neatly folded up—keeping the words hidden from view. She didn't want to read them, not quite yet. She just wanted to find out how they felt in her hands, and if she felt like the same girl again while holding them.

But they only felt like paper, and the faint smells of tobacco and ink no longer fascinated her with their hints of a life so mysterious and arcane. In fact, they only made her nose itch with the need to sneeze, and she dropped them into her lap in relief. No, these letters had lost all their power to bewitch. She now knew that life of tormented words punctuated by cigarettes and wine, knew it and hated it.

Now she only wondered if she was bold enough to get rid of these last physical mementos—permanently.

You might regret it, whispered the part of her mind that always doubted, always worried, always fretted. *You might wish to look back on them years later, when they would no longer hurt to read.*

But the rest of her suspected the ache would never completely fade, that it wasn't the type of wound that would ever heal pain-free. The words would haunt her just like their owner, and so would the love she'd once held, so laughably adoring and fervent.

Slowly, she rifled through the letters, opening them up to find one in particular. Words flashed before her eyes, syllables woven in the gorgeous rhythm of a wordsmith that knew her skill. Weathered paper and faded ink couldn't dim their glittering nature, and Alice soon found the paragraph she'd sought out.

I think there's some part of you that will always love me, even just a little. It's the key to eternity, being held in someone's heart long after vanishing from their daily life.

Alice looked up to where Colton sat at the edge of the hearth, watching her. A few feet of space separated them, and she leaned over the box to offer the letter. As he took it, face expressionless, she said, "That turning point I told you about earlier, where she left with someone else... She wrote me this letter when she came back the next morning. Slipped it under my coffee cup."

He read through it quickly, teeth flashing in a silent snarl before he handed it back. "It's not even a fucking apology."

"Well, she wasn't good at those." Alice's thumb ran over one corner of the letter a final time, and then she folded it and set it with the rest.

"I want to burn these," she said, and was proud that she sounded so certain.

He added a few small branches to the fire, dry, knobby ones that burned bright and hot while she gathered the letters in order. She still knew every crease and smudge on each one, still knew at a glance how to order them from first to last. With Colton bare-skinned and her wearing nothing more than an oversized shirt, it felt both too casual and strangely ritualistic to be in such physical states for what she was about to do. The wolf at ease and the witch girl not quite able to strip herself down to raw, vulnerable flesh.

Nerves fluttered through her as she knelt across from him, the letters crinkling in her grip while the flames cast up sparks and smoke. "You once said I seemed to be under some kind of spell from her. I don't think breaking it is as easy as burning some letters. But I think it could help. Is that my witch blood speaking or just a silly hope?"

He gave her that shrug he used toward anything inexplicably human, body relaxed even while her fingers tightened against the paper. "It's your idea to do it. That's all that matters."

She smiled a little, understanding what he didn't say. Her idea, when she was so used to following the ones thought up by others. "You've never decided things for me."

He just gave her that sly look before feeding the fire another small log. It popped against the hunger of the flames.

When the glowing heat reached her face, she finally pulled the first letter free from the rest. The paper was thick, almost velvety, and still the color of cream. Magdalene had never spared any expense on writing materials. Alice ran fingertips along it, remembering how hot her cheeks had felt the very first time she'd read the letter, hair twisted into a messy bun and dog hair covering the scrubs she still wore from her shift as a volunteer at the vet clinic.

Hello, sweet Alice...

Her gaze skipped a few lines, finding the sentence that had filled her with something so sweet and radiant that she had felt sure she glowed.

I see something in you that died in me. It gives me hope.

She didn't read any further. Before she could think, her fingers crumpled up the letter, the thick paper folding into edges that bit at her palm. And before she could hesitate, her hand swung toward the fire in a throwing motion clumsy with rage and desperation. The balled-up letter rolled into the heart of the flames.

A dark thrill rose within her as the paper withered and blackened, a shock as strong as when she'd been forced to watch the same thing happen to the wolf pelt. The sight of this, however, brought a small smile to her face. She really hadn't thought she had it in her to destroy anything. Not *her*.

The next letter went into the fire as a ball, too. By the third, that thrill pulsing in time with her heart had bristled into something savage, and she ripped the paper in half before flinging both pieces at the flames. Another sheet of paper, and then another, the words leaping out at her in the instant before the fire devoured them whole.

When the final letter crackled in the fireplace, she looked at Colton, breathing as heavily as if she'd spent those past minutes running. "Those would have been worth a lot of money, considering how everyone is building her reputation. Especially in a few more years. But I don't care. I just wanted to..."

When her voice trailed off, Colton raised his eyebrows. "To get a bite in."

"Yes." The word came out as half a laugh. "Especially since I can't burn *everything* away."

Then she looked back at the flames, watching the fire dim in an exhalation of sparks. When Colton moved in and pulled her close, she melted into him, feeling his chin rasp against the top of her head. "Even after Samhain comes and goes, she'll keep trying. She'll never leave."

And now she, the witch girl, would have to fight and keep fighting. Suddenly, she better understood the horror that immortality could bring. Of what made Colton sound so tired whenever he alluded to it. How many times had he woken up, the same pattern of fight or flight stretching out before him while years blurred into a meaningless flicker of seasons? How did one make peace with an eternal struggle?

Ah, but beasts know how to endure. If they can walk despite a wound, they walk. If they must run, they run, and don't hesitate at the pain.

Even as her calm attitude threatened to slip, his arms tightened around her. "If the bitch keeps coming back, then we keep chasing her off."

The words reassured her in their very simplicity, a granite bedrock to build on, and she nodded, falling quiet while they both watched the blackened remains of the letters flake into ash at the heart of the fire. No, burned paper wasn't much, but it was still something, and she felt lighter for it.

"What else did she do that morning?" said Colton, suddenly. When she blinked up at him, startled by his rare curiosity, he added, "To make it up to you."

"Well, nothing. I stayed."

"Make breakfast?"

"Magdalene never cooked."

"Brew the coffee to go with that bullshit letter?"

Alice shook her head. "She was already in the shower when I got up. Why?"

"Just curious. You get hungry in one way or another when you come back from a tough blow. Figures the bitch never saw that."

Alice couldn't help smiling. "Is that a hint?"

He nipped at her ear, words turning sly. "Maybe. Feel like some food?"

"I do," she said, surprised at the truth to her answer. She had eaten regular meals since the accident, yes, but with the mechanical awareness that her body needed it to survive. Now she felt more... Awake. Ready to find the pleasure in food again.

Even as she tried to think of what to cook—breakfast in the past few days had simply been toast with jam or butter, and they'd finished the last of the bread yesterday—Colton said, "It won't look pretty like yours, but I know how to make oatmeal."

"You can cook?" she said, twisting around to look at him in full.

"A little. Sometimes, there's no forest or field to hunt in while I'm living like a man."

It was too much to resist, glimpsing this new side of him, and she nodded eagerly.

In the kitchen, he ignored measuring cups and ripped open bags with his teeth. The coffee pot burbled away while a lump of butter melted in the pot. Oats went in by the handful, the flakes sizzling as soon as they hit the hot butter. Colton eyed the results before shaking in spices and giving everything a cautious sniff.

To Alice, who carefully weighed and measured ingredients and immediately returned them to their places in the kitchen, it was a fascinating chaos. And yet the smells already filling the small kitchen left her mouth watering. "You have hidden talents."

When she inched closer to the stove, feeling more ravenous by the second, he said, "I just do what smells good. And I know what to eat to heal faster."

That sobered her somewhat, and she had to reach out and touch him, to feel the solid warmth of his arm flexing against her fingers as he splashed in milk straight from the carton.

At that, he glanced over, shaking his head. "I'm fine, Alice. I always turn out fine."

With the oatmeal now simmering away, he moved over to her, hands bracing against the counter behind her as he leaned in until their noses brushed. She found herself thinking back to the time when he'd been the wounded one, nothing more to her than a wolf dying from a gunshot.

"You laughed when I asked if Magdalene could hurt you," she said, softly. "But that bullet did."

"Misery's different from dying. It's difficult, getting a bullet out. Slows me down."

When she bit her lip, he licked at her mouth, coaxing her teeth to release the tender flesh. "I'm no beaten-down dog. Don't feel sorry for me just because there's roughness to my past. I figured out ways to keep going."

And that was the crux of things, wasn't it? To keep living despite it all. She thought of the uselessness of her nails biting into her own skin earlier. Of Magdalene's refusal to move past Indigo, and Darby's refusal to move past Magdalene. Samhain lurked ahead, yes, but right now it was a bright morning and there were things to enjoy in it.

When she nodded and licked him back, he teased her, his hips pinning her against the counter while he reached behind to pour them coffee.

She knew how to tease back. "What makes you decide whether to live as a man or a wolf?"

His hand squeezed her thigh before reaching above her head to grab bowls. "They're just different ways to find shelter. And things change. I had to hide in the woods when people still knew what I was. Then they started putting different names to me, started thinking I was just a spirit instead."

He paused to rip open a bag of frozen fruit and shake some into the bottoms of the bowls. Raspberries, blackberries, and blueberries immediately began thawing as he poured the oatmeal onto them. Alice sipped at her coffee, trying for patience, and then gave in when he remained silent, dropping spoonfuls of peanut butter on top before finishing it all off with a handful of mixed nuts. "You can't stop there. What did they call you?"

"Different things. Churchyard beasts. Or hairy ghosts. Gravewolves. Black devils." Then he handed her one of the bowls. "They'd leave food at the edge of the woods, sometimes. Offerings for safety, or in thanks if I decided not to rip open their bellies whenever they crossed my part of the woods. Mostly little cakes or iced buns."

"Sweet things," she said, satisfaction rippling through her. She'd wondered for some time how a wolf in the forest had developed a taste for pastries and confections.

Then her gaze dropped to the bowl in her hands. The rich smell of peanut butter and pecans mingled with the warmth of cinnamon and toasted oats. Her mouth watered even before she took her first spoonful.

Colton watched, head cocked to one side. When she hummed and took another bite, he said, "Even little things make you happy."

"There's nothing little about this. It's fantastic."

He didn't acknowledge compliments like a human, simply shrugging them off.

They ate in comfortable silence. She savored every bite, unable to remember the last time someone had cooked for her once she'd left for college, and insisted on helping him clean up, still licking traces of peanut butter from her teeth while tucking things back in the cabinets.

It was while they lounged on the couch, their second cups of coffee in hand, that she asked, "What makes you leave the woods?"

Her voice had fallen slightly shy, slightly cautious. He always bore her questions even though he rarely answered them in detail, but this was something she had puzzled over for some time. Surely, she wasn't the only sympathetic person he'd ever met. And from his carnal appetites, she flat-out *knew* she couldn't have been the only woman.

He studied her, and something in her expression drew a straight answer from him. "It's not enough, being a wolf. I can live as one for years, decades even, but I'll still remember what it's like to be a man. Who I was. Not much, but enough."

Then he glanced over at their faint reflections in the nearest window, sounding slightly surprised. "Even now, things sometimes come to me. Like knowing that I used to be clean-shaven."

His knuckles rasped against his beard as if he tried to remember what his face even looked like.

Alice hesitated, sensing the deep roots behind those simple words. "And now you're not."

He looked at her, faint amusement slipping into his eyes. "No. Now I twitch whenever you cut my hair."

His hand rubbed at his jaw a final time before falling away. "It is what it is."

Alice was naturally curious, but she also knew when to let something drop rather than press forward, and only nodded. When she rested her head against his shoulder, she felt the muscles there relax. Whatever had happened, it was something he didn't want to talk about.

In a few more days, her bruises started turning yellow and she grew stronger, able to clean around the house. Colton cooked a few more times, but she didn't miss his look of relief when she felt well enough for them to shop for groceries that could be turned into a few meals.

She began taking walks in the woods, Colton loping alongside in his fur. Something about the height of the trees and the endless gloom of thick woodland excited her, made her blood pulse hard and fast. Perhaps it was simply a faint memory of her time spent wearing the wolf pelt; perhaps it was only the thrill of seeing Colton bound between trees, at ease with himself despite what she now knew lurked in his past. The ache of following along on two human feet was a small yet persistent one, but she kept it locked away as best as she could and enjoyed what was still left to her.

Sometimes, Alice's stepmother called, and Alice would make agreeable sounds in response to the reassurances that her father wouldn't hold out forever. In truth, she hardly listened, because it was old pain, dull pain, and in between Denise's words was the sensation of Colton lazily playing with her, taking her tension and transforming it into a different, sweeter type. Eventually, Denise would hang up and they would be left to themselves again, stretching those precious final days of safety to their fullest.

Could one call it a honeymoon of a sort? Their wedding being one of blood and hauntings, of near-drowning and savage teeth. Their vows made in flesh and torn sheets, in the raw reveal of her thoughts and the lack of his concern when she kissed scar tissue on his skin.

Yes, a honeymoon, one where sunlit days rimmed them in gold while they shared bites of succulent roasts and delicate pastries, and star-strewn nights draped them in shadow while she lay his head on her lap to pull burrs from his hair, the taste of blood heavy on her tongue from licking it off him.

He did remain silent over one thing—that detail from his past about being clean-shaven and how it now seemed to needle at him. Alice often caught him glancing at mirrors he had previously ignored, always with his hand scratching at his scruff. Since he never said anything, neither did she, but it was easy to see that it bothered him not to remember something as simple as how he had once looked.

And then one afternoon, while she was baking a batch of pumpkin turnovers, it got the better of him. He disappeared into the bathroom despite the buttery smell of puff pastry, and a little while later, just as she whisked together the cinnamon glaze, the clatter of metal against the porcelain sink rang out.

"Fuck!" Colton's snarl echoed.

Alice ran for him, already guessing what had happened. The bathroom door waited ajar, and she pushed it all the way open to find him growling at his reflection in the mirror above the sink. A trickle of red ran from the single patch of shaved skin on his throat. The rest of his scruff was hidden behind a lather of soap.

Without looking at her, he said, "I don't remember everything about the ritual. Just when they slit my throat. It's fucking stuck with me."

Then he raised one hand enough to show how it still trembled, and growled again. It was a ferocious sound, a mauling sound, but Alice drew close without fear, pressing a towel against the cut as he fell quiet again. She couldn't imagine what it must have taken him to even bring the edge to his skin.

But what good is pity to a nightmare creature? Sing their praises in whispered tales of terror, honor their ferocity with gifts of appeasement, worship their strangeness by weaving their existence into the mundane fabric of the world—give shadows teeth and claws, lust and hunger. Pity is not for those who are feared.

Even as Alice ran comforting fingers through his hair, she considered the razor lying in the sink, and then the spots of blood dotting the porcelain. "Do you want me to do it?"

When that drew a searing glance, she added, "I won't cut you. I shave a lot more of me, and every day at that."

The muscles in his back remained bunched with tension, but his voice sounded calmer. "You don't grow it on your face."

"No, but I've felt *your* face over every inch of my body, and I know exactly what I'd be working with."

Despite the surly twitch of his shoulders, he didn't stop her when she turned on the water, testing it until it ran warm from the faucet. "Here. Wash off the shaving cream. We need to soften the hair first."

While he did that, she brought over the pre-shaving oil she used on herself. He gave it a dubious sniff and then let her rub it on, still scowling.

She began talking, aware of how sometimes the very lull of her voice eased him into a calmer state. "You have rough hair, which means you'll scrape yourself when trying a close shave. This oil will prevent that. Let it sit for a minute, if you can. The smell shouldn't be too bad."

His response was another shrug, but he had already come back into himself enough to sit on the edge of the bathtub, leaving it easier for her to reach his face.

"You're not the first man I've shaved," she said, cleaning the razor. "The salon I worked at offered that, too. I won't hurt you."

"I know." But the words were terse, and a frown line was still etched deep between his eyebrows.

She studied him while lathering his face with shaving cream, her fingers careful yet confident. He never trusted words. What were little huffs of breath to a creature like him? Teeth used or restrained, now... Yes, he understood that. And the softness of a body against his own, or the sweetness of a tongue. If she wanted to put him at ease, words weren't the way to go about it at all.

He had tensed up again, realizing it was time for the razor, but the look on his face changed as she settled into his lap, and his hands instinctively caught her by the waist to keep her balanced.

She had dressed in one of his shirts for the day and *only* the shirt, leaving her bare cunt pressed against the rough denim of his jeans. His eyes dilated when she shifted to take the razor from the edge of the sink, slyly using the movement to rub against him. Then he swore under his breath, and she felt one of his hands leave her waist as he readjusted himself. When she licked her lips, not entirely exaggerating her excitement at his virility, he growled. "You're playing with me now?"

"Don't worry, I'll concentrate," she murmured. "I'm just hoping to make things a little less tense. Raise your chin and trust me."

His mouth went grim beneath the lather of shaving cream, but he did as she asked, revealing the strong lines of his neck. Her hand remained light and steady as she made the first stroke, satisfied that the razor's edge slid smoothly without a hint of snagging.

He kept still as she continued, following her gentle touch to angle his head this way or that. The fingers digging into her hips relaxed little by little as she fell into a rhythm, interspersing the strokes of the razor with occasional brushes of her guiding hand through his hair or along his shoulder. When she checked his sideburns to make sure they were even, she risked squeezing her thighs against him and felt his grip on her tighten. The line between his eyes had disappeared, smoothed out by a new type of frustration, and she bit her lip to keep from laughing.

Her strokes were careful yet efficient, and she finished quickly. After setting aside the razor and wiping his face clean with a towel, she looked him over. This time her legs clenched against him unconsciously. "Jesus, Colton. You look *good*."

Without the scruff, the strong line of his jaw was undeniable. He still looked rugged, and his eyes still held the gleam of something feral, but now the sharpness and hunger in his face were revealed in full.

He remained silent, intent on her, and when she started to slide off to let him get up and take a look at her handiwork, he only held on tighter. "You're done with that part of me."

The tone to the words made her shiver. Without thinking, she stroked at his freshly-revealed face, still marveling at it.

The glint in his eyes changed, and then he was kissing her. He had lost none of his roughness, devouring her with every slide of his tongue and every nip of his teeth, but she gasped at the new sensations of skin on skin, of hard bone magnified.

The prickle of hair had been replaced by smooth power and she was desperate for more, already grinding against his jeans as a silent form of begging.

He ripped open her shirt with a single jerk of his hands. Buttons popped and clinked on the tiles, and she had a moment to feel the cool rush of air on her exposed breasts before his hot mouth found her. She arched her back, panting even before he found one nipple and caught it between his teeth. It was both too much and not enough, and she writhed, digging her nails into his shoulders. At that, his hand slid up the length of her back, snarling into her hair and pulling her head back. It left her gasping, left her chest thrust out and vulnerable to his hunger, and he acted on it, sucking and nipping and biting. Working her into a frenzy until she begged his name and dampened his jeans with her slick, grinding cunt.

He could snap her neck if he wanted. He could make his bites maul instead of tease. But even as his growl rumbled against her skin, she only urged him on. She had met with sadism before and couldn't find an ounce of it in his appetite. And she was as hungry as he...

Then his other hand slipped from her waist to her swollen cunt and rough fingers pushed against her tender flesh, finding her clit and rubbing at it, drawing out her panting into moaning. Then his fingers pinched and she howled, thrashing against him in quick, overwhelming release. The aftershocks hit just as hard, and she would have slid to the floor in a boneless heap if he hadn't continued to hold onto her.

He seemed content to just rub his cock against her cleft while she shook and panted, the hand at her neck now stroking along her skin, calming her down. She pulled herself together enough to shoot him a puzzled glance, surprised that he wasn't balls deep in her.

He understood it, and without his beard, his smile was more obvious. "Not nearly finished with you yet. Just letting you catch your breath. Teasing me while I can't fucking move." But the words sounded wry instead of angry, and his eyes held a lazy promise instead of a threat.

"If we're going to do this a lot, it might as well be fun." She stroked along the side of his jaw and then twisted enough to give him a clear view of the mirror. "Have you seen yourself?"

He remained quiet, but his grip on her tightened as he stared at his reflection in near-bewilderment. Then his knuckles ran against his newly smooth chin. "I'd forgotten. It's been so long that I'd forgotten what I looked like beneath all the hair."

Then his gaze flickered back to her, the green of his eyes gone dark with surprise. When the struggle for words entered them, she shook her head and nuzzled at his face, repeating his words back at him. "It's not like I got nothing out of it."

It drew a huff of a laugh from him, but he still looked at her in a way that left her breathless, and when they kissed, his tongue slid against hers like she was nothing he'd ever tasted before.

No, she couldn't change his past or have it weigh on him less heavily, not anymore than he could with hers. But she could show that she'd seen this side of him and still loved him, and she would continue to show that with each day left to them, no matter how many or how few that proved to be.

And for the first time since Magdalene had tried to choke the life out of her, Alice felt ready to do more than survive. She felt ready to *fight*.

CHAPTER TWELVE

THE MARKS OF TEETH ON SKIN

See how the girl appears so silent and sure while walking through the woods? And see how the black wolf lopes nearby —sometimes bounding ahead and sometimes circling back to her side, night-dew on his fur and nose keen. The stars have gone. The sky grows grey with coming dawn. It's time to return home.

The wolf's path steadies, gains purpose. The girl's feet remain light, finding purchase against tangled ferns and fallen, moss-covered branches that would have left her hesitant in the near past. The air between the massive tree trunks is still dark, still untouched by the weak light, but her steps falter only when the wolf growls in warning. His ears prick toward the violent shaking of branches ahead of them, toward a shape emerging from the gloom of the forest.

The girl sees the spread of antlers and hears the snort of breath. Then she ducks behind the nearest tree, keeping the black wolf's teeth between her and the hulking form as it reveals itself in full. It's a buck, aggressive from being in rut and ready to attack anything that isn't the doe it seeks. The girl knows enough to understand the danger of a creature driven mad by its instincts—stay still and the buck will slash and gore. Run and it will chase and trample. Even now, faced with the black wolf's slavering jaws, the buck lowers its antlers and shakes them in threat.

But the wolf only sneezes a laugh before beginning his hunt, dodging those sharp points of bone and snapping at the side of the buck to lure it away from the girl. A rake of teeth drives the deer's frustration into fury, and hooves just miss the wolf's ribs. The wolf only lunges back in and bites the meat of a back leg. The buck twists, slashing at those painful teeth, but the wolf is already out of reach, eyes intent.

It's a test to see which is more nimble, more deadly: wicked antlers or savage jaws. Hooves rip up the ground from the force of each charge. Teeth snatch at convulsing muscle. The buck spins with every bite, desperate to gore the shadow that slips just out of reach.

The girl holds her breath each time the deer slashes, fear mixing with a dark thrill as its antlers cut through air. If the wolf is hurt, she'll be left defenseless against the enraged buck, and yet that fact isn't what leaves her heart racing. There's something pure in this brutality. An ugly honesty can be found in these two beasts fighting each other. Life spills to the ground as blood, shows itself in muscle trembling with power and growing exhaustion. To watch them is to remember that her own heart is simple, struggling flesh.

Finally, the buck stumbles from one too many bites to its back legs. As quick as a thought, the wolf lunges for that thick throat, using all his weight to throw the deer off-balance. Even the girl can smell blood and fear in the air. Then the buck falls in a heap of heaving muscle and flailing hooves. It rises just as quickly, eyes wild while trying to shake free.

The wolf lets go and circles out of reach, silent as he searches for another chance at a bite. But the buck turns and flees, sides heaving for breath as it bounds out of sight, marking the ground with its blood. The wolf doesn't follow, and his tongue lolls in laughter instead of weariness as the forest falls still once more.

When the girl steps out from the cover of the tree, gasping for breath as if she'd hunted the buck herself, he lopes over. Blood stains his muzzle, but she crouches without fear and runs hands over his thick fur while he pants. He takes her fussing with some grace, letting her see for herself that he's uninjured before changing form.

She looks up at the man standing before her, the sunlight now strong enough to burnish his hair and skin until they appear gold. Her heart lurches strangely, but she smiles at him and means it.

Yes, see how the girl remains at ease, her hands already stripping her clothes away while he watches and licks the blood from his mouth. Perhaps it is only the light of the rising sun that gives her eyes such a feral look. Perhaps not...

Even after changing back into human form, sweat ran down Colton's skin. The buck was gone, chased off, but his gaze remained wild and unsated as he looked at Alice. She had already pulled off her coat and shirt, and now matched gazes with him while continuing to kneel there on the ground. They were close to the house but the air between them felt thick with lust and impatience, felt impossible to push aside. Just as her fingers drifted toward her bra, he caught her by the nape of her neck. From his hardening cock, it was obvious what he wanted.

Her grin grew wicked as she leaned in, nuzzling a path along the etched muscles of his lower stomach. She found a vein where the blood beat hard and fast from the hunt and kissed along it until his cock strained. When he caught a fistful of her hair, the noise that came out of her was close to a growl itself. They hadn't been this rough since the accident, and her mouth was all eagerness as she took him in.

She sucked and lathered every inch, humming as musk and sweat filled her senses. Every muscle against her seethed with need, and she coaxed him even further with her sweetness, driving his frenzy as the tang of salt grew in her mouth. Each growl left her sucking harder while she clung to him, fingers digging furrows into the mud on his skin. She knew him well enough to understand the change in his breathing, to understand that he was close... So very close...

The sound of twigs and gravel popping beneath wheels barely pierced her awareness. The slam of a car door, though, sent her jerking away even as Colton's grip tightened. He snarled as she twisted enough to look, cheeks flushing.

A line of firs and their undergrowth shielded them from being seen by whoever had parked in the driveway of their home, but Alice still caught glimpses of pink hair through the gaps between branches.

"Shit," she whispered, still frozen against Colton. "It's Darby."

His only response was to bury fingers deeper into her hair, and his cock remained hard and impatient against her face even when Darby pounded on the front door. When Alice risked glancing away from the other girl, she found Colton's gaze hot upon her, as intent as if nothing else existed for him in that moment.

"Alice!" Darby's voice sounded as harsh as a crow's call, catching her attention once more. "Answer the fucking door. I know what you've been doing."

When Alice shuddered, Colton shifted enough to stroke himself against the curve of her jaw, the lewdness coaxing her to look back at him. His hair was still wet with sweat, and blood spattered his chin and chest from harrying the buck. His teeth flashed as he said, "Fuck her."

She licked her lips, tasting his musk on them, and saw his eyes darken in response. Even as Darby shrieked her name again, Alice felt an answering savageness rise within her. She rubbed her cheek against his cock and felt it jerk as she smiled into it. "No. Fuck *me*."

Another growl rumbled in his chest as he thrust himself back into her mouth. Darby turned into nothing more than a mosquito's whine as Alice gave him her softness and heat, panting in time with the rhythm of his hips. Then her tongue flicked along the underside of his cock, stoking him into release. She moaned around his thickness as heat and salt shot into her mouth, muffling her voice.

Even as she sucked him clean, tongue now slow and soothing, Darby's words echoed from somewhere on the porch. "My house got broken into, you bitch. Rob says he interrupted the two guys who did it and that it was a protest against his work, but he's fucking lying and I *know* it. I know everything."

As soon as Alice pulled away, panting quietly, Colton was on her, pinning her to the ground. The hunger in his eyes hadn't dimmed any, and she gasped as he rubbed himself against the denim between her legs, realizing he'd take her as soon as he was ready.

"What if she hears?" she whispered.

His hand paused at the band of her bra, and he looked faintly amused even as Darby beat on the door again.

"'Fuck me,'" he quoted at her, and she felt herself arch at the sound of those words in that deep, dark voice.

"I know, and I meant it, but I can't keep quiet if we're going this far."

"I'll worry about that." In the brightening light, his eyes looked anything but concerned.

Even as his skin pressed against hers, sticky with blood and dirt, Darby's voice turned ragged. "Your car's still here, so I know you're home. Don't think you can just *hide*. Face me, you fucking coward."

Alice felt her pulse racing in her throat, felt the fear of discovery joined by something hungry and ferocious as she looked at the blood running down Colton's jaw. What was she? Something that would always cower at someone else's anger? Something that would always cower out of the fear of being seen? *Truly* seen? Her heart pounded so hard that she thought her ribs might crack.

"Right after I tell you about the photos, someone breaks in and suddenly everything is destroyed or missing. Big fucking coincidence, right?" The creak of wooden boards beneath footsteps turned into the crunch of gravel, as if Darby now searched the area.

Then Colton's hand cupped the curve of her cheek, surprisingly tender despite the tension in the rest of his body.

"Trust me," he said, the words a low rasp as his thumb ran over her mouth.

One breath escaped her. Another. Darby's footsteps sounded out somewhere near the house, each snapped twig beneath her shoes as sudden and angry as her voice while she kept calling Alice's name. And yet Alice's focus remained on Colton as the frantic beat of her heart morphed into something that bristled instead of quaked. His eyes were still green, still human, but he had never appeared more wild to her.

She licked the thumb still against her mouth, and then sucked at it, her gaze still locked with his. It was the only response he needed, and his hand caught her bra and ripped it off in one quick jerk. It was the same savagery as when he'd grabbed the buck's throat, but she reveled in it, arching as his hot mouth found her nearest breast. The act left her head pressing into the bed of fir needles and moss, but she still heard words cutting through the air, as furious and thwarted as bullets shot in the dark.

"You fooled me, you know. I thought you were just a trust fund baby who got tired of things and went back to your old life. This quiet, meek little mouse."

Just then, Colton's teeth nipped, drawing a muffled yelp from her before he straightened up to rip at her jeans. The zipper gave under his intensity; so did the fabric, and she arched her hips to help him pull the shreds off her legs even as heat began to pulse through her. Her hands scrabbled for something to hold onto as she realized he would be unrelenting, ravenous. Delicious.

"It's all a lie, isn't it? A mask you wear to fool others. You got someone to steal the photos and trash my place. Probably the guy you live with—I can't find out *anything* about him. It's like he doesn't even exist. Who the fuck is he, huh?"

Her panties felt tight against her swollen flesh, and she hummed despite herself as he pulled them down, exposing her to the air. Her legs clenched around him as the bulk of his weight settled against her.

She was still gasping, but he breathed as lightly as when he'd fought the buck, and the light in his eyes remained much the same. A hunter's hunger and yet she offered her neck without fear, her panting turning shallow with lust at the first rasp of teeth against her skin. The finger-shaped bruises had finally faded enough that she felt only the intoxicating threat of his attention.

"But I figured it out. Even though you didn't want me to, I figured fucking *everything* out. And that's why I'm here."

Her heart jumped. At Darby's words? At that dangerous mouth tasting a path along her skin? She didn't know and didn't even *care* as the head of his cock nudged against the swollen, sensitive flesh that protected her clit, leaving her fingers digging into his hair. Some part of her remained aware of the absurdity of this, of how they goaded on the chance of being discovered as the wild, thrashing things that they were.

And yet nothing like fear slid through her as Colton raised his head to hers, licking at her mouth as she panted. If this girl wanted to snap at their heels and chase away their peace, let her dare the forest and its primordial heartbeat. Let her shout at the dark. Let her try to threaten the shadows into cringing before her.

And if she did, she wouldn't find Alice abashed and covering her exposed skin.

Alice tightened her legs around Colton, her fingers now digging at his shoulders as he shifted against her enough to rub the head of his cock along the slippery seam of her cunt. His eyes grew hungrier as they took in the change in her expression, at how she no longer ducked her head as if still nervous of being seen, identified, pilloried.

The lack of response only seemed to infuriate Darby further, and the other girl stalked back to the house, back to the nearest window, peering in at the unlit room while her voice cracked and shook. "Don't think you can ignore me. I found more photos, different ones. The post-mortems of Magdalene. And you know what I did? I took them to a forensic odontologist, one who specializes in animal bites."

Alice jerked as he pushed in, biting her lip at the delicious burn of him stretching her open, filling her inch by inch. Despite the chill in the air, she felt her skin grow damp at the backs of her knees and in the hollow of her throat, felt the dirt on him muddy her stomach and ribs. Her fingers clawed at his back in a silent demand for more.

Then Darby kicked at the front door. "He said that it was a wolf that attacked Magdalene. That *mauled* her to death."

Teeth on her neck. Alice shivered, arching into them as hands dug into the softness of her thighs. He was sweating, too, drops falling onto her collarbones and chest as his hips moved in a hard, unrelenting rhythm.

"But it wasn't just a normal wolf, was it? It was *so* much more than just a starving animal. So much more than a grotesque tragedy, and you knew it all along."

The words nearly pulled Alice away, nearly turned her back into something small and frail, but then Colton growled, shifting enough for his mouth to find the heavy flesh of one breast. She was writhing even before the hot press of his tongue met her nipple.

"Magdalene was practicing at shooting ranges in the last weeks before she died. She was trying to protect herself because she was *scared*. What were you doing, huh? Where were you?"

Alice bit into the flesh of her wrist as she tried to keep quiet, shuddering heat building within her with every movement of his mouth, with every thrust of his cock. Then he shifted against her, pinning her hand back down even while teasing her nipples into sweet points of agony. She rocked against him, panting, flexing her thighs to goad him on. Almost there...

Then Darby's voice turned jagged, vicious, desperate. "I know where. Sneaking behind her back to fuck that mystery man of yours. *Plotting* with him. You're murderers."

Teeth caught her nipple and bit, and she was lost to blinding heat even as a hand covered her mouth, reducing her howl to a muffled whine as she thrashed. Her fingernails dug into his skin so hard she thought he'd flinch. Instead, a laugh rumbled against her chest, and even as she jerked from the aftershocks, the hand covering her mouth shifted until it was only a thumb tracing over her lips, leaving her free to pant and tremble.

"How?" For the first time, Darby sounded broken instead of outraged. "How could you look at the body, identify it, and then go home and keep fucking him? What kind of heartless monster are you?"

Alice panted against Colton for a few breaths before twisting enough to look toward the house, drawn by the true grief in the other girl's voice. The trees remained thick, protective, but she thought she caught flashes of Darby's pink head bobbing, thought she caught sight of artfully weathered combat boots testing the groundcover. The other girl was thinking about entering the forest.

Even as Alice's breath caught in her throat, Colton growled, the weight of his body keeping her from moving in panic. "Let the bitch find us."

"I know what you are," said Darby, her voice now cracking. "I don't care if it's impossible or if no one believes me. She's explained everything in dreams. Showed me what really happened to her. She was mauled to death by a wolf. By *you*."

The footsteps had stopped. Alice caught sight of uncertain boots shifting against the first of the creeping ferns that bordered the edges of the woods. "You're not slipping away from this. Wherever you hide, I'll find you and make you face what you did. I fucking *promise*."

At that, Colton raised his head from the pulse on her throat, finally looking in Darby's direction. Even as the girl retreated, toes pointed in the direction of the driveway, Alice found herself grabbing at his shoulders to keep him close. The hunting look was back in his eyes, and there was nothing playful about it. The buck had been a bit of fun; this would be a kill.

"No," she whispered, drawing his attention back to her even as the car door slammed.

His eyes looked yellow as they studied her face. "She threatened you. I'm not letting that go."

She ran a hand up the side of his neck, finding the stickiness of drying blood. "Neither am I, but if she believes everything she said, then that means she came here with something to protect herself. Or that would reveal us. A gun, a hidden camera..."

He gave her words nothing more than a growl but stayed against her, watching while the car started up and then drove away. She wrapped her legs around his tense body, trying to distract him. He was still inside her, still straining with a load, and once the car drove out of hearing, his focus returned to her face.

"She's a puppet," she whispered. "Just like how I was."

"She's nothing like you." The gleam in his eyes still looked murderous, but she felt only the soft heat of his tongue as they kissed, his hips working against her again. His release was quieter than hers, a snarl into her neck while he pinned her still with his weight.

Afterward, she panted while he lazily licked at the suck marks on her throat and breasts. The rest of his body felt just as relaxed, and the look on his face suggested nothing more than satisfaction filled his thoughts. It was as if he'd shaken off Darby's words and threats as easily as he shook rain from his fur.

For Alice, though, her trembling turned into true shivers, not all of them from the sweat cooling against her skin. Colton noticed, and pulled her up with him. No words were needed while he shook the fir needles out of his hair and she gathered the scraps of her clothes, using some to brush the leaves and dirt off her skin. Only her coat had survived his hunger, and she quickly pulled it on against the cold.

Her phone was in one of the pockets, and it rang even as they walked back to the house. Colton glared at the noise, and Alice knew then that they both held the same thought—that it was surely a call from Darby. Yet when she pulled her phone free to check, Fiona's name flashed across the screen.

"It's not her. It's my aunt." A member of the family calling this early? That was very unusual. She had to answer it.

"Ally, darling." Fiona's voice rang out, larger than life and utterly delighted. "I didn't call too early, did I?"

"No, I've been up." By that point, she and Colton had reached the outside water faucet that they always used to wash off the worst of the forest muck. She waved at him to go first and added, "Is everything all right?"

"Oh, I'm fine, but Tom has been looking *terrible*. He doesn't like your handyman at all." Fiona sounded decidedly wicked about that fact. "How long have you been hiding him from us?"

Alice made a noncommittal noise, her gaze drifting over to Colton as he brushed water from his face. Drops continued to trickle over the hard muscles in his chest and stomach, and she quickly looked away to concentrate on her aunt's response.

"Well, it doesn't matter. Denise says he's very nice, and I'm sure your father is exaggerating about things as usual."

"What's he saying?" asked Alice, her muddied toes flexing against the gravel in a sudden spike of nerves. When she saw that Colton watched her, she managed a smile and another wave to signal that she was fine, and then started cleaning the mud from her calves.

"Mostly how he can't do anything about you ruining your life if you won't accept any help. And he's always called me the emotional one. I keep telling him it's good that you're expanding your horizons with a salt-of-the-earth type. Experiment early and settle down later."

Alice's gaze slid over to Colton again, catching his silhouette through the nearest window as he prowled around inside the house, part of their routine after returning from a walk or a drive. He'd never explained why and she'd never asked, both of them all too aware that he searched for any hint of Magdalene's presence, any hint of that ghostly pettiness that had left Alice so paranoid and panicked.

The thought of Samhain sweeping her up and carrying her away from him felt like a sharp stab to the heart, and she found herself having to sit on the porch steps to stay composed. "He's not a phase," she said, quietly.

"Young hearts always think they know what they want," said her aunt, airily. "Anyway sweetheart, I'm not calling to argue, so let's move on. And *don't* say no to this idea of ours as soon as you hear it, all right?"

The first threads of apprehension wrapped around her. "All right."

"Your stepmother and I have been talking. We all know your father is stubborn as a mule. He'll never make the first move to resolve things even though he's absolutely miserable right now. I have a small party coming up on the 29th of this month, and we think it would be a fantastic idea if you came to it. At this point, we're both sure that things will have to be smoothed out in person."

The thought of facing her father again, of meeting his silence, left her stiff with tension. "But it might just antagonize him even more. You know how he doesn't like family business being brought into the public eye."

"Which also means he won't storm out in front of so many witnesses, or snub any attempt at conversation you'll make."

Alice's teeth rasped against her lower lip at the thought of making him angrier, but she had to admit that her aunt and stepmother had a decent point about having to force him to set aside his silence. Perhaps cold politeness would warm into honest conversation if he had no choice but to talk with her.

But did she want to do this? If these final, precious days before Samhain proved to be her last, did she want to spend one of them on family that expected her to have a whole life waiting ahead, a whole life that they must mold to be sure it fit neatly with theirs?

"It's not for Halloween or anything, is it?" she said, a little proud of herself for feeling out the situation rather than immediately giving in.

"No, no. A friend has started a new catering business and I'm throwing a party to showcase her talents. It won't be very big, only fifty people or so. It begins at seven and includes dinner, dessert, and coffee for afterward. I'll email you the official invitation."

"I see." Alice's fingers picked at the hem of her coat.

When she said nothing else, her aunt added, "I'll extend the invitation to Colton, too, if that's what it takes to get you to agree."

"I appreciate that, but I still need to think about it."

From her aunt's short pause, Alice knew that her sudden resistance was confusing. Fiona's voice sounded uncharacteristically hesitant as she said, "All right, but don't wait too long. It's the day after tomorrow."

Alice, painfully aware of how quickly the days slid by, only murmured something agreeable. When the call ended soon after, she shoved her phone back into a pocket as if it being out of sight could sweep away the snarl of emotions coaxed into life by her aunt's words.

She stood up calmly enough but shook a little while turning toward the front door. Just then, Colton appeared, still in his skin and undressed. Her attempt at a smile faded when she took in the grim tilt to his mouth. "What's wrong? Did you find something?"

"Fingerprints on the window. Made from the inside."

Her trembling swelled into visible shivering and he noticed, pressing close against her while they went inside. The living room windows were clean—she always cleaned them to keep a clear view of the forest outside, which she liked looking at— and their pristine condition made the handprints all the clearer.

Careful marks, narrow in the palm and with graceful, long fingers. They looked like they had been made in ash, and Alice immediately understood the significance.

"The letters I burned. She's saying she knows about that." And that she wouldn't let it slip by unpunished.

A growl bubbled behind Colton's words as he said, "And the human that came here earlier—it's no coincidence."

She nodded, desperation itching at her. "It's only going to get worse, isn't it? Darby will just keep harrying us all the way into Samhain, and then Magdalene will take over and do things for herself. And there's nowhere we can go to keep it from happening."

Strange, how she shook out of anger as much as fear. She thought of Colton's teeth ripping into the buck, of the power she'd felt when she'd had jaws that could crack bone and a predator's body that could run for miles without tiring. Fur lost, fangs lost. How was she supposed to fight back now? The utter unfairness of being so weak and fragile when she needed to be strong and vicious left her struggling not to scream.

Then Colton's hand cupped her chin. Calming her down. Holding her steady. "We already knew this. And you won't be left alone."

She nodded, trying to remain composed even as her heart beat like a drum. "I know. All we can do is wait it out."

They were honest words, which was perhaps why they held little reassurance, but cuts made by the truth left wounds that bled clean and healed properly, and she gave him a wan smile before turning her head enough to kiss at his palm. Then she tried to grasp at something normal, something that had the pleasant dullness of a routine. "We should finish cleaning up."

He smiled a little. "Got a bath ready while I checked things over."

That surprised her. The bathtub was something they'd never played with, for all that it was one of those old porcelain specimens deep enough and big enough for two. Before, they'd always been too impatient, too frantic for each other to enjoy the indulgence of soaking together. "Why not a shower?"

"Always ready with a question." His thumb ran over her mouth before he added, "Haven't gone at you that hard since the accident. You'll be sore."

She felt her smile come alive, and her fingers stopped trembling enough for her to easily undo the buttons of her coat. "It was worth it."

The words kindled a smolder in his eyes, and it stayed there as they headed for the bathroom.

To Alice, sharing a bathtub had always sounded like a romantic idea that would turn awkward once it was tried, and she was surprised at how easy and comfortable it felt to slip in with him, her back settling against the muscles of his chest and stomach. She pulled her hair to the side before fully sinking back against his body, humming at the sensation of hot water after nearly two weeks of lukewarm showers dictated by the doctor's orders.

The tub was deep enough that only her breasts and throat breached the water, and she twisted until she could grin against his jaw, already imagining what he'd do in response to such temptation.

"We'll get to that," he said, the rasp in his voice amused as his hand slid down her arched neck, teasingly stopping just past her collarbones. Then he splashed water over her exposed breasts, and she hummed again at the warmth, anticipation melting into something softer. Her foot absently rubbed against his leg as stray drops from the faucet emphasized the quiet. It felt like the final calm night before a storm blew in with all its wrath and destruction.

"People are finding us," she said, voice soft. "No more hiding."

His hands traced along her body, easy and soothing. "Scared?"

She didn't know the answer to that. She had lived with fear for so long that to be scared was to breathe. It sat in her stomach alongside food and measured time better than a clock. It set the structure of her day and harried her heart in the deep of night.

To ever shake free of it had once seemed laughable, for it had simply morphed into different shapes over the years. The soft, malleable haze of getting into trouble as a child hardened into a pitted hunk of panic over being abandoned in one way or another. The wrong decision made, the wrong words said.

And yet when she thought of what rushed through her each time her thoughts glanced off the closeness of Samhain, each time her skin prickled with the memory of Magdalene's fingers squeezing away her chance at life...

"It's not the fear that I'm used to," she said, the truth of it all leaving her voice breathless. "It's not what used to make me cringe back from things. What I felt there in the forest... Or whenever I see Darby's manuscript and start thinking about ripping her head off... I'm scared because I *want* to fight back."

Colton's muscles flexed against her back as he laughed, a short huff that stirred the hair near her ear. "That's no bad thing. Everyone has teeth, Alice. You're just learning how to use yours."

She thought about it while his hands continued to slide along her body, squeezing at her flesh as if he'd never stop marveling at its softness.

"You're not thinking about the human," he said, after a while.

"Darby? No. I've been expecting something like that ever since we realized Magdalene is visiting her in dreams. Magdalene is too good with words... And Darby never got a taste of her at her worst. She's just an extension of Magdalene and Samhain at this point, and I'm not thinking about those, either. I've been worrying about them for weeks. Darby didn't bring any new threat to us, not really."

Then Alice shifted, growing tense as the truth slowly rose to the surface. When teeth lightly nipped at her ear, she sighed. "I'm thinking about my mother and the way she'd scream at my father. Even though he wants to run my life, I don't want to do that to him. If that's what fighting means..."

There was a soft growl from Colton before he said, "There's yelling and there's fighting. Your mother just hid. Franny Harford wouldn't have been alive by the time I met her if your mother had warned her off with a few bites."

"What do you mean?" said Alice, blinking. "Warned her off from what? We never had any contact with her."

There was a long pause, long enough that she craned her neck to look up at him. He appeared reluctant, even evasive, but when their eyes met, he gave in. "Your grandmother was starving by the time I met her. Too weak to hunt for herself. Too weak to be sly. She let some things slip. Your mother used to be the lure for victims."

Alice sucked in a breath, freezing against him. "Is that what drove her insane?"

"Don't know. Could've been that, could've been hiding among humans without relief, and could've been Franny always calling after her. Most witches don't like being alone. She would've tried forcing her daughter home." His gaze was as steady as ever, but his hands rubbed along her hips soothingly.

Alice shuddered, pieces clicking together as she picked out the implications behind his terse explanation. "So my father was probably..."

"An intended meal."

Three simple little words, and yet they drew another shiver from her while casting light on the shadowy memories of a voice cracking in fear even as it yelled, of fingers trembling against the cigarette pinched between them. "Then my mother saved him and left the woods to live in the suburbs as his wife. As a normal woman. But it didn't work. She hid, so she never got away."

A bitter laugh escaped her. "Sounds like what I learned with Magdalene. Like mother, like daughter."

His growl rumbled against her shoulder blades, soft and brief. "You won't end up like her."

"Not if I fight." Then she sighed, turning her cheek enough to nuzzle him. His jaw rasped at the curve of her cheek. She had shaved him yesterday morning but already felt the roughness of a growing beard against her face. He was always so wild, so resilient, and she bathed in that as much as the hot water.

"I want to see my father," she said, after a while. "I want to try talking to him one last time before Samhain. Just in case."

His arms tightened around her—he never liked it when she implied Samhain might tear them apart—but his voice remained a steady rumble. "This have something to do with the phone call?"

Her fingers continued to rasp against his jaw while she explained her aunt's proposal. He listened without comment as she finished with, "I'm not going to give in or return to how they want me to be. I just want to see if he'll talk. Even if I survive Samhain intact, I don't want my next visit to him being at his headstone."

Colton caught her hand in silence, stroking the palm with his thumb. When it grew obvious he wasn't going to reply with words, she looked him right in the eyes, a question ready. It was one she had asked before, often enough that she already felt sure of the answer. Often enough that he read it in her face before the first syllable left her tongue.

His hand traced the curve of her throat as he said, "I'm going with you."

Even as her body relaxed against his, her voice jolted in surprise. "But you've always said no."

"I didn't feel like it before. Now I do."

Then he lightly pinched at her nipples, drawing a gasp of a laugh out of her.

She caught his hands with hers, not wanting a haze of lust to overwhelm her thoughts just yet. Even as he gave her another teasing squeeze, she managed, "I'm serious. If you don't want to..."

"Do you want me there?"

"Well, yes. Of course. But it's going to be a dinner party with people who like talking about nothing. And they'll all be curious about you."

"It's all right." He already sounded disinterested, instead eyeing the lines of her body.

"But..."

Then one of his hands pulled free of hers, sliding down past her stomach and between her legs. The rest of her words fell away as she jerked, catching his wrist as he found her.

"Relax," he murmured. "You never have to worry with me. If I don't want to do something, then I don't fucking volunteer."

Relax. It was something that should have been impossible for her, and yet she found her limbs falling limp in the steaming water, found her body melting against his as he kept teasing her, drawing her out until the water slapped at the rim of the bathtub from her writhing. Sweat prickled along the areas of her skin that weren't underwater as she shook through her release.

When she fell limp against him again, he lightly stroked between her legs as she panted.

After a while, she managed to say, "We'll have to get you a suit."

"Got one."

She laughed into his neck. "From the same secret place where you kept those sleek clothes you wore to my parents' house?"

He nipped at her ear. "It's no mystery. I store things here and there in case I need them."

"Is it like that old phrase? A wolf in sheep's clothing?"

"Something like that," he said, amused. "I'll tell you more about it. Maybe during the party to give you something to look forward to."

He fell silent again while she sat up and dried her hands on the nearby bath towel. His own hand remained a comfortable weight between her legs while she reached for her phone, still in the pocket of the coat lying crumpled on the floor.

As she tapped her aunt's name, he murmured, "They'll try to coax you back. Put a leash on you. Humans don't like wild things."

In the few moments left before the phone began ringing, her free hand crept back to his. "I'm not wild."

Then she twisted enough to smile at him. "Not yet."

The gleam in his eyes flared into a full smolder, and his fingers squeezed hers just as her aunt answered, her tone already delighted and sure.

"Fiona? We're both happy to go."

CHAPTER THIRTEEN

TAKING OFF THE MASK

The moon glowed red as it rose half-full, casting the road in unfamiliar light as they drove to the party. Alice looked at it through the passenger's window in silence, stomach tightening at how the cool, serene face had transformed into something bloodstained.

When the surrounding trees opened up into wide sky, revealing the eerie sight in full, she found herself saying, "A lot of folklore warns about a blood moon. It's supposed to be an ominous sign."

Colton didn't seem impressed, remaining intent on the road ahead without so much as a glance upward. "Never found it any worse to hunt under."

The very indifference of his voice steadied her. It was solid rock against shrill winds. It was rope anchoring her to time and place while currents threatened to pull her into the suffocating past and chilling future. It was a shadow that never fled in the face of light, as magnetic as any malevolent moon, and she found herself looking over at him.

The black suit he wore hadn't diminished any of his danger, instead emphasizing broad shoulders and lean strength. And the crisp collar of his white shirt only drew attention to the sharp hunger of a jaw already dark with stubble despite how she'd shaved him an hour earlier. There was nothing tame about him at all, nothing sated, and even as the glittering lights of civilization appeared in the distance, his eyes continued to gleam like a beast's.

She wanted to see his teeth. "You don't believe in supernatural signs?" she teased, feeling her shoulders relax. "Or that nasty things might come alive under strange moonlight?"

Now he glanced over. "Whatever's out there worries about me. Not the other way around."

She should have laughed. From the quirk to his mouth, he expected her to. And yet something about the way he looked at her, gaze unguarded, made her lungs squeeze until it hurt to breathe, and a thought came to her with all the clarity and mercilessness of a mirror: she would never stop grieving if she lost him.

It wasn't the old panic that had been instilled in her from the moment scrubby grass and shadowy oak had swallowed her mother whole, the one so easily stoked by Magdalene once she'd found out about its existence. It wasn't even the slow-creeping form she felt whenever she looked at her father and saw a gravestone of unspoken thoughts and confessions. The terror of separation, the agony of abandonment... No, this was much different.

There in the flickering darkness, she watched this beast who wore the clothes of a man without taking it to heart, and realized what she felt had nothing to do with fear. She loved him.

Could a witch die of grief? Perhaps not. And she, the incomplete girl, the so-called doll, was quite used to scar tissue filling in the missing pieces. She would endure, as she somehow always did, but the beat of her blood as it sang through her veins would fade into a drone, and the hunger in her heart, so demanding even as the rest of her hunched in silence, would dull into a vague pang. She would exist without living, and a howl in the night would be as unreachable to her as a half-remembered dream.

To lose oneself in a beast—to go into the forest and offer tender heart to slavering jaws—is to learn the grief of not what is given but of what might become lost.

A short growl brought Alice back into herself, brought her senses back to her seat in the car and the bracelets on her arms and her neatly pinned hair. Colton stared at her, and she realized they were at a stoplight—already in town. The red light glared across them both as she shook her head, trying to clear it. "I'm sorry. I don't know what came over me. I..."

When her voice trailed away, his thumb ran over her cheek, wiping away the wetness.

She gasped, realizing she'd been crying. "That's not waterproof mascara. God, it must be running down my face."

"Fuck the makeup." The words held his usual bluntness, but his hand remained gentle as it caught her own and kept them from fumbling at her clutch for a tissue.

"But we're only fifteen minutes away. If I don't clean up fast enough, we'll be late."

"Fuck being on time."

It drew a watery laugh out of her. "You keep saying that."

"It's a good answer."

When she made a sound somewhere between a hiccup and a sniffle, he cupped her chin, coaxing her to look at him. "What's wrong? Worried about the bitch showing up?"

That fear... Yes, it was present in her heart as well, but enormous enough that it had become something stable even as it drew an ever-closer path toward her. It hung in her world like the blood moon now above them, looming large at night and maddeningly visible even in the day. How much thought could she give Samhain and Magdalene when it was all so *inevitable*?

And so in a strange way, she found it easier to obsess over the little things, to pick at the fringe of her worries and magnify them until they blotted out the true menace. Worrying about her father when she might be dead within a few days. Such a fool.

She shook her head, more at herself than as an answer to his question. "It's not about Magdalene. It's just that... I'm not good at this, Colton. At being defiant."

The light shining over them flickered to green, and he pulled away to resume driving. But even as the car slid forward, he glanced over at her again, a line of concern still etched between his eyebrows.

It was difficult to explain, but for him, she tried, fingers tangling together as she searched for the right words. "I don't like crossing my father face-to-face, and going to this party will be doing exactly that. My aunt and stepmother feel this is the best chance at a reconciliation, but all I want to do is make him see me instead of my mother."

She half-expected a *fuck him* in response, but instead Colton seemed to think about it all, eyes as inscrutable and piercing as whenever he hunted in the woods. Then he said, "The worst he can do is threaten your money. Probably thinks it'll scare me off. Scare you back."

A test of sincerity? She could see that. A stabbing at the heart to see whether it held true. "He's wrong. I'm sure I've been cut out of his will since Magdalene happened, so all he can do at this point is take away the trust fund."

"If he pulls that fucking move, you won't go hungry or homeless." Colton's teeth flashed with each word.

Despite the lingering burn of tears, she found herself smiling. "You're very sweet, you know."

When he shrugged it away with a brief growl, eyes still dangerous, she insisted, "You are. All of this is meaningless outside of one little social bubble, but you're still coming with me. You don't even like being around people."

His hand found hers again, twining their fingers together. "Doesn't matter."

She felt calmer now, breath hitching only a little as she said, "Still... Magdalene can't do too much at the party. I won't mind if you need to slip away and take a break from socializing with me."

"Alice." The dark edge to his voice turned wry as he squeezed her thigh. "We've gone through this. I'm not the one to worry over."

"It's just that everyone there will be curious about you. Who you are, where you're from, what you do for a living."

When he only shrugged, she insisted, "My aunt will never stop asking questions. And my father will probably—"

The hand on her thigh slid further up, pushing past the folds of her plain black dress, and the rest of her words dissolved into a sharp breath. Colton kept watching the road, but she heard the distinct roughness to his words that was his version of teasing. "Whatever he does is his problem, not mine. My problem is stopping you from fretting over me."

"I..."

Then his hand slid between her legs and she instinctively grabbed at his wrist, already feeling that first spark of heat as fingers found the thin fabric of her panties. If her mask was still in place, if she still cared about such things, she might have protested that she needed to look her best at her aunt's and that he needed to be careful while driving.

But she didn't, instead clutching his wrist close as her thighs squeezed against his hand. Goading him. Begging him, even, to help her forget for a few sweet moments.

He growled softly in response, rubbing along the seam of her cunt until the fabric there grew damp. Her entire body already shook, straining and disheveled even as he remained cool and sure.

When a car in the next lane drew close, she flushed, grip tightening on his wrist at the idea of being seen.

"Want to stop?" he murmured, voice giving no indication of what he thought either way.

As she panted, each breath shifting her body just enough to add to the delicious friction of fabric against swollen flesh, she thought of what she must have looked like. Legs askew, hair spilling free against flushed skin. Frantic. Alive.

"Don't you dare," she managed, and arched her back in an attempt to press his hand closer to her clit.

He continued to tease, fingers changing rhythm until he found one that made her hips jerk beneath the weight of his arm. She found herself bracing against her seat as if they were about to crash, the very roughness of his touch drawing her close even while it maddeningly avoided her clit.

Just as the other car passed by in a harmless flash of tail-lights, the driver's face lost in the darkness, Colton pushed aside the soaked scrap of fabric that kept his hand from completely finding her. At the first rasp of his calluses, she bit down on her lip to muffle a cry, trying not to scratch at his wrist.

A rumble of a laugh reached the edge of her senses. "Stop holding yourself back. You can't hurt me."

Then his thumb pressed in and she howled, nails digging into his skin even as the road remained straight and steady in front of them. Her bracelets jangled as if they were about to fall apart; her heartbeat sang in her ears. And for one long, agonizingly delicious moment, everything slid away, even the sullen light of the moon.

Then she fell limp, gasping as fingers slowly rubbed along her folds, drawing out aftershocks. As the world slipped back into her senses, she looked over at him. He still appeared intent on driving, alert yet relaxed while guiding the car into a turn. Then he glanced over, and the intensity of his eyes once more took her breath away. Something flickered in them, gone too quickly for her to understand, and she instead sank into the sensation of his hand now gently rubbing along her thigh.

Spent, satisfied, all she could think to say was, "We'll arrive looking like I've just been fucked."

"Do you care?" Amusement tinged that dark voice, as if he already knew the answer.

She laughed. "Not right now."

Even so, she took care to at least smooth down her hair and fix her makeup as he pulled into a driveway circling around a mammoth water fountain. Other cars had already been parked in a neat line, their preening surfaces reflecting the strung lamps that glittered among the box hedges, and he followed suit while she studied what waited for them.

Her aunt didn't believe in understatement and her home reflected that, with lush gardens coaxing visitors down the hand-cut stone path to a sprawling, two-story mansion of wood and brick. Countless windows kept the architecture from looking dreary, their polished panes breathing golden light that lit up the air. A line of trees spread out behind the house, tall firs that marked where the back lawns ended and the lake's edge began. It was all very imposing and elegant, but as the night closed in, its endlessness marked out by glittering stars, Alice couldn't help thinking that it looked as fragile as a spark in the dark. It was a constructed world that they were about to step into, a doll's house exquisite enough to make one forget how easily it could be crushed.

Then Colton opened the door on her side. Even in the surrounding light, he remained a column of black in his suit, solid and unshakeable. Whatever he saw in her face made him offer a hand to her.

"Words," he said, eyes gleaming at her. "That's all they can use. You've got teeth."

Alice pressed her tongue against them, taking in the bluntness of their shapes. They were an understated signal of good living, straight and aligned thanks to an orthodontist's skill. Suited for a smile that invoked delight, or encouragement, or just the base idea of well-groomed beauty. Glittering, useless abilities compared to fierceness of true fangs. But without the pelt to transform her body to match her hunger, they would have to do.

With a final nod, she placed her hand in his and let him pull her to her feet. As her heels lightly rapped against the pathway, matching a pace with his own hunter-silent stride, his hand brushed the small of her back.

It kept her going even when they stepped through the front entrance and light and conversations washed over them. Alice blinked, reorienting herself to airy rooms and the people that filled them. White walls and hardwood floors reflected the warm lights, turning the very air gold. She could already see where dinner would take place—in the room that overlooked the deck and then the lake beyond. Her aunt stood near the gorgeous rosewood table, studying the centerpiece with one of the hired waiters. From the pinched skin on Fiona's forehead, Alice guessed that there was a slight problem.

Before she could find any other familiar faces, a waiter approached with a tray of cocktails. Alice took one that had been poured in an old-fashioned copper mug, and clutched at the chilled surface even as Colton shook his head to send the man on.

She took a sip, hardly tasting the sweet burn of whiskey and ginger beer while searching the faces around her. Colton also remained silent, studying the clusters of people with equal care.

Who would appear first? Magdalene or someone from her family?

Then Colton's head snapped toward their right, and Alice looked over to see a woman approaching them, a practiced smile already on her face.

"It's all right," Alice murmured to him, her fingers flexing against his arm. "She's an old family friend. One of my father's business associates."

Then she put on her own sociable smile and raised her voice. "Mrs. Fraser, how are you?"

Barbara Fraser looked much the same as what Alice remembered—tall and thin like a greyhound, with startling blue eyes. True, there were now streaks of grey in her hair, a proud gesture of how she would be as no-nonsense about aging as she was in all other matters of life, but it was still pulled back in the same neat bun. And her jawline was still pointed, the skin at her neck drawn thin instead of sagging with middle-aged fat. Her dark brown dress was as understated as the muted gleam of gold at her ears.

But her expression looked relaxed and unfeigned, and there was no hesitation in her voice as she said, "Little Ally Corrigan. I'm surprised I recognize you. It's been ten years since we last met."

Alice offered a polite laugh. "I must've still had braces on my teeth."

"You did. I remember because Gretchen got them at the same time. She's here, too, and will be very excited to see you."

Then her gaze flickered to Colton, and she held out her hand. "Barbara Fraser. A friend of the family."

He shook it, voice bland. "Colton Graves."

The name drew a slight arching of the brows from Ms. Fraser, and Alice suspected the other woman was trying to connect it—him—with anyone she knew.

"We met while I was on vacation this past winter," said Alice, deciding to end the other woman's struggle.

Ms. Fraser nodded. "That's right, your family has a cabin somewhere near the coast. Close to Point Reyes, isn't it?"

"No, it's further north," said Alice, feeling a slight twinge at how something from her maternal line had been neatly clipped of its mats and brought into the family fold. "Deep in the forest."

Something flickered in the older woman's eyes, something Alice couldn't quite name. Surprise? Suspicion? Whatever it was, Colton saw it, too, because Alice sensed him coming alert, some of the disinterest leaving his expression as Ms. Fraser said, "So, you met through serendipity and decided to see where it would lead? That's how it goes for many people. Personally, I never saw the appeal in trusting anything so superfluous."

"What's better than chance?" said Colton.

Ms. Fraser regarded him. "You don't seem like a romantic at first glance, Mr. Graves."

When he only shrugged, she added, "Careful judgement. Planning. All the things people throw aside when they're young and in love."

"When they're foolish, you mean," said Alice, hearing the ghost of her father's sentiment in the other woman's words. In a way, it was unsurprising. Ms. Fraser held a career as a CPA, with her own accounting and tax preparation business, and she was *good* at it. Precision, attention to detail, and excellent time management and organization were traits she'd lived by and thrived on for decades. She understood the world as data and paperwork and problem-solving, and was rewarded for it, too.

Little wonder, then, that her voice held such surety as she said, "It's natural to want to follow your heart, but where does it actually take you? Divorce rates are through the roof. When people talk about wanting a good life, what they really want is security. We're all just creatures of comfort."

"All of us?" said Colton. Alice didn't miss the sudden gleam of amusement in his eyes but didn't understand it either. He must have heard more from Ms. Fraser's words than she had to take such interest in them.

And Ms. Fraser must have heard more from *his*, because her face suddenly smoothed out, gaining the chill and sharpness of an icicle. "It's stability that sees you through something as fickle as life. Nothing else."

Then her gaze flickered past Alice's shoulder. Alice followed it and found herself looking at a young, heavily pregnant woman at the other end of the room, one with the same proud cheekbones and stubborn mouth as Ms. Fraser.

Even as familiarity clawed at Alice, Ms. Fraser spoke again, now sounding almost weary. "Gretchen went through a similar phase, Alice. The amount of planning I had to do for her even after she grew out of her whimsical moods and tried to settle down... The wedding alone would have been a disaster."

Gretchen Fraser. Alice blinked rapidly, too shocked to say anything even when Colton shifted beside her, also turning to look. *That* neatly-groomed socialite, so reserved that she seemed to be speaking in a whisper, was the squalling, angry-eyed Gretchen she'd known?

Yes, Gretchen, one of the handful of girls around Alice's age that had always been pushed by their parents into becoming a group of friends. And yet Alice couldn't say that she knew much about her; the other girl had always been rebellious against the nest her parents had built, a green-haired renegade that had frankly terrified Alice with her merciless tongue and disdainful sneer.

What a shock, then, to see how Gretchen had transformed into someone as well-kept as her mother. Her hair returned to its natural darkness and done up in a soft bun. Her blue dress falling in soft folds around the swell of her belly. The scowl transformed into a diamond-bright smile.

Realizing her silence would become rude if it stretched on, Alice quickly said, "I didn't know she got married. Or that she's now expecting."

"Yes, she's doing very well now." Then Ms. Fraser returned her focus to Alice. "I'm sure you'll get there, too. Have you made any plans to go back to school?"

Before Alice could answer, Colton spoke up, still studying Gretchen. "Where's her husband? She's been standing there alone since we've been here."

"Brad is in D.C. on business for the rest of the month."

Colton looked back at Ms. Fraser, that strange amusement still lighting his eyes. "So he travels a lot."

"He's a lobbyist. It's a hazard of the trade." Ms. Fraser's tone dared him to question it or anything else, but he didn't.

When the older woman continued to study Colton, a slight frown pulling at her lips, Alice murmured, "I'm glad things are going so well for them both."

"Yes." The terse word suggested there were volumes more left unspoken.

"Alice!"

All three turned in the direction of her name, Alice immediately recognizing her aunt's voice. Fiona called it out again, delighted and bubbly and merciless in slicing through the conversation as she approached their group. "Sweetheart, you look *wonderful*. Your skin is almost glowing."

Fiona herself looked resplendent in an ombre dress of brown and gold that magnified the green of her eyes. Her smile grew slightly knowing at the sight of Colton, but her first action was to pull Alice into a firm hug, and even when they straightened up again, her hands held on to Alice's, squeezing them reassuringly. "I'm so glad you came."

Then she smiled at Ms. Fraser. "Enjoying the party, Barbara?"

Ms. Fraser nodded, but the tightness remained in her face as she said, "I'm sorry, but I should see if Gretchen needs help with anything. She's at that point where even waddling is hard work. Alice, please keep in touch. Both Gretchen and I would love to see more of you. Mr. Graves, it was nice to meet you."

The lingering chill in her voice suggested otherwise, and the way Colton's mouth twitched in reply told Alice that he was still amused.

After Ms. Fraser drifted out of hearing, Alice's aunt sighed. "She's always so stiff. I've tried to be kinder toward her after her heart attack—it must be *so* traumatic to have such a dire health problem while you're still so young—but she doesn't make it any easier. Enough about all that, though. I'm thrilled at how well you look. Denise told me all about the accident and sent me pictures of the car. I couldn't believe you came through it in one piece."

Before Alice had a chance to answer the burst of words, her aunt turned toward Colton. Her smile remained brilliant, but her eyes were no less appraising than Ms. Fraser's as she said, "And you've been taking care of her for us. It's so nice to meet you, Colton, and to know that you exist! Alice has told us absolutely nothing about you."

"Didn't want to make things complicated when they didn't need to be," said Colton, voice easy and glance significant as he turned a little toward the deck. Alice followed his gaze and started at the sight of her father, who spoke with a man she didn't recognize. They both looked relaxed, chuckling a little while holding half-empty glasses, and a fit of guilt squeezed her heart at how her very presence would disrupt that.

Then her aunt said, "I understand. Tom can be very bullish, which is why we had to concoct this whole thing. Has Alice already explained it all?"

At Colton's nod, she brightened further. "And you don't think of us as horrible manipulators?"

"Not horrible."

That drew a delighted laugh from Fiona. "It's a start anyway. I'm so glad you're willing to work with us to help smooth things over between Alice and her father. Alice, honey, Denise is keeping her distance tonight to make sure you have some privacy with him, but we're both hoping you'll have everything cleared up before dinner so that we can *all* enjoy talking to each other."

"I'm not sure talking to him will help at all..." began Alice, but Fiona didn't let her finish.

"Just try." Then her aunt patted her hand and released it, an unspoken signal to go on and get it over with. "Give him something that makes him feel like he won. Agree to a part-time job, or to go back to school."

"Or to find someone more suitable?" said Colton, voice bland.

Fiona didn't even pause. "Well, you know how to dress for the occasion. That's one mark already in your favor. While Alice talks with her father, how about *we* have a nice, long conversation where you tell me all about yourself. I have *so* many questions to ask."

Colton's expression didn't change, but Alice read the reaction in his eyes as he realized his comment had backfired. *Shit.*

Alice felt her mouth twitch toward a smile while Fiona's arm settled firmly around his, tugging lightly when he kept his hands in his pockets and remained unmoving. When she tugged at him again, he said, "You'll be disappointed. I don't talk much."

"The strong, silent type? I already guessed that. How about just a drink? Alice needs some privacy with her father anyway, and I'll make sure you get something stronger than the Autumn Harvest cocktails going around the rooms." Then Fiona gave Colton the winning smile that always charmed people, or at the very least resigned them against resisting the force of nature that was her personality.

Colton looked unswayed either way, instead glancing at Alice with a clear question on his face. *Do you want this?*

She nodded, ignoring the prickle of nerves. It was what she had come for, wasn't it? "I'll be fine."

His eyes narrowed, as if he'd sensed her discomfort at being alone, but when she smiled at him, he finally let Fiona tug him away in a different direction.

Her aunt laughed when he continued to look back at Alice. "Of course she'll be fine. Her father's a grump, not a monster. Anyway, I promised you a drink. We have a minibar set up just through here. I believe there's also some scotch left in my late husband's liquor cabinet, although I don't know where the key is by now. I think it's scotch. Maybe whisky. I never learned the difference between the two. Do you know?"

"Yes," he mumbled.

"Good, then you can tell me all about it. I think I remember hearing that it has something to do with where it's made, but that..."

The rest of Fiona's words were lost to Alice as they moved further into the room, Colton's expression rapidly dissolving into quiet misery just before they disappeared behind a group of people.

Alice ran sweat-damp fingers over the fabric of her dress, glancing around as the murmur of voices entwined her like a net. Before nerves could get the better of her, she moved, letting the natural flow of bodies guide her way toward her father.

The deck had been as carefully designed as the rest of the house when it came to a mingling of the rustic and the elegant. Built right over the lake, with the wood stained a dark cherry, it gave visitors a sense of stepping right into the wild without losing the comfort of a home. Waves lapped at the support posts while strings of lights shimmered gold against the deep blue of the sky and the pale perfection of the moon. The cold gleam of lake water churned all around. It was a beautiful sight in all, and Alice wasn't surprised to find the deck as crowded as the house despite the chill in the air.

Her father stood near one corner, still talking with that same man. Still relaxed and jovial. As Alice stepped outside, skin already prickling against the breeze that pulled at her hair and dress, she felt the same mute dread swell in her and the same old tics lock down on her mind. A smile pasted itself on her face before she could even think about the need to look pleasant, but her fingers curled and uncurled against her cocktail.

She even twisted around, some part of her begging to run back inside, run back to the forest with Colton, and ignore any attempts from the outside world to reach her. Within seconds, she saw her aunt, now lost in conversation with two women even while she absently held on to Colton, who looked ready to die.

Before their eyes could meet, she faced her father again, heart now pounding for a different reason. She had to do this. If she didn't, her family would continue to prod her to play along with things, and she wasn't willing to anymore. Not when it meant pulling Colton into the mess with her.

With a final, calming breath for courage, she let her heels announce her presence, their light rap magnified against the wooden boards of the deck. As it so happened, the man who had been in conversation with her father chose that moment to leave, adjusting his tie absently while giving her an equally absent nod and smile. Alice glanced around, taking in how the other people on the deck remained a discreet distance away, and then took the final steps toward her father.

A sense of weightlessness stole through her when his head swung in her direction, that dizzying feel of bone and meat holding little sway against the ground, like when an elevator plunged downward. She watched shock flash across his face, and then hardness replace it.

The sight didn't pause her footsteps, but the tremble of defeat already lined her words as she said, "Hi, Dad."

"Alice." His voice remained neutral. Measured. "I wasn't aware you were invited."

"Fiona added me to the guest list when she found out I was fully recovered from the car accident."

Ah, there. A flash of concern, there and gone again too quickly for all but the most familiar of people to notice. It gave Alice enough hope to add, "I wanted to see you. To talk about things."

"Alice, I don't appreciate this," he said, voice stiff. "There are more private ways to have a conversation than at a party."

"I know, and I'm not trying to embarrass you or make a scene." Her hand had begun to sweat against her glass and so she set it on the railing, keeping her face angled toward the fast-moving water that gleamed like an oil slick beneath the scattered lights.

There was a pause before her father asked, "Have you changed your mind at all?"

"No."

"Then everything that needs to be said has been said."

She hesitated, still unable to face him. What she heard in his voice was painful enough. "I just wanted to see if it was possible to disagree on something and still be a family."

"Alice, you already know where I stand. What part of that is unclear?"

"The part that makes it necessary." Then she finally looked at him, taking in his grey hair and wrinkles. Taking in how he looked like a normal man instead of the imposing, rigid figure who had always towered above her, dictating life as he saw fit.

When he said nothing, she added, "What if I do everything you say and still end up miserable? What if none of it makes me happy? The last time we talked, that's what you said it was all about."

"A home, a good education and career, and a family." He ticked them off on his fingers, lines of irritation deepening on his face. "How could a life like that make you miserable?"

Because it was nothing more than a leash. But she didn't know how to explain that, and so only bit her lip before saying, "It's not what I want."

"If not that, then what? You're twenty-five and pushing for independence as if I'm a dictator. Very well. What do you want, Alice?"

She didn't know how to answer that either, not when the answer was blood in her mouth and Colton between her legs and the moon hanging above sweet and rich. *Freedom*.

"I want to choose things for myself," she said, aware of how weak it sounded.

Her father rubbed at his head. "You've done that before, and now you can barely say her name."

When she flinched, something like regret slipped into his expression, but his voice remained steady as he said, "I just want to keep you from hurting yourself. From feeding destructive tendencies."

Aware that she wouldn't be able to speak without trembling, she remained quiet, eyes now fixed on her hands as they clenched at the railing.

"There are rumors that I'm about to cut off your trust fund," he said, abruptly.

"Are they just rumors?"

"I haven't decided." Cruel words, but he only sounded tired again.

"So, what you mean is, you'll do it if I keep seeing Colton." Her palms stung from her nails biting into them. "Well, it won't work. He doesn't care about the money."

"I'm sure he's told you that."

How strange, that she would only cringe at scorn directed at her and yet bristle at any meant for Colton. She found herself straightening up, her voice now shaking out of defiance. "Ask him yourself, if you'd like. I didn't come here alone."

Then she glanced back toward the house, knowing her father would look, too. Colton had escaped from her aunt and now stood at the minibar, a shot of whiskey in hand while he watched them both. He winked at her father before emptying his glass in one swallow and reaching for the bottle again.

"He doesn't care about this type of life," she said, quietly. "And neither do I. But I *missed* you during the years I was away with Magdalene, and wanted to see if things could be different this time."

Her father looked like he didn't know what to say. For a moment, Alice hoped that he might unbend, just a little, just enough to even consider her words.

Then someone from inside called his name, and his expression smoothed back into a blank mask. The chance was lost. "You already know my answer, Alice, and there's nothing else to say about it."

Even as she nodded, her shoulders sagged.

"Goodnight," he said, the word terse and formal, and then walked away, leaving her to blink at his back.

She felt stiff, too shocked to even absorb the pain as he disappeared among the other guests, and for several breaths she only stood there, stupidly holding her drink. Before she could take a step after him, or even numbly seek out Colton, someone on her left spoke her name.

"Alice?"

She turned on instinct, still too frozen to attempt a polite smile, and found herself under the attention of...

"Gretchen. Hi." Alice realized how awkward she sounded and quickly added, "It's great to see you."

The other girl tilted her head, dark eyes flashing above her grin in a practiced show of excitement. "Alice Corrigan. God, we haven't seen each other since high school graduation. Can you believe it's been six years?"

Alice murmured something agreeable, still struggling with a sense of disbelief at how Gretchen had changed.

"I'm surprised you're here. Last I heard, you'd gone off to the city to be an artist."

Alice twisted her cocktail around in her hand, the same old lies waiting on the tip of her tongue. But for what? Her father wasn't about to compromise his view on things, and she felt... Raw. Perhaps even angry herself.

Her gaze returned to Gretchen's face. "Not as an artist. I went *with* an artist. A writer."

Gretchen's smile froze on her face, and then something about it changed, something that drew out hints of the sardonic girl that Alice remembered. "So, you're finally admitting it. It was a badly kept secret, you know. When it's Magdalene Bishop your name is attached to... She was the youngest to win a Pulitzer Prize, wasn't she?"

"For fiction, yes." Alice felt goosebumps rise from hearing Magdalene's name out loud, but she didn't look away in shame while drinking from her glass, and didn't try to change the subject either.

"And now you're back in the fold." Gretchen sipped from her own bubbling drink.

When she saw Alice's gaze follow the glass, she rested her free hand on the swell of her belly and added, "Don't worry, it's only sparkling cider. I'm a good girl now."

"Your mother told me about your wedding. Congratulations."

"She tells everyone about it. It's the first thing she could be proud of when it came to my life. Bradley Grant. Lobbyist. Always flying to D.C. because he's so busy and important." Then Gretchen laughed, but the sound was bitter, black as tar. "God, I haven't been honest like this in years. I didn't know I still had it in me."

"You sound like you hate him," murmured Alice.

The other girl shrugged. "Way too strong a word. We're apathetic about each other. It looks good for him to be married and with a baby on the way. A happy family."

Then Gretchen took another sip from her glass, studying Alice all the while. "What about you? Are you happy?"

"Much more than I used to be." Her gaze drifted over to the house once more, this time finding Colton in an empty room upstairs, his figure unmistakable through the shining window. He had found the liquor cabinet. There was no sign of a key in the lock, but the glass door was open anyway. He poured a glass of scotch for himself calmly, obviously uncaring if anyone found him, and knocked it back with the smooth viciousness of jaws snapping shut. Then he reached for the next bottle.

Alice's mouth twitched toward a smile just as Gretchen said, "I don't recognize him."

"You wouldn't. I met him on my own. My father and I just had a fight about it."

When the words were met with silence, Alice looked back at Gretchen and found the other girl staring at her. The smile had left her face, and for the first time, she seemed to really *see* Alice. "So that's it. You're not here with your tail between your legs at all. You just came back to rub people's faces in the fact that you escaped this life."

Alice shook her head, ready to explain, but Gretchen's attention had already jumped back to Colton. "It's always easier when there's a fucking hunk to help you feel better about things. He's going through every bottle in there."

"He's insatiable," said Alice, feeling her mouth curl into a real smile for the first time since she'd left him with her aunt.

Gretchen hardly seemed to hear. The bitterness had left her face and in its place was something softer, something vulnerable. "He reminds me of someone I once knew. Not the way he looks, but... Where did you meet him?"

"He did some work on a cabin I inherited up north."

"Cabin. So it's rural area? I met Shane close to the woods, too. Back when I used to hike a lot, pretending I could disappear into the trees and never come out again."

A chill ran through Alice, and she found herself wondering if her own expression looked that pained and bewildered when she thought of the burned pelt—of something wild that had been lost to her. "What was he like?"

"Savage. He scared me and I liked that. He would catch and gut things to cook them over a fire. Did you know that wild animals are seething with parasites? You could see the intestines writhing on the ground from the worms inside. I used to throw up at the sight of blood before meeting him. Now I don't even flinch."

Then the other girl abruptly turned away, as if the sight of Colton had grown too painful. Alice joined her at the railing, and for a few heartbeats, they simply looked out over the lake. Lights glittered in the distance. Laughter from the party reached them in waves as Gretchen said, "The sex was fantastic, but what really got me was how he made me laugh a lot. Made me laugh about *myself*, which I've never been good at."

"What happened?" said Alice, voice soft.

Gretchen seemed to realize where she was, because her eyes sharpened and then she shook her head, the movement causing her diamond earrings to dance and chime. "It's easy to guess. An ultimatum from my mother to behave or else. She knows me too well. I'm good at rebelling as long as I can still live in comfort, but I don't have the backbone to reject her money. In the end, I'm just a coward."

Then the other girl looked at Alice, a strange light glittering in her eyes. "It's almost funny, isn't it? You were such a little ghost compared to me. Always there, watching and listening. Always so obedient. Did you ever even sneak out of your parents' house at night?"

"No."

"And now you're the most daring one here."

"I wouldn't call myself daring," murmured Alice.

"No. You wouldn't."

Before she could respond to that, Colton looked over, his eyes unerringly finding them both. They looked sharp, alert, and unaffected despite him being on the last bottle of scotch. Alice didn't know what he saw in her face, but it made him drain his glass and then set it aside, all attention on her as he left the room.

"Just like Shane," murmured Gretchen, and again Alice saw something like pain cross the other girl's face.

But by the time Colton appeared on the deck, Gretchen's smile was already back in place, and she drifted toward another cluster of guests before he was close enough to be given an introduction.

Alice continued to watch her until Colton's hand brushed the back of her neck. As it stroked down the length of her spine, rough calluses rasping against the thin silk of her dress, she relaxed enough to twist and look at him. "How are you?"

He shrugged, casting a glance around the deck before returning his focus to her. "Found the scotch. It was a good selection."

She tugged at his tie, already feeling herself relax. "I can't believe you're still standing. Does alcohol even affect you?"

He gave her a sly look before his eyes turned serious again. "Saw your father's face as he came back inside. Hasn't cracked yet, has he?"

She shook her head, but the pain was an old one, a known one, easy to bear in the way of an faint scar that can barely be seen on the skin. It was only the chilly night air making her shiver, or at least that was what she insisted to herself.

But when Colton pressed close against her in a silent offer to usher her inside, she stopped him with a hand to his chest. "Colton, answering questions is probably your worst nightmare by this point, but there's something I want to ask."

That drew a growl of a sigh from him, but as he shrugged off his suit jacket and wrapped it around her, he nodded.

"That girl I just talked to said you reminded her of someone she knew. She met him in the wilderness, too, and something about the way she spoke about him made me wonder if..." Then she hesitated, not wanting to sound ridiculous.

"If she met someone like me?" There was no change in his expression as he glanced out at the choppy waters of the lake. "Sure. He probably told her his name was Shane."

Alice started. "How did you know...?"

"I caught his scent right away. Didn't take long to find where it came from."

"No, she's married to someone else. We talked about that."

"I didn't say anything about the human who gave her that rock on her finger. Though he probably doesn't know anything. The mother does. Saw how she glared at me? I reminded her of him." Then he began moving, following the perimeter of the deck. Testing the boundaries like any wild thing.

As they walked together, his hand still light against her back, Alice whispered, "You can't leave it at that. How many of you are there? Do you have any sort of... Society? Pack? And what do you mean you can still smell him on Gretchen? Even if he's seen her, she hasn't seen him. She talked about him as if he was dead."

He shot her a sly look. "You ask more questions than your aunt."

"Colton."

"There are some of us here and there. Never in groups. You couldn't even put two of us in a room together."

"Why not? Too territorial?"

His eyes gleamed at her. "Too aggressive."

Such tantalizing hints of a world. Such vivid glimpses of his mysterious nature. Alice could think of a million questions to ask, but as she looked at the amused quirk to his mouth, at his clean-shaven jaw already shadowed with stubble, her voice fell soft. "She left him."

He didn't look surprised. "It happens a lot. He'll hang around until there's nothing left to her but the grave."

"Are you speaking from experience?" Alice ran her hand along his arm, trying to convey that it was only curiosity that drove the question.

"Alice." His sideways glance was easy, relaxed. "You know that's a dangerous question. It has the type of answer that sticks."

She bit her lip. "I've asked you similar questions before, and you only slid around them. I really don't mind learning the truth. I wasn't innocent at all when we met, and knowing your appetite... I can't see being the first girl to ever catch your attention."

He remained quiet for a few breaths. "Why do you want to know?"

She knew the answer heart-deep, but crystallizing it into words still felt painful. "I deified Magdalene into someone she never was. I don't want to do that with you."

At that, he met her gaze in full. In the warmth of the lights, his eyes appeared nearly as yellow as when he was a wolf. "There have been others. None like you."

Despite the cold night, she flushed. "Oh. I didn't expect to be that... Distinct."

He leaned in until their noses brushed. "Alice, you're fucking stunning."

Then they were kissing, his mouth impatient and rough. Intoxicating. She let him in willingly, eagerly, ready to lose herself in his heat.

A distant bell shattered her haze, and the sound of her aunt's voice calling guests in for dinner dissolved it completely. When she tensed up, Colton broke off with a short snarl, eyes now dark and feral as the taste of scotch lingered on her tongue.

She panted up at him, not yet ready to put on a mask and join the rest. "I don't want it," she found herself saying, feeling lighter with each word. "What Gretchen has. What I could have. I don't want *any* of it. It's not the right world for me."

"There's another one out there." So close together, his dark voice rubbed against her like velvet.

"Your world?"

He nodded. "You can reach it even without teeth and fur. I'll show you how."

She drank in the words like champagne, absorbing their sweet promise. Drank in the sight of him, wild and ravenous and untouchable.

As they approached the house, she looked up at Colton with a smile, already eager to get through the meal and leave for home, but he wasn't looking back, all attention instead on the room where they would be dining. Then his shoulders stiffened.

Recognizing the unsaid warning, she scanned the area. Then she sucked in a breath, a pit forming in her stomach. An unmistakable figure stood among the guests, waiting by the ornate table while people took their seats. Even at that distance, the sneer of her crimson mouth pierced Alice's heart like a needle.

"Magdalene," she breathed, and heard Colton growl softly.

Someone crossed in front of them, blocking their view, and when it cleared again, Magdalene had gone. Before Alice could even hope that nothing more would happen, glass shattered and a scream rang out.

A woman she didn't recognize shrank back from her place setting, laughing a little breathlessly as her shaking fingers picked broken shards from her lap.

"Already making a fucking scene," said Colton, a rasp entering his voice.

Alice felt goosepimples rise on her skin as remnants of red wine spilled from the shattered crystal on the table, pouring to the ground as Alice's aunt rushed over, hands fluttering in distress. "Would she leave with us?"

"You know the bitch better than me."

She nodded, knowing he was right. Knowing the answer to her own question. "No, she wouldn't. She always enjoyed dramatics. And they won't understand... They won't realize."

"What do you want to do?" His hand caught hers as they continued to watch the guests react to the mess.

It was all on her now. If she wished to flee, he'd lead her to safety. If she stayed and tried to grapple with whatever petty violence Magdalene wrought, he'd fight with her.

Her fingers tightened against his, already sweating from nerves, but her voice came out sure and strong even as a whisper. "We'll stay and fight against whatever she tries. I won't let her torture anyone else if I can help it."

Colton said nothing in reply, but his eyes took on a hunting light as they hurried toward the house. Alice just bit at her lip, wondering if she remembered enough about Magdalene's tactics to anticipate the worst of them. She was about to find out.

CHAPTER FOURTEEN

THE DROWNING WATERS

See how the girl sits there so stiff and proper, posed like a mannequin? She fits in perfectly with the other guests at the table, sheltered from the surrounding night by the warmth of candlelight and glittering like the crystal wine glass she holds. And yet, while the rest chatter over chèvre-stuffed figs, forks as arched as their eyebrows, her expression fills with something much darker than pampered delight.

She's afraid, this girl. Look how her eyes dart this way and that, studying the faces of those surrounding her as though one will at any moment twist into something else. As though a knife will slash at her own flesh instead of the delicate ribs of lamb served as the first course. The tight line of her mouth eases toward a smile only when she glances at the man beside her.

If one could call him that. Even in his fine suit, he carries the calm of a hunter. His jawline holds the lean strength of something hungry, and his glance reduces people down to vulnerable flesh. The other guests don't know what he is, but they recognize him all the same. He's the looming mountain that has no road cut into its sides, the prick of starlight in unending sky. He's the quiet in the woods when one is lost and panicked, desperate to hear anything above the frantic thrum of their own heartbeat.

He works in forestry, go the whispers around the table, and the responding nods carry satisfaction, even relief at putting a name to what separates the man from them even as his cufflinks wink with the rest. At putting a name to what makes him so *different*.

Still... Don't heap too much scorn upon them. They're blind in the way of humans ignoring the darkness beyond the firelight, and all they can sense is their own hunger and the sating of it. They're lost in the succulence of duck breast crisped in its own fat, in the bright burst of pomegranate against their tongues. Wine brings its soothing warmth, and even as the sky above glitters coldly, their laughter rings out across the churning waters of the lake.

Sweet, foolish creatures. They don't perceive the thinning of the veil between worlds, or understand the power of the night so close to Samhain. Only the man, eyes gleaming as if he's still in the woods, and the girl, shivering as though she already feels ghostly fingers upon her skin, realize that the shadows loom larger than normal. That from the surrounding darkness stretches something hateful. Something hungry itself...

"I don't understand," murmured Alice, shoulders rigid while her fork prodded at the uneaten miniature cake left on her plate. Even as her aunt's voice roused the rest of the guests, she leaned closer to Colton and added, "Why hasn't she done anything? I thought she'd spend the entire dinner tormenting people with her tricks."

There were only crumbs left on Colton's plate, and he'd already settled back in his seat to watch the others leave. His expression revealed nothing of what he thought as people drifted over to the sliding glass doors leading out to the deck. Waiters stood there with trays of dessert cocktails, smiling politely as each guest chose a drink. Everything seemed perfect. A sugar-crusted end to a pleasant evening.

"She's still here," said Colton, voice flat. "Not *right* here, but nearby."

Alice once more searched for any hints of Magdalene's presence. The rap of a heel, perhaps, or the flash of a familiar silhouette among the confusing mingle of pretty dresses and dark suits. A flickering from the lights strung all around the deck to indicate her presence. Even just a glimpse of that wicked smile while faces turned this way and that, seeking out old friends and new conversations. But there was nothing, nothing at all.

And yet something about the look on Colton's face, so keen and alert and knowing, drove her to ask, "How can you sense her?"

"This close to Samhain, it's easy to smell her. It's a little like smoke in the air."

Alice nodded, but the answer wasn't satisfying. Something in her silence must have told him as much, for he glanced over. The uncertain candlelight warmed the green of his eyes as his hand skimmed down her bare arm, soothing away the goosepimples there. She dropped her fork to clutch at it, feeling the sick pit in her stomach shrink for the first time since she'd heard the wine glass shatter.

"What are you really asking?" he said, and the roughness in his voice was almost enough to take her away from the glittering corset of society and the sour taste of fear left in her mouth, to take her back to the crackling of a log-fed fire and the warmth of their entwined bodies.

"What does she look like to you?" she asked, hating how vulnerable she sounded. "I always wonder how Magdalene appeared to people who weren't..."

"Caught by her bullshit?"

It startled a laugh out of her, but she quickly fell serious again. "Yes. Sometimes, I just want to know how I might have seen her if she hadn't become my whole world."

For that was the hardest thing to grapple with, wasn't it? She could easily find examples from her time spent with Magdalene that would be more shocking, more horrifying, or even more pitiful in the eyes of others. She could pluck the memories that would always haunt her and then cast them like rune stones for any curious observers and say, *here—here are the strands of the web I helped wrap my heart in.*

But how could she possibly explain that even now it proved impossible to view Magdalene as something diminished? That her life had been molded into a shape of her lover's making, that her sense of normal had been distilled into what was necessary to kindle another's happiness? Fear reduced to making a mistake, joy to performing a task correctly. The sun had been Magdalene's smile, and the stars the precious words of praise that had glittered in her heart for years until the emptiness finally became too much. What a contained, neat little existence it had been—easy to understand, safe in the way of having no choice.

And only lately had Alice grown to understand that this world was not *the* world. Magdalene had long loomed above like a goddess in all senses of the word—terrible, divine, wrathful, benevolent—and Alice still struggled to see her as something lesser. Even her rebellion had been that of a believer rejecting core tenets, of turning away rather than casting out. She still could not face the rules burned into her heart and declare them false.

And so she looked at the wild beast beside her, at the nightmare creature that saw others without fear, and begged, "How do you see her?"

For a long moment, he studied every inch of her face. Then his hand caught the back of her neck, and the rasp in his voice softened into something that rubbed against her like velvet. "She's a fucking parasite. And one day you'll pull her away like one."

At that, her chin started trembling, and she turned fully in her seat toward him, already raising her face to his in a wish to erase the metal-heavy fear still in her mouth. Wishing to lose herself in him for a brief, precious moment. A flicker in his eyes showed he understood.

Just as he leaned in, nose brushing hers, Fiona's voice cut through. "Ally, there you are!"

Her aunt sounded some distance away, probably out on the deck with the other guests, but Alice still pulled back, muffling a sigh while Colton shook his head at the interruption. His heat lingered against her skin as she watched Fiona hurry over. Her aunt still looked sleek and sparkling, not one hair out of place, but worry pinched at her mouth and drove an artificial bubbliness into her words.

"Sweetheart, why are you sitting at the empty table? It's almost time for the group photo."

"I..." Alice glanced over the groups of people, quickly picking out her parents. Tension lingered in the set of her father's shoulders, and her stepmother's smile looked forcibly bright as they chatted with another couple. "I don't think I should."

Fiona's expression turned startled. "I know things didn't work out like we'd hoped with your father, but that doesn't mean you should make it *worse*. He's already grumbling to Denise that you're making a scene by not being out there."

"I'm sure he is," murmured Alice, and her fingers squeezed against Colton's in a fit of panic over what she was about to say. Yet she still looked directly at her aunt, and still added, "But I'm past acting like everything is fine when it isn't."

"Ally..."

"No." She kept the word firm, unflinching, and after a moment her aunt sighed.

"Well, no one can force you into something. But at least get some drinks for yourself and come out to the deck, just to show everyone that you're not upset."

That seemed fair enough, and Alice nodded.

Her aunt brightened again. "Try the Autumn Harvest cocktail. There's apple butter in it. I remember you adored slathering that on your toast when you were little. And Colton, you seem like a man who would enjoy the Burning Witch. It's cinnamon whiskey with pumpkin liqueur and a dash of cayenne."

Colton muttered his disgust, but Fiona didn't notice, already pivoting away from them to return to the deck.

As her aunt disappeared among the other guests, Colton's voice rumbled in Alice's ear. "Hard to believe you two are related."

She smiled wryly. "Which one of us are you complimenting?"

He gave her a sly look that suggested in a safer time and place, she'd be bent over the nearest object with his teeth against her neck. "You know which. You're less pushy. More aware of things. Your father won't stop his fucking pouting because of a group photo."

"She just wants everyone happy," said Alice, watching his thumb run over her knuckles. Then she sighed. "I just want everyone safe."

There was a soft growl from him before he rose sure and easy from his seat, drawing her up with him. "Always so sweet."

The words kept her steps sure as they approached the lingering waiter. Colton gave all three options a shake of his head, but she dutifully picked the recommended cocktail, and the smell of cognac and apple soon filled her senses as she held it without sipping, wishing to keep a clear head. She couldn't help notice how many guests had flushed cheeks from the alcohol and rich food. Their movements had grown a little careless, a little looser. The laughter had stopped sounding so restrained.

A few people lingered inside the warmth of the house, but most had positioned themselves in the center of the deck, right where the strands of lights would best reveal them. As Alice twisted her glass back and forth, watching the photographer fuss with his equipment, Fiona saw her and made a quick *come over* gesture.

Alice hissed in a breath, eyes instinctively darting to her father as he stood so close and yet so impossibly far away. He hadn't once looked over at her, and his expression remained jovial as he spoke to the people surrounding him while they all waited to take the photo. Even so, she knew that in his view, she was making a mess of things with her hesitation—drawing their dispute out into the open. The chance to step into the fold before her reluctance grew too apparent was rapidly shrinking.

And now that all of her family had settled together, people were beginning to glance at her. She shifted, years of social training coaxing a step out of her. Then Colton's hand caught her arm, surprising with its tightness. It jolted her awake as thoroughly as a sharp nip, and she looked up at him.

He wasn't looking back. Instead, he studied where they stood, at the edge of the concrete foundations of the house, and then where the wooden boards of the deck began, just after one stepped through the glass doors of the dining room. His mouth had gone very grim. Then he glanced around the perimeter of the deck, taking in the massive wooden supports that kept the entire construct steady above the pitch-dark water. The strung lights swayed slowly in the air.

"Colton?" she whispered, realizing he sensed danger.

"She didn't want to fuck with you," he said, turning to her. His eyes had darkened with rage. "Just keep you still long enough to make a trap."

Just as the implication hit her, Fiona hurried over once more. Even in the uncertain light, her exasperation was obvious. "Ally, your father looks like a vein in his forehead will explode any minute. *Please* join the rest of us. It's only one photo."

As soon as Fiona's hands reached for Alice, Colton pushed forward, keeping himself between them. The lines of his body had gone hard with tension. Alice squeezed his arm, heart now pounding like a drum. "Fiona, we have to get everyone off the deck."

"What?" Her aunt sounded distracted more than concerned, glancing back over her shoulder at the others.

"It's about to collapse." Panic drove her voice high as she tried pushing past Colton, but he held her still, continuing to stare at Fiona.

"Alice, don't be silly." Fiona turned toward her again, this time stepping closer until the light from the house hit her full in the face. Her normally green eyes had changed into a striking amber. "That's just what I want."

Alice's blood froze in her veins. Her tongue felt dead in her mouth. At her silence, her aunt's mouth twisted into a familiar smile. Magdalene's smile.

"What did you do?" she whispered, voice shaking.

The answer came in her aunt's voice, but the inflection, the purring delight, was all Magdalene. "Everything necessary to see you again."

Then Colton snarled, eyes flashing. Alice knew the sound, recognized that it meant blood and death. In the heat of the moment, he would save Alice over anyone else even if it meant attacking her aunt—ripping at her to drive Magdalene and her threats away.

And from her growing grin, Magdalene planned exactly for that.

"No!" Alice lunged, shoving Fiona—Magdalene—out of Colton's reach. Even as he roared her name, Magdalene's fingernails bit into her arms, keeping her close as they both fell onto the deck in a sprawl of limbs and fabric.

"Got you," breathed Magdalene's voice into her nearest ear, and then the wood beneath them cracked.

As if watching from another world, Alice saw the boards around her buckle. Glass shattered as people stumbled and dropped their drinks. The entire deck lurched like something alive.

Beneath the first chorus of screams, Alice heard the ghost of a laugh as Magdalene's grip tightened against her flesh. Then the deck crumpled in on itself, sagging like a dying beast as splinters of wood stuck into the air like snapped bones. In the last flicker from the strings of light as they toppled through the air, Alice watched the boards open up into swirling water. Then her screams joined the rest as they all fell.

Frigid water slapped the breath out of her. Slapped Magdalene's hands away. In her sudden freedom, Alice scrabbled, heels slipping against broken wood as bubbles swirled all around. All was blackness as currents rushed over her head and tugged at her dress, and she thrashed on instinct, kicking away anything that might be fingers.

Just as her lungs began to burn, she broke the surface with a gasp, sodden fabric already threatening to pull her under again. Her surroundings had turned into a sightless hell. Screams and splashing filled her senses as she groped at the water, searching for something solid to hold onto. A shoe kicked her in the side. Nails scratched along her arm. Once, hands even flailed against her, the weight of a body lurching over her own as if to use her to stay above water. She bit until she tasted blood and found herself free again.

Finally, her fingers latched onto wood and she pulled herself onto it, heedless of splinters or sharp edges.

As she coughed and gasped for breath, Colton's name nothing more than a croak from her mouth, bodies continued to struggle all around, splashing and screaming. Wood bobbed uselessly. Smoke rose from where the strings of lights had exploded in the water.

In the distance, the house winked at her like a beacon. A few people struggled up the remnants of the deck, fighting against the mud and exposed concrete foundations until they could climb to safety. Several others looked dry and focused as they pulled sodden guests from the water, bundling them in towels and getting them inside.

As Alice paddled closer, shifting against her makeshift raft until she could keep all but her hand out of the water, she caught sight of her aunt among those rescued. Just as she opened her mouth to call out, a wave slapped over her, blurring her vision and leaving her coughing.

Before she could recover, a hand locked around her own, fingers somehow colder than the currents swirling around. Alice choked on a gasp, skin prickling as pain—fingernails—bit at her wrist, trying to wrench her off the wood. The water lapped at her limbs as she fought back, struggling to stay above the surface.

Hair fell into her face, and then there was nothing to see except dark, churning waters smoothing out into nothingness. The splashing around her suddenly looked like fish leaping, panicked and bulging in the eyes, and the lights in the distance had already hardened into the cold shine of stars.

"No!" Her voice came out raggedly as the raft beneath her shifted, sliding her further into the water. She could see a figure beneath the surface now, hair swirling gracefully and smile vicious as a knife stab. Magdalene was waiting.

The broken boards buckled further, and for one moment she had the sickening sensation of them flipping on her. Then an arm snaked around her waist and yanked her back, centered her weight on the raft. A jaw rasped against her neck until it found her ear. "Stay calm. The bitch won't get you."

Tears hot as fire ran down her cheeks at the sound of Colton's voice. Then the hand around her wrist tightened, desperate to keep her. Alice screamed as it dug into her flesh.

Colton snarled as he pulled her arm free of the water, revealing Magdalene's hand as well. His teeth flashed before sinking into it, ripping open the skin. A familiar scream ran through Alice's head, and then the hand flinched back. Disappeared.

Ragged screams continued to slice through the air while Colton remained in the water, guiding the raft toward the house.

"You think she'd fucking expect it by now," he said, eyes feral as blood ran down his mouth.

Alice's teeth chattered too hard for her to speak.

They quickly found a twisted area of the deck that could be climbed like stairs to reach dry ground. He pushed her up most of it, but when clipped grass finally tickled at her toes, her knees still buckled.

His hands felt nothing like Magdalene's as he pulled her upright to keep her out of the mud, brushing sodden strands of hair from her face. Still silent, she clung to him, dimly aware of how his teeth had grown out as sharp and fearsome as a wolf's fangs. She had never seen them like that while he was human, and when she tried to numbly touch them, he caught her fingers and warmed them with his own, staring at her all the while. Furious. Seething that he'd almost lost her again.

Somewhere in the distance, she heard a frantic voice call her name. Then Colton's growl rumbled against her. He was ready to rip apart anyone that tried getting in between them. And yet the voice persisted, clearing the fog from Alice's mind.

"There's blood on your mouth," she whispered, taking in how he would appear to an outsider. Bloody. Feral. Inhuman.

He only leaned in, still looking at her as if he never wanted to see anything else.

When her name rang out once more, she reacted without thinking, tugging at his shirt collar to bring their faces together. Then she licked the traces of blood from his mouth, making his hands tighten against her. She didn't stop, quick only from not wanting to be discovered.

Someone was watching them when they separated. Panic rippled through Alice until she recognized the figure. Gretchen stood on safe ground, dark eyes wide with shock and phone forgotten in her hand. As she stared at them, something new filled her expression. Something like hunger. Something like grief.

Without a word passed between them, Alice sensed that the other girl *knew*. Such a look only came from someone who had seen a wolf's fangs before, who had felt their thrill as much as their threat. For a long moment, Gretchen's expression crumpled as if she were about to break down. Then she forced herself calm and nodded at Alice, a stiff jerk of the head. Other people appeared beside her, their voices hoarse and unclear in the night air. Whatever they said sent Gretchen into the house with her phone once more at her ear.

Before Alice could do more than blink, her father was there and sweeping her up into a hug, breath hitching as if he could hardly breathe. He was soaking wet, with a thin trickle of blood running from one eyebrow, but it was the look on his face that truly shook her. He was *crying*. As her arms slowly wrapped around him, first uncertainly, and then fiercely, Colton remained nearby, eyes inscrutable. When she looked at him over her father's shoulder, though, he understood and stepped away.

As she rested her cheek against her father's shoulder, an action echoing back to her earliest memories as a child, Fiona's voice—her *real* voice—announced her presence.

"Ally! Thank God. Then we're all safe."

She had never seen her aunt look so shaky, ankles trembling in their heels as if she might collapse at any moment. "Fiona, are you all right?"

"My dress is ruined. And I must have hit my head against a board because I have the *worst* headache in my entire life."

Her father's voice sounded rough. "You're fine. There are others that have broken legs, and Gregson's wife has been bleeding from the nose since she was pulled out of the water."

From the way his arms tightened around Alice, she knew that he'd worried about finding her in such a state. Or worse.

As her aunt continued to tremble, Alice glanced at Colton in a silent plea. His expression told her that he understood, and that she was the only reason he'd agree to do it. Then he briefly disappeared into the dining room, soon returning with a chair.

When he offered it to Fiona, she sank into it with a smile that was only a glimmer of itself. "You look the best out of all of us. I bet your job leaves you in far more dangerous situations than a collapsed deck."

"Sometimes."

"Tell me about them. I need distraction before I burst into tears over what's happened."

Alice thought she heard him smother a sigh, but then rest of the world faded away, for her father's grip tightened around her. When his hand cradled her head, she realized he wasn't about to speak any words. That perhaps he would never be able to. Perhaps, for them, it wasn't even necessary. The desperation in his grip told enough; for all his bluster, he didn't want to lose her. For all his bluster, he was *terrified* of the idea.

Alice held onto her father and let him cry long after her own tears had stopped.

Later, she continued to feel strangely calm while waiting in the hospital parking lot. She and Colton sat on a concrete curb that bordered some young maples and their bed of mulch, and her fingers absently played with a fallen leaf while they watched the horizon glimmer with coming dawn.

"She possessed Fiona," she said, finally.

It was such a stupidly obvious statement, but Colton still answered. "Samhain's close. Gives her more influence in this world."

She nodded, now silent while looking at the emergency room entrance. For the past several hours, the dinner party guests had trickled out in ones and twos, bandaged up and sent home with instructions on how to care for their superficial injuries. Her heart hurt for them—for their bewilderment, for their fine suits and dresses muddied and wrinkled, for their wounds after a night of what they thought would be good food and good conversation. They looked liked bedraggled peacocks, stripped of all their elegance. She was aware that she herself surely looked just as disheveled, hair snarled and pulled free of its bun and makeup wiped away from lake water and tears.

Only Colton looked unshaken, sitting easy and calm while his eyes picked up the green of the nearby shrubs. His tie had long disappeared and the collar of his shirt had been ripped open, revealing the strong muscles beneath. Scruff already covered his jaw, and his dark hair looked wind-ruffled.

She was just about to reach out and bury her fingers in it when he shifted position, abruptly focused on some thick shrubs that formed a patch of natural landscape between two buildings across the street. In the not-quite-twilight, they remained as dark as shadows, shivering slightly from the breeze.

Then she saw a pointed muzzle as black as its surroundings. Next, a pair of glowing eyes. Her heart beat faster as they flashed at her, but in that very moment Colton growled, his posture stiffening up as he continued to stare at what could only be another black wolf.

Before Alice could breathe a word, voices drifted over from the emergency room entrance, and she glanced over in time to see Gretchen and her mother. Both seemed unharmed, tired instead of traumatized.

Gretchen looked exasperated, and walked barefoot while her mother glared at the shoes dangling in her hand. "I'm fine, Mom. I never even got close to falling into the water."

"You have a condition." Despite her sharp tone, Ms. Fraser looked much older and frailer than from the night before.

Perhaps her daughter noticed it, too, because her voice softened. "And you have an even worse one with your bad heart. I'm fine. Let's just go home."

As they walked off without seeing Alice, her gaze jumped back to the wolf hiding in the bushes. Those eyes now flashed at Gretchen, and that pointed muzzle traced the other girl's direction until she and her mother got inside a car.

As they drove away, Alice sensed the other wolf hesitating— he would have to pass by her and Colton to catch a final glimpse of Gretchen. "He wants to follow her, doesn't he?"

Colton remained intent on the other wolf. "He can do it when he's not in fucking front of me."

"And you really don't like each other, do you?" she said, voice soft.

Now he looked at her, eyes absolutely feral. "No. And I'm not in a patient mood."

"You're..." She hesitated, and then finished her thought. "You're shaken up like me."

He responded with an irritated twitch of his shoulders, but his hand remained gentle as it cupped her chin, drawing them closer together. "Wouldn't say that. Just want to rip something's throat out, and the bitch isn't around."

She dropped her forehead against his, basking in the heat of his skin. Words tumbled out of her, heavy ones that she wished weren't true. "Magdalene used my family against us. If she had made Fiona try to—to strangle me, or something else like that, you would have attacked her."

A muscle twitched in his jaw. "Would've had to. Otherwise she'd have used your aunt's body like a shield and done whatever she wanted."

Alice shuddered at the thought. "She found the weak spot. You'll protect me no matter what, but I'll sacrifice myself for other people every time."

That drew a low growl from him, but he fell silent when she raised her face enough to look at him. "I won't put my family in danger again. Until Samhain's come and gone, I'll have to stay away. Shut myself up at home. It's her same old trick of isolating me from everyone else, but I don't know what else to do."

Despite the tension in his body, his voice remained steady, his mouth brushing against hers as he said, "She'll have to do a lot more than that to get rid of me."

They coaxed a smile from her, those words. "I know."

Then she sighed, turning her face into his shoulder until his heartbeat sounded strong and steady against her cheek. "Just a few more days of hell."

A few more days... And hopefully not an eternity.

CHAPTER FIFTEEN

THE BEAST THAT FRIGHTENS BEASTS

See how sweetly the girl sleeps. The wolf beside her is just as quiet, their limbs twined together. They are deaf to the world outside and heavy in their slumber. Far above them hangs the moon, returned to an ivory glow that brings to mind wedding lace dulled with dust and bones bared of their flesh. The very night feels crystallized, an ageless, motionless land of black and white.

And yet just beyond the ridge of pine that looks down on the girl in her little house, something stirs. Something that sets the animals running. Something whipped on by the mountain winds. Something that feeds on whatever it can catch.

Sparks appear in the darkness. The air breathes heat. A strange glow casts itself into the sky, devouring star after star. Smoke swells before this beast that frightens beasts, and an entire line of trees blackens as the first of the flames reveal themselves.

The forest is on fire.

Alice woke up choking on smoke, heat prickling at her skin like a sunburn as hands caught her up and pulled her out of bed.

"What..." she coughed out, the heaviness of sleep leaving her stupid and clumsy as she looked up into Colton's furious face.

"Don't talk. Just breathe." Then he shoved fabric into her hands, and a familiar weight that she recognized—her purse.

As he hurried her over to the window, the crackling of wood filled her senses, cleared her head, and she looked at the strange, orange glow seeping into the room with fresh horror.

The air had already thickened enough to stuff her mouth full, and she only panted quietly while Colton ripped off the screening, sweat prickling at her neck and knees from the growing heat. The ceiling suddenly sagged, showering sparks on them. She cringed, a strangled scream working in her throat, but Colton only shook himself as if he were in his fur and slammed the window open.

"It's in the forest. We're fucked if it reaches the road before us." His voice seethed as he helped her climb over the sill.

Survival instinct took over, driving her on even when her bare skin scraped against splintered wood. Gravel bit into her hands and knees, and her next gasp drew in fresh air.

Her wild glance around found smoke and flames everywhere. Embers flew like fireflies. Tree branches popped and curled. The darkness of the night had transformed into a writhing hellscape.

Behind her, the house groaned and leaned. The telltale crackling of flames joined the creaking of strained wood. Alice gasped Colton's name, realizing their home was about to collapse, but he was already at her side, desperation leaving him rough as he pulled her up and pushed her further from the waves of heat.

They ran for the truck together, two dark silhouettes against a wall of fire. Ash stung Alice's skin as they slipped inside the cab, Colton silent behind the wheel. As the truck roared onto the road, embers flying all around, she came back into herself long enough to pull on what he'd given her—one of his flannel shirts. She burrowed into the fabric, taking comfort in the softness and the familiar smell of fur and clean sweat, but couldn't help peering out the window at the billowing smoke. Her panicked breathing was the only sound made between them.

When she looked back at Colton, searching for any sign of reassurance, she found his mouth grim and his eyes utterly focused on the road ahead. Dressed in a t-shirt and jeans, he showed no signs of having been roused out of bed in a hurry, but she knew him well enough to understand the muscle jumping in his jaw. He was worried.

"Have you ever been in a fire before?" she asked, picking at the folds of flannel in her lap.

"Not one like this." Colton gave the rearview mirror a sharp glance.

She nodded and then twisted around in her seat to see how much distance they'd put between themselves and the fire. Then she started. Ghostly shapes jumped onto the road, graceful even in their panic. The oncoming fire reduced them to silhouettes, but she still recognized what they were.

"Deer," she said, numbly. "The deer are using the road."

"Everything's surprised," he muttered. "It grew fast for this time of the year."

"Maybe a campfire got out of control." Alice knew the words sounded too high with fear, knew that placing a reason for the raging danger did nothing to tame it. Knew that trying to attach a sense of normal to the flames licking at their heels was sheer human folly.

Colton only growled under his breath, the sound merging with the rumble of the engine as the truck tore down the road. Neither of them spoke the name that sat between them as heavy and baleful as a rock thrown through a window. Neither of them had to.

When they reached the first turn in the road, Colton took it. Alice understood the significance. "You're crossing the bridge?"

"I'll feel better when there's a river between us."

She nodded, staring once more at the unearthly glow around them. The river would be low and sluggish at that time of the year, with the previous winter's snow melt having come and gone. Still, water was water, and in the steep rises and drops of the mountains, a river between them and the gaping maw of the fire would be the safest thing possible until they got out of the wilderness and back into civilization.

"She took our home," she said, softly, feeling her shoulders slump.

Colton's hand found hers. "We'll find another one."

The sureness of his voice steadied her, and she squeezed his fingers tightly even as the lights of the bridge winked at them in the distance. Safety.

But when they drew closer, Colton swore and slowed down. For all that it spanned thousands of feet to connect the two steep sides, the bridge had only two narrow lanes of traffic. A car sat sideways, blocking both. The doors were open and its headlights stared through the railing of the bridge and beyond. One of the tires looked flat. In the haze of glowing smoke, nothing was sure, but Alice didn't see any sign of the driver.

"It looks abandoned," she said, glancing behind her to check the distance of the fire. Inside the swelling smoke, flames flickered like a great, glowing heart. Her mind reeled at the idea of losing precious time trying to find the driver.

Colton didn't hesitate. "Fuck the truck. We'll cross on foot. It won't jump the river for awhile."

A light tug on her arm was enough to break her spell of uncertainty, and she slid out of the truck, bare feet flinching at how the pavement already felt hot from the approaching fire.

A new wave of smoke blew up from behind, rasping against her lungs and drawing tears from her eyes. Even as she coughed, hair whipping into her face, she turned toward Colton. He slipped around the front of the truck, already reaching for her. The thickening haze reduced him to a dim silhouette.

Just as their fingers brushed, a crack echoed through the air. Alice flinched, assuming a tree had split under the heat of the flames. Then Colton staggered, feet no longer carrying him forward. Red spread over his white shirt as he sagged against the truck's grille.

Alice shrieked, mind whirling even as she lunged for him. Another crack—a *gunshot*—left glass chips pelting her shoulder. Smoke poured into the hole left in the passenger window.

"Get behind the fucking truck," he snarled, making a final, desperate lunge toward her.

But she didn't shy away, not until her hand caught his nearest one. They collapsed together against the bulk of the truck, glass glittering all around as three more shots sounded. When nothing else happened, Alice frantically pushed at his shirt, already intent on staunching the wounds.

He stopped her, sides heaving and teeth flashing as he rasped, "Someone's shooting from across the bridge. A fucking trap."

"We'll get back in the truck," she said, her own voice hoarse, almost inhuman. "I know how to drive it. I can ram through that car."

"The last shots weren't for me. Look at the tires."

She did, choking back a howl of rage at finding two deflated. "Then we won't use the bridge at all. There must be a way down to the river on foot. All we have to do is wait for the smoke to grow thick enough to hide us from view."

In the brief silence that followed, her heart withered into something tight and shivering.

"The bullets did too much damage," he said, finally. "I can feel it." His gaze never left hers, even when blood began running from his mouth.

"No," she said, clutching at his shirt, but her own mind betrayed her, pulling back those early memories of how they'd met. Of how weak he'd been when she'd discovered his slumped body in the mud. Pierced through with a bullet and too injured to do more than twitch in her presence.

"I'll drag you," she said, ignoring how sparks flew past them. "Drag you into the passenger's side and then drive us over the bridge. And if anyone shoots at us again, I'll run the fucker over with two bad wheels."

Smoke blurred her vision, but she thought she saw a ghost of a smile cross his face. The smell of blood hung heavy between them. "There's your teeth. Now start using them for yourself."

The crackle of burning bark fought with the panicked pulse in her ears. Her breath had already started hitching in her chest. "Stop talking like that. I'm getting you out of here."

At her first tug, he caught her arms, his hands still strong despite being slicked in his own blood. "Alice, you can't. The truck's useless and you know it."

Finally, the tears came, and she only shook her head while giving him a useless pull, willing his body to rise whole and strong. His grip against her tightened, and the first hint of desperation slid into his voice. "Out of time. The fire's here."

And it was, embers sizzling all around as the flames exhaled heat strong enough to crisp her hair. When Alice twisted toward the fire, panic licking at her, his hand caught her chin, forcing her to look back at him.

In the smothering smoke, even his eyes were nothing more than a glimmer. "There's a deer trail on the right side of the bridge. Steep but not impossible to follow. The river's thin right now. Just wade across it and follow the current on the other side until you reach a trail that goes back up."

"No. No! I'm not leaving you."

"Alice." A growl entered his voice even as wetness bubbled behind the words. "Witches burn to death."

"And you won't? It's melting metal. You'll be a pile of ash." She gave his shirt a final tug, face crumpling at how his body remained limp beside the truck.

His hands found her frantic ones. Blood turned sticky between their fingers. Sparks fell around them like snowflakes. Despite the line of pain between his eyebrows, he never looked away from her. "I'll find you again, understand? No matter what."

"I love you." Her mouth trembled with the words.

Something flickered in his eyes. "Alice."

"I do." Then she shook him once more, willing him to somehow get up. She couldn't tell whether her eyes burned from tears or smoke. "I can't bury how much you mean to me anymore. Whatever you think about it, it's true. I love you."

"I know." Then he stilled her again. "I tell you the same thing every day. Just not with words."

For one gut-wrenching moment, she felt the heat of his face pressing against hers, felt his mouth against her temple. Then he gave her enough of a push to coax her upright, separating them. "Smoke's thick enough. Remember what I said. I'll find you, Alice."

She shook her head, unable to reply, but the look in his eyes sent her stumbling away. The threat of bullets was only a dim pulse in her mind as she walked backwards, not wanting to look away even when the truck hid him from view. Just beyond, flames crackled greedily.

In a few breaths, she bumped against the railing that marked the edge of the steep drop to the river. Her chest felt brittle, ready to crack like an egg and empty out until there was nothing left. Then a great wave of smoke reached her, swallowing the truck completely.

Even as her mind went blank, her body kept moving, climbing over the steel railing with shaking limbs. Smoke had reduced the bridge to hardly more than a shadow, but a flicker of movement at the other end warned her to throw herself down. A gunshot cracked through the air and then she was on the ground, breathless as rock and root dug into her stomach.

Her fingers curled into the earth, and she began shaking for a different reason. Even in such a brief moment, she had seen who it was. She had *seen* who waited behind the scope of a sniper rifle, face screwed in concentration.

Despite the danger, she scrabbled upright, tears streaming down her face. Her voice shrieked out across the bridge, echoing even in the thick air. "Darby! Darby, I saw you up there! You—"

Then the ground gave out from underneath her, and her words were lost with everything else as she slid down the steep side, hands desperate to grab onto anything. By the time she lurched to a stop against a scrubby bush, embers hissed into the water below and smoke swallowed everything above.

In another state of mind, Alice would have wondered at not falling and breaking her neck. Instead, she only continued the descent, wild-eyed and heedless like an animal, hanging onto scrubby branch or jutting rock long enough to slow gravity's pull. Two more gunshots rang out, but she ignored them each time, something frantic driving her forward.

The river was a muddy, sluggish thing, faintly picking up the unearthly glow of the fire above. The water went up to her calves as she waded across, arms limp at her sides and gaze still mindless. Colton was still up there. Colton was...

Sparks flew here and there as she numbly followed a strip of sandy ground that rose from the water's edge, waiting until the deer trail appeared to start the climb up. Everything felt as hazy as a nightmare as she clawed through wild grass and prickly branches. When a branch slapped her cheek, she let it. When thorns snarled her shirt, she ripped it free. Something urged her on, tireless even when the sky seemed to stretch forever out of reach. Perhaps it was the distant rumble of helicopters, a concrete sign that there was something beyond this hellscape. Perhaps it was the awareness that she'd break down and never stop crying once she slumped to rest. Perhaps it was only sheer numbness.

Flames jeered at her from the other side when she finally pulled herself up to level ground, hands shaking against the metal railing that warned cars of the steep drop should they veer from the road. But there wasn't any traffic at all, and in the eerie stillness, she began walking. The entire world had turned into something ghostly, a rippling mass of smoke that promised the endless hunger of flames.

Then light streamed past her, casting her shadow ahead. Alice flinched on instinct, expecting the screech of brakes, the sickening crunch of her bones shattered by speeding metal.

Instead came the rumble of an engine slowing down, and a woman's voice called out. "Hey. Hey!"

Alice turned, still dazed, and watched the driver open her door to get out and wave. The woman looked about ten years older than Alice, with short blonde hair and a nose ring that glinted as she walked in front of her headlights. "Get in! The fire's about to jump the river. The winds are blowing embers right across. Come on, hurry up!"

The front passenger's seat was filled with bags and suitcases. As the woman pointed Alice to the back seat, she said, "Rufus won't mind sitting with you. He's a certified therapy dog. Very gentle."

Before she could add anything else, Alice got inside and found herself sitting next to a black Labrador Retriever. He sniffed at Alice, ears relaxed, and panted easily as his owner started up the car and sped off.

"It caught you asleep, didn't it?" said the woman, voice falling soft. "All you've got is your purse."

"It's all I have left." Alice couldn't help looking at the dog again. His brown eyes were gentle and calm, entirely unlike the piercing yellow that would forever be burned into her heart, and yet she still found her breaths swelling into sobs.

"Go on. Give him a hug. Rufus likes comforting people, and sometimes crying against a dog helps more than what anyone else can say."

Then Rufus nuzzled at her elbow, just as Colton did while coaxing her into a hug, and she collapsed against him, hands convulsive around his neck. Her fingers clung as if flames still jeered with their nearness, still taunted her with what she couldn't save from them.

And so as fire licked the very sky, Alice cried into black fur and tried not to think of the smell of burned hair.

CHAPTER SIXTEEN

ANGUISH AND ASHES

Alice pulled the blanket closer around herself, trying to ignore how every movement stirred up the stench of ash. It clung to her hair and skin, stoked the pit of nausea in her stomach. Burned at her swollen eyes. Despite the stuffy heat of so many evacuees milling around in one room, she couldn't stop shivering, vacant in thought as the TV bolted in the upper-right corner flickered grim news reported by grim faces.

They were all in a section of a community college hastily transformed into an evacuation center. They were all people who had lost everything in the fire, and showed it in their numb faces and ash-streaked hair. Many cried into their hands or wiped at reddened eyes. Despair etched foreheads and carved the corners of mouths. Panic scratched behind words. They were burned things themselves, cringing at how the bright light of morning hadn't chased away the horrors of the night.

And yet Alice only sat there and watched, her own tears long gone and her own worries evaporated. She felt utterly remote from everyone and everything. A few hours earlier, the part of her mind that still thought had even guided her into texting her parents, letting them know she was okay. She didn't want them to see her, not on this day.

Dully, she blinked at the bowl of Halloween candy set out on what would have normally been the professor's desk. The bowl was in the shape of a gap-toothed pumpkin, and the candy already looked picked through. The day of Samhain had come at last, and Magdalene would be in full power.

The name left her fingers curling against the woolen folds of the blanket, digging into the thick fabric like claws. She felt empty, a mere outline of a person, and yet something dark and bitter beat deep inside. She couldn't name what it was, only sense that it was there, growing whenever she buried her face into her shoulder and breathed into the flannel shirt she still wore. Even after her night of hell, it still smelled like him.

"Alice?"

The sound of her name shuddered awake some part of her mind, rousing it through the prickle of familiarity. She blinked, eyelids feeling like sandpaper, and turned to see who it was.

There stood Gretchen, looking far out of place in her sharp black-and-white maternity dress and precisely pinned hair. She wore large, chic sunglasses that turned her face into something severe and remote, and the faint smell of lavender and honey drifted from her skin. Alice supposed she should have felt small and pitiable in comparison, with her bare feet still showing traces of mud and her hair left in snarls. Strangely, nothing flickered within that hollowness that filled her, and her words sounded only flat as she asked, "Why are you here?"

Gretchen removed her sunglasses then, revealing eyes that looked strangely unsure. "When we talked at the dinner party, you mentioned living in Calico Creek. I recognized the name right away when the news mentioned it this morning."

"So, you heard how everything there was destroyed by the fire."

The other girl nodded. "There's already drone footage. It looks like what you scrape out of a fire-pit. No one's searching for survivors. They're just hoping they can find bones in all the ash."

For a split second, Alice felt her mouth tremble and quickly looked down to hide it. Her hands pulled at the blanket again, drawing the flannel shirt closer against her skin. If Colton had somehow escaped the flames, he would have already found her. She was sure of it.

When she said nothing, Gretchen's voice grew awkward in the way of someone used to ignoring emotions now faced with the possibility of consoling them. "I'm sorry. It's just that... I grew worried."

"Why would you care?" The words fell out like dull pebbles, much too small and worn to be hurtful.

Gretchen's fingers flexed against the cloth bag she carried over one shoulder. She almost seemed embarrassed. "Do you want to go outside to talk? It's stuffy in here."

With a stiff nod, Alice rose with the blanket still wrapped around her. No one looked as they left the room. Outside, the sun looked blood-red from the haze of smoke, and the distant mutter of a helicopter could be heard—faint hints of what raged through acres of land while they walked over clipped lawns and past sedate oaks. The college had a small rose garden still lush and full despite the autumn weather, with wooden benches nestled among the established bushes for privacy. They sat on one, Gretchen still appearing uneasy. Alice didn't make any attempt to smooth things over, instead watching the sun wink through the leaves that surrounded them.

"The man who was with you at the party..." said Gretchen, finally.

"Colton." Alice felt her heart clench.

"He's not here with you."

Such an obvious comment, and yet it cut so deep, drawing tears into eyes that she thought had gone dry. As she fought to respond, fought to spit out even one word, it came to her that it wasn't that she felt nothing. It was that she overwhelmingly felt *so much* that she couldn't even grapple with it.

"He saved me," she said at last, voice strangled and small.

"But got caught in the fire." Something flashed across the other girl's face, something that cracked her flawless makeup and doll-like eyes.

Then she reached out and squeezed Alice's hand. The movement was a little stiff, but her voice sounded sincere as she added, "I'm sorry. You start to think they're invincible against anything because of what they can do. And then something happens, and your heart feels like it'll bleed out."

The implication drew Alice's gaze to the other girl. Gretchen stared back, the set of her jaw going stubborn. Her silence dared Alice to claim that she didn't know what that meant.

Alice saw no reason to avoid the truth. "He told me nothing can kill him. That he..."

There was a brief silence as they both glanced around, furtive despite the privacy. The words sounded so alien in their own mouths, so ridiculous.

Then some of Gretchen's old boldness came back, because she blew out a breath and said, "Shane explained it as him dying as a man and coming back as a wolf."

Alice nodded and watched the wariness fade from the other girl's eyes. "Colton said it in a similar way. And that he's already died and can't die again. But he has a heartbeat. He *bleeds*."

"And he does get hurt," finished Gretchen. Then she looked right at Alice. "Do you believe he'll come back?"

It wasn't her true question. *That* one hung in the air between them, as sharp and snagging as barbed wire. *Will you wait for him?*

The truth of the situation—that she might not be able to wait, that she might end up in hell herself—was too much. It gaped at her like the sky, reduced her to something small and hopeless in the face of the infinite.

"I—I..." Her heart squeezed until it felt impossible to breathe.

Her stammering drew a nod from Gretchen. Then the other girl pulled the bag between them, offering the handles to Alice. "Here, I brought this for you. Go on, look inside."

As Alice did, silent once more, the other girl added, "I figured the fire must have left you with nothing, so I got some clothes and toiletries. A phone charger, too. After you get dressed, I'll drive you to the nearest car rental place."

"I'm sure that my parents..."

"Your parents must have already offered to scoop you up and take you away from your troubles. But you're sitting here instead."

When Alice said nothing, the other girl's eyes turned fierce. "Don't go crawling back to them now that he's gone. Don't start acting like it was all just a silly dream, trying to get away. I'm twenty-five and had to make an excuse to my mom about why I was out shopping this morning. I have less control over myself now than when I was in high school because I was scared to live without luxury. Don't end up like me."

After a final hesitation, Alice pulled the bag onto her lap. "Thank you."

The words sounded too stiff and formal, but more, much more, passed between them as they shared a glance. Alice found herself adding, "You could do this for yourself, too. You still miss him, don't you?"

"You already know the answer to that." Then Gretchen looked away. "I decided on my life months ago. It doesn't matter if it was the right choice or the wrong one. I made it, and now there are people who depend on me."

Her hand spread against the swell of her stomach, emphasizing the words. Snuffing the glimmer that Alice had caught in her eyes for the briefest of moments. Then she looked at Alice again, voice steady as she repeated, "Don't be like me. Be brave and wait for him. What do they know about you? What do they *really* know?"

It was her family that Gretchen referred to, not anything else, and yet the words still hit true, piercing the numbness in Alice's mind. Darby's sneer flashed through her thoughts. Then Rob's hands and camera. And then Magdalene's smile.

What did they know about her? What did they expect? They had shot her lover and burned him to ash, and yet *still* they would only wait for her to cower. Would she freeze like a rabbit until they caught her? Would she only shiver over what they had done?

"Nothing," she said, slowly, Gretchen's question ringing through her head like a faint howl on a frozen night, distant but piercing. Something in her stirred, woke up. Something in her howled back.

She looked at Gretchen then, feeling a snarl bubble against her next words. "They know *nothing* about me."

For a moment, something just as feral glittered in the other girl's eyes. Then she once again smoothed her face into the polished mask of a young socialite and put on her sunglasses while rising from her seat. "I printed out some hotel addresses and put them in the bag. I'm not due back until one o'clock, so we can take a look around if you want to rest somewhere before renting a car."

"It's all right," said Alice, feeling a small, savage smile touch her lips. "I've got the cabin, remember? And I'm going to use it."

To hunt a beast is to court death itself. To hound one for too long without a killing bite? Sheer folly. There are some beasts that will turn and face the threat of teeth even as their blood steams in the air, their very exhaustion giving them a heedless power. They have the ferocity of a wild thing and the recklessness that comes with desperation. Sometimes, the hunter's quarry proves to be the most dangerous of all, for it no longer fears *anything*.

The drive to the cabin passed in strange fits of time. Alice was really only aware of trees, miles of black road stretching before her, and the lingering smell of smoke in her hair. Strangely, even though she now willingly drove toward what would become Magdalene's cage, she no longer felt trapped at all. She was well aware of how it all looked—her home burned down and her lover gone with it, the need to keep distance from her family to avoid putting them in danger again... Yes, she very much appeared like an animal caught in a snare. It was certainly how others would see her.

They were wrong. They didn't understand that the things she quietly endured would never go unpunished when committed against someone she loved. She wasn't about to let that go. Something in her had burned away in the fire—that fidgeting, self-conscious fear of what others would want from her, friend or foe—and now her heart felt like a smoldering lump cradled by brittle ribs, as if the slightest touch would be enough to shatter that protective case of bone.

And yet she didn't feel like she was about to collapse. No, her rage held her steady. This was much different than losing the pelt. Some things could be endured when set upon her own skin, but the same cruelty committed against another? Unbearable. She would not submit quietly. She would not cower in the ashes of her lover. So they wanted her? Well, then. They were about to have her.

Her knuckles looked white against the steering wheel as she entered Perry. Memories fluttered at her mind like blind moths while she drove through the small mountain town, but she shook them away, urging the rental car ever faster along roads that still felt familiar.

The final stretch of trees that sheltered the cabin from the road looked just the same, and for one wrenching moment, Alice allowed herself the idea that what she expected to find wouldn't be there at all. That she would steer the car down the strip of gravel road and find the cabin empty and waiting. That she would park and look at the fixed porch step and the woodpile newer than the rest, and that the shadows among the trees would then shift with life, turning into black fur and piercing eyes.

The wheels spat up pebbles and earth into the final turn, and she craned her neck as the first flashes of weathered wood and stone chimney appeared between the massive redwoods.

Then she hissed out a breath, feeling her heart wither once more at the sight of two cars in the driveway. Both belonged to Darby and Rob. If she had to guess, Rob had probably followed Darby in a panic.

She parked in the shadow of the trees, keeping the car hidden, but got out without any attempt to keep quiet. Voices cut through the chilly air, indistinct yet sharp. She followed their anger, soon spying Rob and Darby on the cabin's porch. Leaves crunched beneath her feet as she approached, unseen for all that she walked openly toward them.

"Are you fucking crazy?" Flecks of spit shot from Rob's mouth with each word. His eyes looked wild behind their thick glasses, and his hair stuck out at odd angles as if he'd grabbed at it more than once.

The dark circles beneath Darby's eyes had grown as purple as bruises compared to the bloodless color of her skin, and the only sign of life in her face was the hateful snarl of her mouth as she hissed back, "You think anyone who cares about anything besides themselves is crazy. She was murdered, Rob. She needs to be—"

"And what the hell did *you* do last night, huh? Where did you even get that gun?"

"It was a sniper rifle."

"I don't fucking care! Last year, you marched against the fucking things."

"He was a *monster*, Rob. He could turn into a wolf."

When Rob just shook his head, she added, "If the fire hadn't been right there, I would have taken a piece just to stop you from freaking out. An ear or something. Whatever form they die in, the body shifts back into its other one. She told me so."

"Jesus Christ." Rob ran his hand through his hair again. "You're insane."

"He had to go, Rob. He murdered Magdalene on that bitch's orders."

"Yeah, the bitch who owns this property and can have our asses hauled off to jail."

At that moment, Alice reached the first step up to the porch. The seething heat that lit every inch of her didn't show up in her voice, and only the lingering grit of ash filled her words as she said, "I wouldn't do that."

Rob jerked like he'd been shot, eyes going wide behind his glasses. Darby's round face fell slack with shock. Both instinctively stepped back as Alice continued up the stairs to join them on the porch.

Alice glanced around, taking in the state of the cabin while Rob tried to stammer an explanation. Darby remained silent, her mouth closing into a tight line as Alice looked between them at the doorway. The door was open, revealing an unlit hearth and unlit candles placed in a large circle on the dusty, wooden floor. There was also a paper bag set off to the side, bulging in a way that suggested it held a lot of things.

"I knew you'd come here to do the seance," said Alice, her voice still flat. "I'm surprised the medium hasn't shown up. It's only two hours until dusk."

"We don't need her," said Darby, eyes burning. "I know what to do."

When Rob's gaze jumped from her to Alice, she scoffed and added, "God, Rob, where are your balls? There's nothing to be afraid of. Her loverboy's dead, and *she's* not going to do anything."

Something twisted deep inside her, snarling, but Alice kept her expression blank. "Darby's right. I'm not here to stop the seance. I want to be part of it."

"What?" Rob looked utterly baffled.

"I want to do the seance. You have my full permission to use the cabin."

When Darby's eyes narrowed in suspicion, Alice brushed past her, heading inside. "Come on. We need to be ready by the time it's dark. How do you want to set things up?"

"What's your game?" said Darby, as they drifted in after her.

The dryness of dust hung heavy in the air, and for one moment, Alice thought she smelled singed fur. It made her voice come out as a throb. "It's time to say hello to ghosts."

Then she turned and looked at Darby, at this girl so caught in Magdalene's web that she was in love with being blind. "Anyway, it's been your ultimate goal all along. Right? Not just to see Magdalene, but to avenge her. You *wanted* me to be here."

"I didn't think you'd come willingly," muttered Darby. "I thought I'd have to pull you out of hiding like a rat."

This time, Alice couldn't hold back a small smile. "Right now, there's nothing I want more than to be here."

Her very calmness seemed to infuriate the other girl. "You think he's coming back to rescue you just in time? He's *dead*."

"Shut the fuck up," hissed Rob.

"It doesn't matter. Who's she going to tell? Who's going to believe her? We're totally safe."

"There's no 'we' to this. I didn't do any of this shit."

Alice shrugged off her coat and dropped it onto the nearest chair before glancing at him. "Hoping to remain a bystander, Rob? You can't. You're in this far too deep to back out now."

As the two looked at her, suspicion and uncertainty etched into their faces, she walked over to the ring of candles and added, "I've got nowhere to run and nothing left to run to. So, let's get this over with."

Darby lit the candles before anything else, and soon greasy wax dripped to the floor. The sky fell grim as the other girl studied from some kind of book while drawing sigils in white chalk inside the circle of light. Rob fidgeted with the pack of pills in his hand, their rattling an intrusion in the thick silence.

Alice watched him like a cat. "What are the entheogens for? Most seances just need you to concentrate."

"There's no medium to guide us," he said, the words terse.

When his gaze slid to the side, refusing to meet hers, Alice realized the true state of things. "You really are here to help Darby. You don't believe in any of this, but you know she shot someone and don't want a medium or anyone else to find out. You don't want *complications*."

When Rob just winced, Alice resisted the urge to spit at him. How had she ever felt cowed by this man? He couldn't even look her in the eye.

"We need to light a fire," announced Darby.

"Do it yourself," replied Alice, not even glancing her way. "You're so good at starting them."

In the brief silence that followed, she added, "Did you think I wouldn't figure it out? A fire just happens to start near my home and just happens to drive us to the bridge where you were waiting in the perfect spot. You didn't even hide your hair."

There was a small groan from Rob, but it was Darby who answered, eyes as flat and heavy as stones. "It doesn't matter if she knows. She's about to get hers."

Strange how those words didn't send a chill through her. Instead, as she settled at the edge of the candlelight and watched Rob clumsily pile wood on the grate while Darby shook a packet of herbs over it all, she found her lips curling into another smile. She hardly even felt like herself.

Yes, she trembled, but not from fear; *that* had been burned away in the fire. It was disgust that left her muscles twitching as she watched the other two mark her grandmother's cabin with their silly little ritual. What did they know? They fumbled in the darkness, cringed away from the shadows. They clung to order, to method, peering into the book as if the words inside could control the forces even now stirring with the first of the stars. Why had she ever feared them?

Her jaw ached with the answer. Because she had believed their threats could trap her. And now they *still* thought the same, here in a cabin where a withered old witch had once lured in victims and eaten every piece of them. Where empty wolf pelts had still twitched with life, and nightmare creatures had emerged from the shadows. And yet they thought they could pull such wildness to them and tie it to their wills?

The wood smoked sullenly, not wanting to light in full. Rob poked at it with equally sullen movements while Darby reached into the bag again. She withdrew from it a copy of Magdalene's *The Chrysalis*, holding it with all the reverence of a holy relic. When she set it in the middle of the circle, her fingers brushed over the cover with a lover's caress. Then she set a hunting knife beside it, an ugly, worn thing with a blade that still winked along its sharp edge.

"Rob, that's good enough. Get the pills out."

They both stared at her as if expecting her to resist taking the drug. Instead, she held out her palm, unflinching as Rob dropped it there, and then swallowed it without hesitation. Once more she felt a writhing, cackling strangeness ripple throughout her body even as she calmly sipped from a cup of water to help the pill go down.

"Check her mouth," said Darby. "I don't want to touch her."

Alice blinked at Rob, absorbing the reluctance in his face. Something struggled in her throat as his hand caught her jaw— a scream? A growl? Something that she fought down to say, "Don't worry. I won't bite."

It didn't ease the fear in his face. Not that she wanted it to. Indeed, even as his thumb pressed at her tongue to see if she'd hidden the pill, she fought with the sudden urge to snap until the bone between her teeth cracked. When he pulled away with a mutter that she'd swallowed it, her jaws locked shut.

Afterward, they all held hands inside the circle of light, the candles guttering in their pools of wax as wind moaned through cracks in the cabin. Rob's hand felt sweaty against Alice's, but Darby's clung tight and desperate like the talons of a vulture. The fire crackled, popping out sparks that never quite reached them.

"We call upon the dead on this night when they can roam free," began Darby, her eyes already dilated from the entheogen. Then she swore under her breath. "Jesus, Rob, this shit is strong."

"You fucking asked for it." His pupils had also grown large.

Darby shook her head and tried again. "We call upon the dead who cannot rest easy in their graves. The... Ones who cry out for justice... And..."

Alice watched the other girl start to sweat, and felt how her grip loosened. Rob also looked horrible, face turning pale and eyes growing unfocused. And yet she herself felt untouched, a simple observer of things. The usual fuzziness and fear that had always clung to her thoughts in previous psychonaut experiences now held no power. Even the thick embrace of the drug couldn't claim her. She cast off the first hints of haziness like an animal shaking water from its fur.

Clear-eyed, she watched Rob and Darby wilt. The firelight flickered over their slumped, unmoving forms, highlighting Rob's vacant gaze and Darby's slack mouth. Alice blinked at them both before reaching out to pick up *The Chrysalis*.

"That's not how you draw her in," she murmured, rising to step out of the circle of candles. "She's always used to being praised. It's her spite that you have to stir up."

Then she walked over to the fireplace and flung the book right into the heart of the flames, hearing an echo of her scream from when Magdalene had done the same to the pelt. Now, though, her voice remained soft and calm as she said, "I'm here. Where are you?"

There came a crackle from the flames that might have been a ghost of a laugh. And then... Nothing. Alice remained patient, letting the darkness of night seep into the cabin.

Letting the candles gutter and spit hot wax. Some part of her sensed Darby and Rob wouldn't wake up until sunrise, that their roles in this little play of Magdalene's had been fulfilled and now she had no more use for them. Judging from the hunting knife, Alice's part was far from over. Strange how the thought made her want to laugh. How satisfied Magdalene must feel in these dark hours. How smug. How sure of herself.

Alice bit at her lip, testing the feel of her teeth, and then changed position, settling more comfortably on the floor. Whatever happened, she wouldn't go quietly.

Eventually, she found herself staring at the flames instead of through the windows. Their dance was hypnotic, silent except for the occasional crackle, and their warmth lulled her. Drowsiness stole over her, pulling her ever closer to a dreamless darkness. Just as she reached the edge of it, instinct warned her to pinch herself hard. The sharp pain snapped her back awake, snapped her back to the firelit room. Then she blinked, realizing dirt gritted between her fingers from the action. Swirls of dried mud covered her arms.

She was as naked and dirty as when she had used to shake the pelt off after a night spent in the forest. Black earth crusted her fingernails. The iron taste of blood rested heavy on her tongue. And across from where she crouched beside the fireplace, stone slabs warm beneath her bare feet, sat Magdalene. Her eyes seemed to catch all the brightness of the flames, leaving the rest of her a column of dark that merged with the shadows.

The fire hungrily ate at something, something that whimpered and twitched. Magdalene's eyes never left her, not even when she lit a cigarette, but Alice's gaze jumped to the seething heart of the flames long enough to see blackened skin and withering tufts of fur.

Alice felt tears stream down her cheeks, but she had now lived with the grief for months, and showed nothing else in her expression while facing Magdalene. "Why did you do it?"

"Weren't you listening before? You would have left me." Magdalene looked just as she had the last time Alice had seen her alive. Whole, unwounded, with dried streaks of tears colored from her eyeliner.

As Alice looked down at her hands, she added, "You know what I feel. It's the same raw agony that fills you during every dream about your mother."

"Am I dreaming now?"

"What do you think?"

"I think you killed Colton. It was Darby's gun but your will."

At that, Magdalene scoffed and put the cigarette in her mouth. Then she pulled up her right sleeve. There, on the meat of her arm between her wiry wrist and sharp elbow, was an ugly, ripping set of wounds aligned in a bite mark. Savage teeth had done that.

As Alice stared, Magdalene said, "I'd say I had just cause. You could at least apologize on his behalf."

"It'd be a lie. He wouldn't be sorry, and neither am I."

"You always turned into a bitch at the worst times."

Alice sucked in a breath, biting back her words like so many times before. But what was left to hide? Her heart had been laid bare. "I loved you. Did you ever know that? Did you ever see how willingly I gave up whatever you asked for?"

"Of course." Magdalene's velvet voice turned gentle, and her fingers brushed the side of Alice's face in a feather-light caress.

"You took too much," said Alice, the words low and shaking. "I want it all back."

Magdalene tilted her head to one side, those lush lips curving into a smile. "But I want you back."

As if it were all that simple. As if it were all that mattered. Alice stared at her old lover, at this woman that she'd once believed she could never understand, and now suddenly understood her all too well. "But what does that matter? *I* don't want to be with you. I *won't* be with you."

The smile faded from Magdalene's face, and when Alice knocked her fingers away, she didn't resist. The shock in her eyes was an exhilarating sight, and Alice heard her voice rise strong and jagged. "You've fooled me, tricked me, scared me, seduced me. You've tried taking everything away just so I'd have nothing else to turn to. But I still don't need you. Not at all."

As panic flickered in Magdalene's eyes, now pitch dark, the other woman said, "You'll always need me. No one will ever understand you like I do."

"No," breathed Alice, still caught in a strange sort of delight. "You don't have to be anything more than old scars."

Then her giddiness flared into something hotter, something that begged to be unleashed, and when Magdalene's fingers snarled in her hair, Alice twisted and bit, catching her unwounded arm.

There was no taste of blood in her mouth. Instead, ash ran over her tongue as she bit again, growling as the other woman pinned her down. The sparks in Magdalene's eyes swelled as they fought, both desperate. Alice snarled up at her, dimly aware of how it sounded like a beast's voice, not a girl's. The last time they had fought like this, Magdalene had held her still with her iron strength and frantic need.

But this time, Alice didn't thrash. This time, she *attacked*.

When Magdalene grabbed at her wrists, she snapped at her face. When hands wrapped around her throat, she lashed out with her fingernails. Rage lit her bones incandescent. They twisted and shook just like the pelt had in the fire. When something popped in her neck, she at first thought it was from Magdalene throttling her. Then her next breath came out as a growl. Her teeth suddenly felt too large in her mouth.

Magdalene's eyes widened, fear replacing their dark desperation as she tried holding Alice down. But Alice was writhing, an agonized shriek wrenching from her throat. It slid into a howl as her body gave one convulsive lurch. Then the world changed, her view sliding and tilting as everything exploded into scent and sound. The pressure in her body grew solid, sure, and now she smelled Magdalene—a dry, thick scent like dust. Like smoke.

Wolf-Alice shook her fur and snarled at her former lover, at the wraith that had promised to never stop tormenting her. Magdalene shrank back, but she was too fast, lunging forward with ready teeth. She bit for everything she had lost, everything that Magdalene still wished to take. Rage bubbled over in her snarls, overwhelming the shrieking and flailing hands that couldn't pierce her fur. When the first taste of blood reached her throat, she only bit harder, determined to rip and tear until nothing remained.

And around her, the shadows flickered, swelling a little with each fresh scream.

CHAPTER SEVENTEEN

A SAVAGE VOW

Somewhere in a lifeless land, the black wolf twitched at the memories of his death as a man. There had been the burning shock of a blade sliding against his neck, sliding *through* it, and then the panic of not being able to breathe. The moon had spun dizzily in its waxing state, throbbing like a heart while chanted words pinned him in place. Kept him still.

Then there had been the darkness of a burial, each shovelful of dirt soaking up his blood and leaving him lost in silence. But he didn't die. Didn't rot. And when the moon next rose full and heavy, it cast ivory light upon a wolf shaking grave dirt from fur as black as pitch, tongue lolling with the effort of digging himself out. The hole left behind bore scraps of human clothing like some grotesque version of a cradle and its blankets—outgrown, unneeded.

As he panted there in the frigid air, the wolf smelled everything. Sharp remnants of magic. Old blood that had soaked into the earth like rain. His own rage. Then he caught hints of sweat from the ones who had buried him there.

Memories flickered at the edge of his mind, as dim and vexing as peering through frosted glass, but he remembered their faces at least. Yes, each and every face that had stared down at his mutilated form in a mixture of disgust and relief. That and their scents were enough to track them down. Enough to drag them into their own graves.

But when revenge is fulfilled and the ashes of determination are blown away, what then? To lust over another's death is to be left empty once the last traces of blood are licked from satisfied teeth. Such a hollow existence, living as a monster in the shadows, and the black wolf soon realized it to be the true horror of his punishment.

For what is left to a nightmare creature that can slip between two worlds without belonging to either? His teeth. His hunger. His loneliness.

Until... Alice.

Alice.

Embers still glowed near the bridge, and the air there still breathed ash among the warped metal of what had once been cars. The fire had devoured everything down to the skeleton, yet the black wolf lunged up from the cinders whole and furious, his yellow eyes the only color in a grey landscape. Reformed, eternal, untamed.

His ears swiveled against the utter silence of the burned forest, finding no hint of life. It didn't matter. He still felt the strength of the shadows. Still understood that on this special night, the two worlds he knew had no barriers. The veil had lifted, and Alice would be alone with the bitch and her human puppets.

He ran, hardly more than a shadow himself. On a night when the dead could touch the living, all barriers fell away like dust. Nothing could stop him. Nothing *would* stop him. As the black wolf tracked Alice beneath the long reach of the moon, unrestrained by distance and time, his teeth flashed in a silent vow. If he had to, he would drag her back from death itself.

CHAPTER EIGHTEEN

A TERRIBLE BEAUTY

Wolf-Alice's jaws frothed with blood and spit as the smell of smoke from the fireplace stoked her frenzied attack, a choking reminder of all that Magdalene had taken. Every flicker from the flames deepened her snarls as she tore at the figure beneath her, this fallen idol of her heart who had once loomed so high above. Eyes as golden as honey flashed at her, but they held none of that knowingness, none of the mystery and lush promise that had once so entranced her. All they showed was *fear*.

"Alice!" Magdalene's voice was a shred of its former velvet seduction. "Why are you doing this?"

No words could emerge from a mouth so savage, but her answer still passed between them, as true and merciless as her bite. *Because this is what I am. Something you can no longer control. Something that is no longer yours.*

And once more she attacked, unstoppable in her rage. Blood splattered the floorboards as arms that were as substantial and vulnerable as living flesh on this one special night now flailed, stripped of all grace.

"No! I need you." The words were hoarse, broken things, as feeble as the fingernails clawing at Wolf-Alice's muzzle to fend off her teeth.

She ignored the words like a sprung trap, ignored the hands like a ripped net, all too intent on reaching Magdalene's throat. She wanted to crush the windpipe that had formed all those poisonous words. She wanted to destroy the voice that had promised love but instilled obedience, the voice that had mapped out the most vulnerable parts of her and then reshaped them like clay.

"I *love* you."

Wolf-Alice paused, her muzzle still wrinkled into a growl. She stared at Magdalene with burning eyes, daring her to say it again. Daring her to reach out and embrace with strangling arms while whispering tender words. Magdalene's appetites always ran to the fragile little things that reminded her of Indigo; could she pretend to cherish a girl now transformed into a beast, sweet face and red-tipped breasts now foaming jaws and coarse pelt?

When Magdalene flinched, Wolf-Alice's growls renewed. She had never been Indigo, that precious girl locked inside Magdalene's ribcage, forever frozen as an image of obsessive love. The girl who had never lived long enough to do wrong, to disappoint. The girl who had long been a silent grave. Hers was the perfection of bones cradled in a mourning shroud, the loveliness of possibilities that could never crumble into bitter reality.

And Alice... Ah, she had been that bitter reality trying to shape itself into that perfection, determined yet doomed to fail. Even when her love for Magdalene had been at its most fervent, she had found herself unable to transform into a living Indigo.

Now there was no idea more horrifying. She no longer wished to be the adored muse, the cherished dream. She no longer wished to be so obsessed over that even her name would be taken away and replaced with something better crooned at a pet. She could become something free. Something that didn't have to be perfect.

She wanted to live—and she would.

Wolf-Alice lunged in, throwing all her rage and strength into driving past Magdalene's frantic hands. This time her jaws locked onto a throat, and when she bit down, vertebrae cracked between her teeth. Blood shot from Magdalene's lips as she shrieked, and then gushed from her ruined neck as she choked.

When Wolf-Alice let go, she looked at the woman who had once meant everything to her with a face stained red. Such a terrible beauty, bared teeth in a mask of blood, and Magdalene shrank from it.

"Who are you?" she whispered, each word drawing more blood from her gaping throat. "What happened to my sweet Alice?"

Wolf-Alice only snarled and bit at her again. And yet this time, her teeth snapped together as if passing through mere air. Then the desperate grip on her fur slipped away. Amber eyes darkened into cinders, and those sharp, clever lips that had once so entranced her now disintegrated into a faceless shadow. All that remained behind was the uncertain outline of a woman, the ragged darkness of something that had always needed others to define its own shape.

Wolf-Alice growled, suspecting some trick yet to be played, but instead the lingering shadow rushed for the fireplace, leaving trails of blood in its wake. With a wail that still sounded like Magdalene's voice, it slipped into the flames and disappeared, causing the fire to hiss and crackle.

The flames flickered wildly, revealing glimpses of the shadowland that Magdalene had pulled Alice to before, that strange land where the moon hung too heavy in the sky and the trees stood in silence. She had given up. She was *fleeing*.

As Magdalene's presence seeped away from the cabin, as invisible and yet palpable as shadows shrinking beneath the face of the rising sun, Wolf-Alice howled a savage promise that there would only be furious teeth for her should she ever dare return.

And yet even as the flames settled, now revealing nothing except the bricks of the fireplace, she knew that Magdalene wouldn't. Not now. Her tender morsel had turned into a frothing monster.

The fire brightened as the last echoes of Magdalene's keening faded. Then came the tick of the clock on the mantelpiece, its delicate arms precise and steady as they marked the passing seconds. The night was drawing to a close.

Wolf-Alice felt herself shake and shiver, felt herself collapse as the seething rage vanished as thoroughly as Magdalene. Instinct drove her body back to the shape it best knew, drove her convulsing even as her consciousness dipped in and out, leaving her scrabbling against the floorboards first with claws, then with fingers. A final, agonized wrench left her slumped on hands and knees, blood still dripping from her mouth.

Magdalene was gone. Truly gone. She should have laughed in amazement, but instead her heart shivered, cold even while the rest of her felt inflamed from changing form. Tears ran down her cheeks, and she couldn't even say why. Unbidden, words from one of Magdalene's letters filled her mind even as she panted for breath, the taste of blood overwhelming against her tongue.

There's some part of you that will always love me, even just a little.

"No," she whispered out loud, fingers curling against the floor. No, not love. Now she only grieved. Even with the threat of Magdalene's presence finally—*finally*—settled, she still felt empty. Carved out. She had lived so long with Magdalene as her focus, first as an object of worship and then as a terror that refused to be locked away into mere memory, that to be rid of her was to be vacant. As if it took her complete absence to understand the sheer amount of damage left behind by her appetites.

Alice felt her next breath hitch out as a sob, but she still raised her head toward the windows to watch the sky lighten. Samhain approached its end, and she was still there to see it. Damaged, yes, but alive. Free to take that emptiness and fill it full again. Even now, she would endure.

As the firelight played over her shuddering body, a muffled noise came from the circle of candles, now snuffed out from melting into their own pools of wax. Alice looked over at Rob as he slowly pushed himself up, eyes bleary behind his glasses and drool crusted on his chin. She watched him take in the sight of her, hunched over like an animal and covered in blood. His face paled.

"Jesus Christ." His wild glance found the opened cabin door and then the porch beyond. Darby slumped against the worn wooden boards there, as if she'd roused at some point during the night before slipping under again. Perhaps to get something in her car that would have helped Magdalene against Alice's teeth. Perhaps merely confused under the influence of Rob's hallucinogen.

Whatever the cause, her motionless form—untouched, still breathing—didn't calm the panic in Rob's face. "What happened?"

"Magdalene came and left again," said Alice, voice flat. Her body was exposed to him and covered in the proof of her violence, and yet she didn't care at all.

"What?" He stumbled upright, swallowing as if he felt like throwing up. Outside, Darby continued to breathe slow and steady, but he made no attempt to rouse her, no attempt to even check on her.

Alice eyed him, taking in the sheen of sweat on his face and how his clothes had picked up dust from the floor. She had never seen him so disheveled. In the past, he had always snapped out of their psychonaut sessions effortlessly, as smooth and smug as an illusionist who had just pulled off a trick in front of his gape-mouthed audience. Now he seemed very... Diminished. Human.

"Why did you just stand by, Rob?" she found herself saying, gaze steady even as her limbs continued to tremble. She settled her weight onto one hip to ease the strain, not looking away as his uncomprehending gaze fell upon her. "You weren't afraid of Magdalene. So why do nothing while she used up people and threw them away? Why let her do that with your own wife?"

"Are you serious?" He ran a shaking hand over his hair. "Who gives a shit about Magdalene? She's *dead*. You're covered in blood like you took a fucking bath in it. What the hell did you do?"

"What did *you* do, Rob? What did you get out of watching her play with people? Out of fucking me while I was half-conscious and too scared to say no to anything Magdalene told me to do? I know why she wanted it—to watch me and make sure I didn't enjoy any part of being with a man. But what did you take away from it? The amusement of seeing little dolls break without having to clean up their shards?" A growl had entered her voice.

Something in her face sent him edging backwards, stepping on the nearest candles. "Forget it. I'm out of here. Darby can clean up her own fucking mess."

Alice raised an eyebrow. "You're just going to leave her with me? You know we hate each other. Who's to say I won't go after her next?"

When he only shook his head, she spat, "I can't believe you used to intimidate me. Now I see exactly what you are."

Something in his expression changed. "What are you talking about?"

"You're pathetic. Just a grubby user who hides behind his camera so that he can claim everything he does is for the sake of art. You're nothing to be afraid of."

Her words froze his feet to the floor. "What's that supposed to be? A threat?"

"It's a plain fact," she said, voice flat despite the disgust welling up in her.

But he began approaching her again, each footstep heavy, and the panic in his face quickly crystallized into something more dangerous. "Are you saying you're going to open up about Magdalene? About me?"

In his eyes, Alice saw the potential consequences of his actions unfold. Oh, she could reveal so many damaging things about him now that she didn't care. How he had given her

drugs and fucked her half-conscious, photographing the
results. How she hadn't been the only one. Even with her
original blurry consent, the facts would be enough to ruin him
in his precious art circles. Work would dry up; galleries would
close their doors. He was good, but he wasn't great enough to
bare his sins and still rise above public outcry.

And yet these worries had never bitten at him because he'd
always been so assured that she would never dare bring things
to light and face her family's disdain. No, she was merely quiet
Alice, the trust fund baby who had gotten in over her head.
Only now, when she might open her mouth and speak, did he
finally regard her, that arrogant aura of his slipping away in
favor of the base instinct of self-preservation. Rob never liked
getting his hands dirty. But he liked being in trouble even less.

When he took another step closer, Alice bared her teeth at
him and said, "As much as I hate her, Darby's right about one
thing. You don't think about anyone except yourself."

From the way his mouth hardened, she might as well have
said nothing, and so she fell silent as he crouched before her,
the bulk of his body blocking the rest of her view. He grabbed
the back of her head, giving her hair a hard jerk as if warning
her that he wasn't fucking around, but she bit back a laugh
instead of a yelp. As if he could give her a wound as painful and
thorough as anything Magdalene had ever inflicted. As if he
could make her scream with the same raggedness as when
Colton had crumpled against the truck, bleeding.

She continued matching gazes with him as he hissed, "You're not going to say a fucking word about anything involving me, understand? To anyone."

"I'm not afraid of your threats. Not anymore."

"Are you even listening?" He let go of her hair and shoved her up against the hearth, the rough bricks biting into the bare skin of her back.

"I am." She shook, but not with the same fierceness that had twisted her flesh into a form that could bite and savage. Her disgust had gone, too, leaving her with only a bone-deep weariness. This man was nothing to her, not even an enemy.

His arm pressed against her throat, pinning her still as he leaned in. His eyes looked wild behind his glasses, but his voice remained slow, emphasizing each word with care. "I don't know what happened tonight, but it doesn't matter. You're not going to say anything about it or any other night we spent together. Got it?"

"Or what?"

His slap cracked her full in the face, snapping her head to the side. The sheer shock of it left her speechless even before pain overwhelmed her senses.

Then Rob caught her chin and forced her to look at him. "Or I'll fucking crush you."

The words drew a noise from her, one that startled them both. It was a laugh. She swallowed the rest of it down and said, "You can't. You've got nothing to hurt me with. Go on, punch me until my nose breaks, or until I can't see out of both eyes. It doesn't matter."

Rob stared at her for a moment before stepping back. Alice watched him walk over to the circle of melted wax, remaining still even when he picked up the knife. She didn't care enough to try wrestling the weapon away. What was he going to do, cut into the gaping emptiness that filled her? She'd still survive. There was nothing to fear from him.

And so she only raised her chin, feeling the pull of drying blood on her skin as he approached again, the knife already pointed at her.

"If you're awake, then the shit we took is out of your system. I know you can understand this, you crazy bitch." He crouched before her once more, the blade now inches from her face.

When she drew in a breath to speak, the tip prodded against her throbbing cheek. "No, enough with the bullshit. You don't have the upper hand here. Your hitman of a boyfriend is dead, remember?"

The words were a lash of agony against her heart, and she jerked as some of the raw hurt came back into her. When she remained silent, the blade moved to where her pulse beat hard and fast, just underneath her jaw.

Then the window shattered inward. A snarl filled the room, shivering Alice's bones with its familiarity, and she jerked toward it despite the knife still against her throat. Rob flinched, expression turning bewildered as a dark, lethal form landed behind him, silent among the glass scattered across the floor.

Yellow eyes flashed at Alice an instant before the black wolf lunged, jaws locking onto Rob's arm to drive the blade away from her neck. Bone snapped, and then Rob screamed, the knife falling from his hand as the black wolf pulled him down. Another bite, then a vicious jerk that sent bone splintering up through the skin of Rob's arm, and then the black wolf let go and lunged for the throat, choking off the man's frantic voice.

Alice found herself gulping for breath as the wolf's teeth tore into vulnerable flesh, but she didn't flinch and she didn't look away. His attack wasn't that patient, suffocating bite that Alice had seen him use on hares and deer but instead something furious, something mauling. Something that splattered flesh over Rob's twitching hands as his blubbering cries thickened into gurgles. Blood spread over the floor.

Despite the savagery, Alice found herself slowly reaching out, nothing like fear in her heart even as vertebrae cracked between teeth. Something that had died with her in the fire now throbbed painfully, something raw like hope but paralyzing like terror. He was right there in front of her, his ferocious jaws proof enough that he was still solid and tangible.

And yet... Magdalene had also felt very real. Had also bled and held the ability to make others bleed. What if this was just another temporary feat of Samhain? Had the fire reduced him to something more ghost than flesh, here before her only because of the strange power of this one night when the dead could roam free? What if the black wolf faded with the rest of the shadows once the sun rose, leaving her with nothing more than ash and memory?

Tears burned down her cheeks at the possibility, and she drew back again, suddenly afraid of her fingers slipping through him like air. As the windows lightened with coming dawn, she found herself rising up, pressing against the lingering warmth of the hearth as the final moments of Samhain slipped away.

Just as the sky glimmered with the sunrise, the black wolf circled away from Rob's unmoving body. As soft light spilled into the room, gaining strength with each passing breath, he shook the blood from his fur and changed.

Alice made a sound that might have been a sob, might have been a whimper as Colton rose from the floor, his gaze never leaving her. Once more, her hands reached for him even as they trembled with fear. Would he disappear with the final traces of night? He had found her, but could he stay with her?

The blood on his face made his eyes appear even greener as he approached. He looked feral, unstoppable. Alive.

"Please," she whispered, remembering how their fingers had brushed just before the first bullet had struck him. "Are you really here?"

Then his hand caught hers, callused and warm and solid, and she felt her expression crumple into tears even before he pulled her close.

"Alice." He buried his face against the side of her neck and breathed in deeply. Losing himself in her scent. Then his hands ran along the length of her body, caressing her as if she was the most precious thing alive.

"You were caught in the fire," she managed, fingers digging into his shoulders. "You *burned*. And when you didn't show up at the evacuation center the morning after, I started thinking that..."

He tested her skin with teeth still bloody, the heat of his body melting hers. "Told you before. Nothing can keep me in the grave."

A hiccup of a laugh escaped between her shuddering breaths. "You found me."

"Always." Then he pulled back enough to look at her. His eyes still glittered viciously, but his thumb remained gentle as it ran along her lower lip, finding the drying blood there.

When his head tilted to the side, she answered his unspoken question. "I fought off Magdalene. I... I changed into a wolf and fought her off."

He almost smiled at that. "You used your teeth."

Then he cupped her chin, giving her that look that meant he was about to fuck her senseless, and when he leaned in, she raised her face to his.

But instead of a kiss, his hot tongue licked at the blood on her mouth. "You never lost your wildness, Alice. She never took it from you."

Tears blurred in her eyes then, and her grip on his shoulders tightened to draw him close. She needed to feel him against her, needed his sweat and teeth and semen marking her body after those agonizing hours of uncertainty left by the fire.

His low growl told her that he understood, and now they kissed, his tongue savage, impatient, savoring her as she arched into him. When her hands fisted in his hair, he growled again against her mouth, hands running up the small of her back and teasing along her ribs. When he cupped her breasts, she felt the stickiness of blood on his fingers.

It drew a shiver out of her, but not one of repulsion, and in the next moment she tugged him even closer, boneless as he eased her down to the floor. The dying embers in the fireplace cast their final warmth over her skin as he pinned her to the ground, hard body stretching over hers. His eyes picked up the lingering light from the last little flames, glowing at her as if peering out from the gloom of the forest, and a sweet ache ran through her heart as she opened her legs to him.

The mere hint of his fingers tracing along her cunt sent her hips jerking, impatient for more. Normally, he would have laughed at her greed, but in that moment he only studied every inch of her face, the grim line of his mouth almost tender before he leaned in to lick away the blood trailing down her throat and breasts. His teeth were still sharp, teasing her flesh with their danger, but she only arched into them, panting as his hand stroked her again. By the time his thumb pushed in and found her inner folds, she was wet and ready. She clenched her thighs against his wrist, never wanting to let him go.

"I love you," she breathed against his mouth, her nipples in sweet agony from his attention.

"Words," he murmured, sounding amused, but the look in his eyes said something else entirely. Then he was kissing her again, swallowing her scream as his thumb rasped against her clit.

They thrashed on the floor like wild things, sticky with blood and slick with their own sweat. His hips were hard and relentless, but she only laughed against his neck, her fingernails digging into his back in a silent plea. More, more. She would never get enough of him even as he filled her full with every thrust.

Her teeth once more felt dull and human, but as she panted in time with his rhythm, squeezing her thighs against him to make him shudder in need, she felt as wild, as *free*, as when she'd run through the forest as a wolf. And when he bit the side of her neck, right where the knife had threatened it, the raw heat of her climax sent her arching up in a howl.

He growled through his, thrusts still hard and furious, but after their panting had faded back into quiet breaths, his mouth turned tender again, telling her everything in his kiss that he wouldn't put into words.

Later, as the sun glowed through the windows, he pulled her upright, settling her onto his lap. She dropped her head against his shoulder, still feeling slightly boneless, and murmured, "I wish you'd seen me as a wolf."

"Who says I won't?" He squeezed at her hips, the lazy smolder in his eyes suggesting he already thought of taking her again.

She blinked at him. "But Samhain is over."

"Samhain's got nothing to do with it. You found your wildness, and your witch blood did the rest." His hands now skimmed along her spine, running along her skin as if marveling at her very softness.

"My grandmother couldn't do that."

"No wildness to her. Just a lot of hunger." He ran a thumb over her flushed nipple and then gave it a tweak, already looking disinterested in the conversation.

His touch sent a sweet throb throughout her, but her curiosity was roused, and when her own fingers hesitantly ran over the hard muscles of his chest, finding no signs of his old scars even as his heart beat strong and steady against her touch, he growled softly, already sensing her impending questions.

She glanced up at him. "You can't expect me to accept things without wanting to know more about them."

He sighed, nuzzling at her earlobe. "Ask whatever you want."

"You *did* burn in the fire."

"Yes. Then I came back."

"But not as a ghost." Her palm pressed against his heartbeat.

"No. I can't die, Alice." Then he kissed the curve of her jaw before pulling back enough to look at her again. "Takes time to recover from whatever fucked us up, whether it's a bullet or a fire. Sometimes a day, sometimes more. I don't know why."

"Your scars disappeared."

"Well, I was fucking ash." Despite the terse words, his hands ran along her back in soothing patterns. "My body had to reknit itself from nose to tail."

Such strangeness before her, and yet she didn't flinch away. Instead, her thighs squeezed against him, reassuring him with her softness, her acceptance. When she fell silent, absorbing everything he'd told her, he studied her face. Then his expression changed, and his hand moved to tilt her chin until the morning light caught the side that had taken Rob's strike.

"He wasn't worth fighting," said Alice, voice soft yet steady. "His threats didn't matter."

Colton growled, rage bubbling beneath his words. "He had a fucking knife against your throat."

"But that wouldn't have killed me. Witches only die from burning or drowning."

"I said nothing else kills a witch. I didn't say nothing else *hurts* her."

Alice only shrugged. "As long as I can survive it, I don't care. As screwed up as it sounds, I don't mind another scar."

Then Colton's fingers coaxed her to look up at him. "You're not getting any more of them. Not if I can help it."

She met his gaze without shame or fear, her mouth relaxing into a smile as her hands slid down his shoulders to find the light dusting of hair on his chest. To feel the absence of scar tissue she had memorized. "I feel the same way about you."

The light in his eyes changed, especially when she reached up to stroke away the tension from his jaw, but just as he leaned in, a cough on the porch interrupted them. Alice turned her head enough to see Darby twitch and then fall still again.

"She's still alive," murmured Alice, surprised at how calm she felt.

Colton followed her gaze. "I could smell she'd be out for awhile. Decided to leave her for your teeth."

Alice drew in a deep breath, aware of the tang of iron still in her mouth. It gave weight to the sudden power she had to decide this girl's fate. Had she lost her hatred? No. Had she lost her rage over what Darby had done to Colton? Never. And yet now that the true threat—Magdalene—had faded with the night, in the bright light of day Darby only looked pathetic. Someone so obsessed that she had lost herself. Someone as blind as Alice had once been.

And yet Alice felt her lips twitch toward a snarl, not a pitying smile. Although she knew full well how Magdalene had been a brilliant puppeteer to any girl unlucky enough to fall in love with her, Darby had still made life hell on earth for Alice. Threatening to humiliate her through that book, threatening to reveal sordid secrets to her family... And then shooting Colton. Leaving him to burn alive in a fire.

"Do we have to kill her?" she said, not looking away from the other girl.

Colton's voice revealed no trace of his thoughts. "Doesn't matter either way when it comes to staying safe. Dead, she's one more body to hide. Alive, no one will believe her."

If it had only been her own head that Darby had gone after, that would be one thing. But she hadn't, and now Alice felt ready to bite again.

"She hurt you," she said, voice low but steady. "I want her to regret that. I want her to realize exactly what she did. Magdalene's gone and now she's got nothing left but herself to live with. I don't want her to get anything as satisfying as a martyr's death. I want her to go through *hell*."

Colton nodded, that feral gleam back in his eyes. Then the corner of his mouth twitched toward a smile. "Got any bleach?"

Alice blinked at him. "I thought forensic science could still find blood traces."

"There are ways around that." The look on his face implied that he was used to employing them, too.

"You're still so mysterious," she murmured, as he stood with ease and offered his hand to her.

As she rose, he pulled her into a lingering kiss. "Plenty of time to figure me out. But first, we finish what these fuckers started."

CHAPTER NINETEEN

ONE LAST BITE

Alice clutched at the steaming styrofoam cup that had been given to her, expression blank while she sat on the hood of the rental car and watched deputies step in and out of the cabin. Sunlight glittered on their badges and holsters, but the air held a chill that tinged their shadows blue and tightened their grim faces. Some of them could be heard in the forest, calling out for Rob. They had been looking for nearly an hour while waiting for a search and rescue unit to arrive.

Vaguely, Alice wondered where Colton had left the body, but the question snuffed itself as soon as she glanced at him. He was busy devouring his third donut, every line of his body conveying a complete disinterest in the deputies scouring the property. The thin afternoon light burnished his dark hair, emphasized the hard line of his jaw. Gave his eyes a yellowness that they normally only held while he was a wolf. It turned her heart into something hot and throbbing to see him so rough-edged and unshakeable, to know that no matter what happened next, he would be there with her, steady and vicious and unrelenting.

As if sensing her thoughts, he looked over at her. The flatness in his gaze shifted into something tender as unspoken words passed between them. *They don't see us. They see what they expect.*

Not wanting to appear happy at a crime scene, she resisted smiling and instead sipped at her coffee, returning her focus to the activity all around her. Between him and the deputies, she was well aware of being the odd one out: with the sleek dress, wool coat, and high heels Gretchen had given her, she must have seemed immaculate and posed to any observer. But her hair fell around her in untamed waves, and her face was free of makeup, free of the mask that would complete the illusion of perfection. She must have looked like a girl who had gotten herself lost in the woods. Like a doll left in a place where it had no purpose.

And yet she didn't feel that way at all, not even when her tongue pressed against the dull, human shapes of her teeth.

"Alice! Oh, there she is! *Alice.*"

The familiarity of the voice broke through her thoughts, and she looked down the driveway to find her father parking beneath a cluster of young redwoods—the only level ground not taped off or taken by the deputies' cars. Denise already leaned out the front passenger's window, frantically waving at her.

"Your father looks upset," said Colton, taking the final bite of his donut. "He'll want to scare you back onto a leash."

"Maybe, but it won't work," she said, waving back at her parents while rising to her feet. "I've tasted too much of the wilderness."

How strange, the calmness she felt in her heart as he stood with her, eyes burning with that same light they held whenever he pulled her close and kissed at her pulse. How strange, the calmness that filled her voice as her parents hurried toward them, their faces etched with worry. "It's all right! We're both all right."

"Thank God," gasped Denise, sweeping her up into a hug. "We saw all this and expected the worst."

"There was a break-in at the cabin, that's all," said Alice, returning the hug. "We're fine."

Her father's brief glare toward Colton suggested he only gave a damn about one of them. "What exactly happened?"

Alice drew in a breath and repeated what she'd already told the sheriff. "After what happened with the fire, we decided to drive here and stay at the cabin until everything settled down. As soon as we arrived, we saw it'd been broken into and called the sheriff's station. They've been investigating ever since."

"You should have *driven* there," said her father, the lines of concern on his forehead deepening. "What if the intruders had still been inside?"

"One was. I recognized her." Then Alice turned toward one of the deputies' cars.

And there in the back sat Darby, mouth set in a fixed line while she stared straight ahead at nothing. Even through the darkened window, it was apparent that her skin was clammy with sweat and that the front of her shirt had been hastily wiped clean, as if she'd thrown up from the aftereffects of the drugs.

"Who is she?" Her father sounded baffled.

Such a simple question, one that Alice could have answered easily. *Darby Reeves, a friend of Magdalene's.* Ah, but she was so much more than that, wasn't she? A girl obsessed, a girl blinded by pretty words and sudden love. A girl whose heart ached in adoration and trembled in gratefulness at being the object of love for such a brilliant, otherworldly creature. A girl much like the one Alice had been, once upon a time.

And yet Alice felt nothing gentle toward her, this sharp little tool of Magdalene's. This girl had hounded her, frightened her, threatened her. On their own, such things might have been easy to sweep aside with a heart clean from purging Magdalene's shadow. But after what she had done to Colton? No, Alice would *never* forgive that, and only the knowledge that the other girl would suffer far more alive than dead kept her from crashing through that car window.

Just the mere memory of her smile beside the stock of the sniper rifle ignited a fury that left it hard to breathe, and Alice's jaw began to ache. Then her teeth pricked at her lips, and even without a mirror she knew they had grown into fangs. A single word would be enough to reveal their new sharpness.

As if sensing her sudden trouble, Colton answered her father's question in a bland tone. "She's someone Alice used to know. An author from the city."

Her parents both understood the significance—that this girl they didn't know was someone Alice had met through Magdalene.

As the confusion faded from her father's face, he stiffly said, "Is she still a friend of yours?"

Just as quickly, her teeth shrunk back to normal, and Alice bit back a bitter laugh. "No. She just knew that this was the cabin where Magdalene spent her final days. It looks like she broke in and performed a seance."

Denise shook her head while giving Alice's shoulders a comforting squeeze. "It all sounds completely bizarre, but at least it's got nothing to do with you. I'm sure the sheriff will take care of everything. She's certainly not your problem."

That last sentence seemed more directed at Alice's father, who had a rare moment of hesitation.

When he said nothing, Denise's voice brightened as she reached into her purse and withdrew a manila envelope. "Oh! Here's a little bit of good news. People were allowed to return to Calico Creek this morning, so we drove to your house to see what was left."

"There was nothing," said her father.

Denise smacked him on the arm with the envelope. "Tom, I said this was *good* news. Although it was true that everything looked like an apocalyptic wasteland. But we still found where your house had been and recovered the papers from your fireproof safe. Everything inside it is now in here."

It was a dizzying sensation to be handed all remaining possessions in something thinner than a notebook. "Oh. Thank you. I didn't even think about..."

"Needing your birth certificate, social security card, and other important papers? I guessed as much, which is why we got them for you." Despite his words, her father's frown eased away. At least until he looked at Colton. "I don't see your truck here. Was it lost in the fire?"

"Everything important to me survived," said Colton, not missing a beat. His brief glance held as much dismissal as her father's entire expression, and Alice had to muffle another laugh at seeing them all but roll their eyes at each other.

"Thanks," she said again, drawing both of her parents' gazes. "I'm glad these survived the flames. It'll make everything a little easier."

Her father nodded. "The only thing left to discuss is where you'll be staying until you find a new home. Not here. This cabin looks like it should have been condemned years ago."

"It's in great condition," said Alice, and then threw a swift glance at Colton before adding, "The roof doesn't leak at all and the porch was just checked for rot."

Denise looked torn. "It does look very cozy, and we're not arguing against your need for independence, sweetheart. It's just that it's so very far away."

"I know," said Alice, still composed. "But we'd rather stay here while planning what to do next."

When her father sighed, she waited for the final curt words that would signal an end to their shaky attempt at a discussion. To her surprise, he only rubbed at his neck and then said, "All right."

"All right?" repeated Alice, glancing from him to Denise, whose expression had eased into one of relief.

"If I can't change your mind, Alice, then I won't try. It's obvious that we're past the point of seeing eye-to-eye on your decisions."

The words drew a scoff from Colton, and her father's stiff expression took on a tinge of irritation as he added, "Some more than others. But I... I want to work past that. I don't want you to disappear for another five years. Or more."

"Neither do I," said Alice, her voice soft.

Then she closed the gap between them to give him a hug. It already felt less strange, more familiar, and now her voice shook as she said, "I still want to see you, too. Just on my own terms."

Her father said nothing, but his arms tightened around her, not loosened.

They had just pulled apart when shouts rang out from the forest. Alice jerked, startled even though she knew what must have happened, and Denise gasped, eyes wide as a deer's. When the expressions of the nearby deputies changed, Colton stepped closer to Alice, the movement sharp and smooth.

"What's happening?" said Denise, as they all turned toward the gloom of the trees.

Alice's father, no stranger to search parties, provided the grim answer. "They found something."

Rob's body, as it turned out. As soon as the first mutters about it being in pieces reached them, Denise covered her mouth with a hand. "Tom, I do *not* want to be here when they bring him out."

"We won't be." Her father's hand already reached out to usher her back to the car, but his next words were for Alice. "We're staying at a hotel in Perry to avoid driving throughout the night. We'll visit again tomorrow morning before leaving for home."

"Let's go out for breakfast," said Alice, her smile small but real.

Surprise flickered in his eyes before he nodded. "Be careful while you're here. And call us if you need any help, day or night."

Even as Denise gave her a quick but fierce hug, face turned away from the direction of the forest, the tone of her father's voice stayed with her. There was a sadness beneath the iron-rigid syllables that hurt to hear, and as they walked off toward the driveway, she found herself sinking back onto the hood of the car. Despite the sudden ache, she managed to wave goodbye until the taillights winked out between the trees.

Then Colton's hand brushed the curve of her cheek, and she looked up at him. "He knows he's lost me."

"He hasn't. Just his control of you."

His calmness steadied her like an anchor, and when he sat beside her, she sighed, raising her face for a kiss. His mouth was hot and unhurried, coaxing her tension into something sweeter, something savage. Coaxing it into something that left her murmuring, "Did you tear apart the body, or was that from scavengers?"

He nuzzled at her hair before answering. "Bit of both. Wanted to make sure the bites were too messy to identify."

His heartbeat reverberated against her skin, and she squeezed her eyes shut, wishing the day was over and that they were alone with the night. She was *not* a doll, but flesh and bone and wearied heart, and she wished to rest.

"But they'll at least know it was an animal attack, won't they?" she said, aware that the less they understood about Rob's death, the longer they would linger at the cabin and document any possible evidence.

"We're about to find out."

A growl had slipped into his voice, and she looked over to find the sheriff approaching them. She recognized him—it was Sheriff Danvers, the same man who had announced Magdalene's death to her on that strange evening that now seemed an eternity ago.

As she straightened up, he offered Colton a brief nod and then focused on her. "Ms. Corrigan, you're probably tired from going through hell for the last few days. I appreciate your patience and cooperation with our investigation."

"It's all right." Then she smiled a little. "It's nice to see you again, Sheriff."

"It would be nicer if the circumstances were better. I'm sorry to tell you this, but we've got no reason to hold Ms. Reeves for anything other than breaking into your cabin. There were no drugs found on her, the knife we found wasn't in her possession, and her husband's body looks like it was torn apart by animals."

"Another animal attack?" It wasn't hard to dip her voice in surprise.

"Yes, ma'am." Then the sheriff raised a hand as if to ward off any further questions. "We won't know anything more detailed until the coroner's report is finished."

When she said nothing else, he added, "It's all up to you, ma'am. Do you want to press charges? If not, she's free to go."

Alice shook her head. "No, I don't want to press charges. Whatever she did last night, it's over now and none of it affects me."

Strange how so little had to be an actual lie. As the sheriff walked off toward the car that held Darby, Alice resettled against Colton, her fingers absently flexing against the manila envelope Denise had given her. With nothing else to do but wait, she found herself opening it up and rifling through the contents.

When her fingers brushed a familiar packet bound in black velvet ribbon, her expression froze. Colton noticed and growled softly. She answered his unspoken query by pulling it out to show him. "These are Magdalene's letters to Indigo. All of them."

They had survived. Alice checked the envelope again and found the photo of the girl as well. Conflicting emotions beat within her heart. Should she keep them? Burn them just as she had burned the ones Magdalene had written to her? They held no interest for her, these obsessive letters to a dead girl.

Just then, Darby's voice rose in a shriek, the words unintelligible as she faced Sheriff Danvers. The man remained impassive, his own voice low and soothing even as she glared at him.

Alice blinked at the scene, and then the awareness of what to do slid into her as swift and sure as a blade between the ribs. She looked at Colton, unsure if she was smiling or simply baring her teeth. "I need to talk to her one last time."

Even as the realization glinted in his eyes, Darby's voice shifted into a final scream as she stormed away from the sheriff, who just shook his head.

"Probably told her she has to identify the body and give a statement at the station," said Colton. When Alice only nodded, he leaned in until their mouths brushed, until the hint of his teeth could be felt against hers. "One last bite, hm?"

Her words weren't quite a growl, but they held a ferocity all the same. "The killing one."

Darby fumbled into her car and slammed the door shut just before Alice reached her. For a long moment, they only stared at each other through the opened window. Two girls, so unalike even though they had been caught in the same trap.

"You bitch," said Darby, finally. "Bet you're feeling pretty smug right now."

"No."

"Why not? You won."

"Won what?" said Alice, quietly. "Do you still think Magdalene needs to be avenged?"

"They said you aren't pressing charges." Darby's voice fell flat, and Alice then knew that she wouldn't bring up things like ghosts and murderous wolves in front of others. Already, she feared being doubted. Ridiculed. Ignored.

"They're telling the truth. I don't like you and I never have, but frankly, still having Magdalene in your head is punishment enough."

"Fuck you, you don't know—"

"I do, and that's why I'm about to give you these." Then Alice drew in a breath. "There was something missing in that manuscript you showed me. Something that *needs* to be in any biography about Magdalene."

When she offered the photo, Darby didn't take it. But she did look, and the hatred in her face slowly transformed into confusion.

"Her name was Liberty Bower. Magdalene called her Indigo. Did she ever tell you about her?"

From the twist to Darby's mouth, Alice knew she hadn't. "Here. These will clear it up then."

She pulled the packet from the pocket of her coat and then slipped a letter free, revealing Magdalene's distinctive writing. "They're love letters to someone she knew in high school. To the only girl who ever mattered in her eyes."

"Why should I believe you?" snarled Darby, but her gaze remained on the sheet of paper hanging between them.

Alice shrugged. "Don't. Believe Magdalene instead. You've studied her for months. You'll know if these are a forgery or the real thing."

When the other girl remained silent, Alice replaced the letter with the rest, some part of her dimly aware of how steady her fingers were. "You were never special to her, Darby. Neither was I. She just used us because she was empty. And since you won't believe anything I say, I'm giving you Magdalene's own words to go on. Indigo was the first girl she loved. The *only* girl she loved. It's the final piece of your book, you know. Showing how happy Magdalene was, and how she never felt that way again. With anyone."

"Fuck you," said Darby, but her voice trembled, and she didn't resist as Alice dropped the packet through the window.

"No, fuck her. This is the last time I'm ever talking about her. And this is the last time I'm ever talking to you." Then Alice walked away, knowing she had just discarded the final piece of Magdalene. It made her eyes burn with tears, made her heart buck in her chest. Made her want to howl at the freedom.

In a few moments, Darby roared off in her car, the packet of letters clutched in her hand as if she couldn't decide whether to tear them to shreds or press them to her heart. She would hate Alice all the more for them, but also herself. And then, one day, perhaps she would even hate Magdalene before letting it all scar up into ugly, misshapen tissue. It was the best she could hope for, surviving her own hell.

Later, once the sheriff and his deputies had left and the sky glimmered with the first lavender hues of dusk, Alice sat on the porch steps, fingers trailing over where Colton had replaced a rotting board back in those strange, wondrous days when they had just met. Back then, she never would have dreamed of escaping for good, or finding a life where her own keloid heart received tender kisses instead of fresh scars.

Twisting around, she watched him prowl around the cabin, expression alert as if he sought out one final trap, one final twist from Fate's knife. Her heart squeezed almost painfully at his silent stride, at the dark scruff already grown back on his jaw and the way his eyes absorbed everything in a glance. Each time she looked at him, it felt like she fell in love a little more.

She smiled as he joined her on the porch, two beer cans in hand. "Where did those come from? The deputies cleared out Rob and Darby's mess."

He winked while popping open the tabs for them both. "I'm good at scrounging for things."

When he offered one, she took it with a mock-suspicious look. "Always so mysterious."

His amused growl hummed between them while she sipped at the beer, hardly even tasting it. Instead, she found herself looking out over the trees as the first stars winked into life. Yellow caution tape fluttered in the wind. Tire tracks could be seen in areas of mud. They were the silent remnants left from the day. They were the last sparks of her old life, finally burning out.

"It's over," she said, voice soft. "I can't believe it."

Warm fingers ran along the back of her neck. She understood the silent signal and melted against him with a sigh, eyes still on the sky. For awhile, they drank in silence, listening to an owl screech somewhere in the woods. Crickets called, and a bold raccoon crossed the road. Behind them loomed the cabin, shadow-black and still faintly smelling of burned things.

And yet Alice felt no fear. This was her world now, and she loved it.

The sound of punctured metal caught her attention, and she looked over to find Colton biting the bottom of the can with his fangs. When he caught her watching, he said, "Quickest way to get the last swallow."

She laughed. "Is it really that easy for you? Just growing them out whenever you want?"

"Sure. You'll soon do the same," he said, giving her that one look that always left her a little breathless.

But she only glanced away, self-doubt prickling through her. Would she? Would she be able to fully change again without all-consuming rage to guide her instincts? Could she find that inner wildness even when there was no need to protect herself?

Then Colton's hand caught her chin, one thumb running over her mouth before he tilted her face toward his. Their noses brushed as he murmured, "Trust me?"

"Always," she breathed.

"Then think of how much you want to bite."

Her response was swallowed by his kiss, a long, teasing one that that let her feel the press of his fangs as much as the velvet of his tongue. When he nipped at her lower lip, something within her came alive—playful instead of seething, thrilling instead of dangerous. As her fingers dug into his shirt, her jaw began to ache.

Beasts understand rapture as much as bloodthirst. The bite that reveres instead of mauls, the exquisite pressure of teeth that catch and hold close rather than choke... Ah, what is more joyful than to feel the tenderness of a mouth that worships when it could kill?

When Colton broke off, still holding her chin, she panted, feeling her teeth press against her lips with the sharpness of fangs. Then she laughed, and he gave her one of his rare smiles.

"It's always there," he said, licking at his own teeth before they shrunk back into human form. Then he licked at hers. "And I'll bring it out of you whenever you doubt it."

UNLEASHED

See how the girl smiles while shaking the pins from her hair? It makes her entire face glow in the warm lamplight of the bedroom. Her high heels are the next things discarded, kicked off with a few disdainful flicks of her feet and left to wait on the plush carpet.

The man watches her intently, leaning back against the dressing table as his eyes devour her every movement. He's already half-undressed, his suit jacket shrugged off and his black tie tugged loose and left to hang. His unbuttoned shirt reveals what a sleek tuxedo has hidden all evening—powerful muscle at ease, hair marking a trail down past a lean, hard stomach. A predator's body with its insatiable appetite.

When the girl slips off her shimmering gown to reveal herself in full, he can't resist any longer, lunging for her with that feral quickness. But she only laughs at the pressure of his teeth against her throat, arching into his hands as they slide down the sweet line of her back. Her own fingers pull at his remaining clothes, tearing them off with equal hunger until they are both stripped down to bare skin.

"I want to see you," he breathes against her neck, and she shivers, half-afraid that she won't be able to show him.

A final, tender bite and then he pulls away, eyes gleaming at her. For him, shifting out of human form is as effortless as ever, like the flicker of a shadow. There's a quick shake to settle his black fur into place, and then the wolf pants open-mouthed, still watching the girl.

Another tremor of self-doubt passes through her, but she crouches down with a smile, twining fingers into his thick pelt as a cold nose snuffles at her cheek. Then she closes her eyes and concentrates, feeling the first cramps of change start from deep inside her ribcage.

Her shift isn't as easy as his, hands scrabbling against the floor as they morph into paws and a whimper of pain sliding between sharpening teeth. But the black wolf presses close, steadying her shaking body until bone locks in place and muscle reknits, until new fur stops writhing and yellow eyes flash.

And from where the girl crouched, a she-wolf now rises, yelping in excitement while shaking herself from head to toe. The black wolf sneezes a wolf-laugh, but his ears prick in pride at his beautiful Alice, still graceful even as she bounces in raw delight.

She rubs against him, smoke to his charcoal, before they both move for the open window and the night that waits beyond. The moon has turned the world into bone and shadow, and yet they join it without fear, the she-wolf as swift and sure as her lover while they run into the deep gloom of the trees. Dawn will find them human and sleeping in muddied bed sheets, but for now the forest is theirs.

Hist! Hear how they howl.

About the Author

I've always loved writing about monsters and the girls who love them, which means I write a lot of werewolf romance. In my spare time I like to do things where I don't have to take myself seriously, like bike riding with my husband, baking anything that sounds good, and painting monsters and horses.

I like scotch, wine, and cats.

Enough about me; if you want to know more about my work, my personal website is juliemidnight.com, and my Instagram handle is @juliemidnighter